Darling Son,

Not a single day has gone by in the past fourteen years that I haven't ached for you, or imagined how things might have turned out if I had raised you. Even though I was young and naive, I never regretted having you. I consider you my greatest achievement, my most precious gift. But I wasn't strong enough to stand up to my parents when they insisted I give you up. I just thank my lucky stars that you found a wonderful family to love you. Simply knowing that you are happy and healthy provides me with such solace.

Son, I've stayed away all these years because I know it was the right thing to do. But now I wonder if it might be possible for me to see you, even from afar, and somehow be there to watch you grow up. I would never try to take your parents' place, but this yearning in my heart can no longer be denied....

Love,
Mom

Please address questions and book requests to: Silhouette Reader Service
U.S.: 3010 Walden Ave., P.O. Box 1325, Buffalo, NY 14269
Canadian: P.O. Box 609, Fort Erie, Ont. L2A 5X3

TEXAS

GINNA GRAY

The Heart's Yearning

Silhouette Books

Published by Silhouette Books

America's Publisher of Contemporary Romance

SILHOUETTE BOOKS
300 East 42nd St.,
New York, N.Y. 10017

ISBN 0-373-47193-9

THE HEART'S YEARNING

Copyright © 1985 by Virginia Gray

Printed in U.S.A.

Dear Reader,

One of the great things about being a writer is that you can take any situation, no matter how horrendous or hopeless, and *make* it turn out the way it should have.

In the case of this book, I recall seeing a TV interview with a woman who had been forced to give up the child she had borne at the age of fifteen. Now the woman was in her seventies, and the child was the only one she had ever had. Her yearning and heartbreak, particularly since she had never wanted to give up her baby, wrenched my heart.

I began to ask myself things like: What if she had broken away from her dominating parents and married a loving man, but still felt this awful void? What if, after her husband died, she found out where the child lived and moved to that town, not to tell him who she was or try to take him from his adoptive parents, but just to be near him, to watch him grow from afar? What if her son's adoptive mother had died and the heroine falls in love with the boy's adoptive father? What if the boy resents her, thinking she is trying to take his "mom's" place?

I do hope you enjoy sharing Laura's struggle to fulfill her *Heart's Yearning* as much as I enjoyed creating it.

Happy reading,

Ginna Gray

To Pam Zollman.
She shared my disappointments,
encouraged me when I was down,
and rejoiced with me when I succeeded—
a true friend.
I don't even mind her
"I told you so's."

Chapter One

Laura's nerves were screaming. She stood for a moment, her clenched fist pressed against her stomach in a vain effort to stop the tremors that raced through her, and stared at the neat gold letters affixed to the door.

ADAM KINCAID
ATTORNEY AT LAW

She was so close. So very close. All she had to do was step through that door. The thought brought with it a fresh wave of panic that caused her chest to tighten painfully.

Laura closed her eyes and pressed her lips together. This is stupid, she told herself bracingly, drawing in several slow, deep breaths. There's no reason to feel guilty. You're not doing anything illegal or immoral. The appointment has been set up for weeks. You have a legitimate business reason for seeking out Adam Kincaid. *And a very personal one also*, her conscience prodded mercilessly.

Laura opened her eyes and looked at the door again. It

wasn't too late to change her mind. She could return to the inn, call and cancel the appointment, and drive back to Houston tonight, and no one would be the wiser.

A heavy sigh escaped her. She could...but she wasn't going to. She'd come too far. Waited too long. She couldn't go on wondering. Longing. Lord help her, she simply couldn't.

Without giving herself further time to think, Laura swallowed hard, squared her shoulders, and reached for the doorknob.

The woman behind the desk looked up when Laura entered the office, an expectant smile forming on her face. She was in her early thirties, fair-haired, blue-eyed, with freckles and a fresh, guileless look that spoke of small-town wholesomeness.

"Hello. I'm Laura Phillips. I have an appointment to see Mr. Kincaid," Laura said as she approached the desk, wincing inwardly at the shakiness of her voice.

"Oh, yes, Mrs. Phillips. We've been expecting you," the woman replied in the slow drawl common to central Texas. "If you'll just have a seat, I'll go find out if Mr. Kincaid can see you now."

Calling on every scrap of the poise she had carefully cultivated over the years, Laura managed to appear calm as she sat down on the wine-colored leather sofa and watched the young woman disappear through the door, but her heart was pounding so hard against her ribs, it felt as though it were about to burst. No matter the outcome, the next few minutes were going to have a profound effect on her future.

Adam's hand moved steadily back and forth across the page, rapidly filling the yellow legal pad with his bold scrawl. His strong-boned face was set and intense, and an unruly lock of sable brown hair fell across his forehead. He was aware of Carly Sue entering the office and closing the door behind her, but his eyes remained fixed on the paper and he continued to write furiously. When he reached the end of the paragraph, he looked up and cocked one dark brow.

"Mrs. Phillips is here." His brow rose a fraction higher at the air of suppressed excitement he detected in his normally down-to-earth secretary, but before he could respond she went on in a rush. "Oh, Adam, wait until you see her. She's *beautiful*. And so elegant and refined looking. A real lady. And, if that bronze Continental she's driving is anything to go by, she's rich, too."

Adam tossed his pen down on the desk and leaned back in his chair, his broad shoulders flexing beneath the white cotton dress shirt. Amusement glinted in his hazel eyes and a hint of a smile tugged at one corner of his mouth. "Well, at least now I know why you didn't use the intercom to announce her. Is there any other little tidbit you feel I should know about my prospective client before I meet her?" The hint of a smile blossomed into a teasing grin as he laced his fingers together behind his head and relaxed in an indolent pose.

Ignoring his little dig, Carly Sue crossed the room. With elaborate casualness, she propped her hip against the desk and traced a smudged spiral across the glossy walnut surface. She cut her eyes at Adam and gave him a sly look. "According to Dink, she's also a widow."

Though he had been born there and had lived there most of his life, Adam was continually amazed by the speed with which news traveled in the small community. There was no such thing as complete privacy or anonymity in Oakridge. Your neighbors tended to know your business almost as soon as you did. Sometimes sooner.

It could be a bit annoying at times, but Adam considered it a small price to pay for the privilege of living in a small town where you knew most of the people by their first names and life wasn't a continuous frantic scramble.

Adam knew that Carly Sue's second cousin, Howard Pettigrew, otherwise known as Dink, worked at the Oakridge

Inn. No doubt he had called her with all the pertinent information before the ink had dried on the register.

With irreverent amusement, Adam wondered how Mrs. Phillips would react if she knew that within minutes of checking into the inn everyone in town knew her name and marital status and had a fairly good estimation of her net worth.

"I see. Well, thank you for telling me, Carly Sue. I'll be sure to give the lady my condolences when I see her. *If* I ever see her, that is," he added pointedly.

The look Carly Sue leveled on him was one of pure exasperation. "I swear, Adam Kincaid, I don't understand you at all. Don't you even have a speck of curiosity about the woman?"

"Sure I do. And if you'll show her in, maybe I can satisfy it." Grinning, he weathered another of Carly Sue's glowers.

Head high, she stalked toward the door in a huff, and Adam knew that he was going to have to endure her sulks for the next few hours. But what the heck, he thought, chuckling softly as he combed his hair back in place with spread fingers. It was worth it. He got a charge out of teasing Carly Sue, watching her ruffle her feathers like an old banty hen. Hell, he'd been doing it since she was a skinny, knobby-kneed kid, trailing around after him and her brother, Dan. It was too late to stop now.

As he rolled down his shirt cuffs and refastened them, Adam's mind turned to the woman waiting in the outer office. He had to admit, he *was* curious. He had been since he received her letter three weeks ago. Why on earth would a woman who owned and operated a successful string of very stylish Houston boutiques want to open one in a small, sleepy town like Oakridge? San Antonio or Austin he could understand. But Oakridge? Shaking his head, Adam rolled to his feet and plucked his suit coat off the wooden rack in the corner. He had just slipped into it and was adjusting his necktie when his secretary returned and announced coolly, "Mrs. Phillips to see you, Mr. Kincaid."

Adam looked up, a ready smile forming on his face, but as he caught sight of the woman entering the room his eyes widened slightly and his breath seemed to catch in his throat. Laura Phillips was not at all what he'd expected.

He had been prepared to greet a brittle sophisticate, a polished, glossily turned-out big-city career woman, the kind he and Carol had encountered so often during their disastrous sojourn in Dallas. Not this exquisite, delicate beauty.

Hold it. Don't be fooled by the packaging, old man. The woman's probably made of cast iron, with a voice that cuts like Toledo steel.

Suddenly he noted the wary, almost frightened look in her eyes and realized that he had been staring. Clearing his throat, Adam resurrected his smile of greeting and stepped forward, his hand extended. "How do you do, Mrs. Phillips."

After the briefest hesitation she nodded and gave him her hand. It was small and warm and soft against his calloused palm, and trembled ever so slightly.

"Won't you sit down," Adam suggested, gesturing toward the chairs in front of his desk as he returned to his own on the opposite side. When they were both seated he propped his forearms on the desk top and gave her an encouraging smile. "Now, how may I be of help to you, Mrs. Phillips?"

Laura swallowed and cleared her throat. "Well, Mr. Kincaid," she began nervously, unconsciously twisting the ring on her little finger, "as I explained in my letter, I plan to open a boutique here, and I would like for you to take care of the legal end of things for me."

Adam's eyes were fixed on her, his expression serious, but inwardly he was smiling. Her voice was as soft as velvet.

He glanced at the letter which lay on the desk in front

of him. "According to this, you own seven shops in Houston, so I must assume that you already have an attorney. Surely it would be better if he handled this expansion for you?"

"Ordinarily, yes. But you see, since I plan to move to Oakridge and live here permanently, I prefer to have legal counsel close at hand. Of course, the firm of Jacobsen and Birne, working through my assistant, will continue to look after my business affairs in Houston, but I feel it would be best if you handled my personal legal business and anything pertaining to my new store."

Her voice wasn't the only thing soft about her, Adam mused as he watched her mouth form the words. The exquisitely curved lips were full and lush, and very tempting. Assuming a thoughtful pose, he leaned back in his chair and studied her from beneath half-shuttered lids. Her skin was like whipped cream and those warm, topaz eyes and long sweeping lashes gave her the look of a wary doe. Her hair was an unusual color, like honey—not brown, not red, not blond—but somewhere in between. And he'd bet his last dime that it was natural. It wasn't plastered in place with hairspray nor frizzed out like she'd just stuck her finger in an electric socket, but billowed in soft waves around her shoulders, shining and silky. He liked the way it swung freely with her slightest movement. And that mouth. Adam's eyes switched to its soft, pink fullness. Oh, yes. He definitely liked that mouth.

Shifting in his chair, Adam cleared his throat. "I see. I didn't realize that you were going to be moving here."

"In the last year, since my husband's death, I've become more and more disenchanted with city life," Laura explained with a quiet smile. She made a vague gesture with her hand. "I don't know, the fast pace, the pressure—it's all become too much for me. I find myself craving the quiet that a small town offers." Hesitating, she smiled wryly and spread her hands, palms up. "Of course, though I intend to take things easier, I couldn't just do nothing, hence the shop.''

Dissimulation did not come easy to Laura, and she lowered her eyes to her hands, not quite able to meet his interested gaze. She wished it could have been different, but as much as she would have liked to tell him the truth, she knew it would only be met with suspicion. Maybe even outright hostility. It was naive to think otherwise, and though her conscience bothered her, it was a risk she could not afford to take. Not that she had told him a lie, she hastened to assure herself. Well...she had and she hadn't. She *was* sick of the pressure and the frantic pace and she *did* look forward to the quiet of small-town living. They just weren't her main reasons for making this move. But Adam Kincaid didn't need to know that, she told herself stoutly. Pushing aside the irritating twinge of guilt, Laura lifted her eyes and returned his look with a weak smile.

"I see. And how did you come to pick Oakridge?''

"I, uh...I found it by accident when I took a wrong turn off the freeway, and I fell in love with the place on sight.''

"And myself?''

"Your name is listed in the phone book,'' Laura replied quickly, after a brief hesitation.

Adam chuckled and shook his head. "Not very bolstering to the ego, but at least now I know that listing is worth the fee.''

Laura smiled sheepishly, feeling like a fool for not having anticipated the question so that she could have a better answer ready, but Adam merely cocked his head to one side and contemplated her over-steepled fingers, seemingly not in the least put out.

"Do you really think that a shop like the ones you have in Houston will succeed here? I mean, Oakridge is just a sleepy little town, and the lifestyle is hardly cosmopolitan.''

Taken aback by the question, Laura gave him a faintly startled look. She had thought he would be glad to have a new business open up, and that he would welcome the possibility of acquiring a new client. She certainly hadn't expected him to try and discourage her. Had she annoyed him in some way? Had he taken a dislike to her? The thought sent a cold trickle of fear down Laura's spine. Adam Kincaid's good will was absolutely essential.

"Yes. Yes, I do," she rushed to assure him. "I realize that I'll have to adjust my stock, concentrate more on casual clothes than on formal, but even those will be of a much higher quality than anything that is currently being offered here in town. And it's my belief that all women, regardless of their lifestyle or where they live, want to look nice and to have nice clothes."

Slowly Adam's hazel eyes skimmed over her elegantly simple teal dress and the supple taupe suede belt that encircled her tiny waist. Drifting downward, they took in the way the soft, lightweight wool lovingly outlined the slender curves of hips and thighs, the nylon-clad legs, and narrow feet shod in taupe suede sling pumps. Even more slowly his eyes retraced their path, lingering briefly on the gentle rise and fall of her breasts.

"Yes, you're probably right," he murmured as his eyes returned to her face, and Laura's breath caught as she read the hot look in their hazel depths.

Panicked dismay swept through her, creating a sickening knot in the pit of her stomach. Oh, my Lord! she thought frantically. Surely he's not going to make a pass? Adam Kincaid is a married man!

But in the next instant the passionate look had left his eyes, leaving Laura to wonder if it had been there at all or if she had just imagined it.

"What size and type of space will you need for your shop?" Adam asked in a cordial, businesslike voice. Laura breathed an inward sigh of relief as she noticed that his expression was one of mild interest, nothing more. "I know quite a few people in town. Perhaps I can help you in locating something suitable."

"Why, thank you. That would be a great help." Her

spirits soared in response to his offer. It was exactly what she had hoped for. Eagerly, she told him the approximate square footage and the type of facilities she required, then added hopefully, "Actually, I would like something on the square, if there's a vacancy."

Adam's gaze followed hers out one of the tall, old-fashioned windows beside his desk and he nodded. "Yes, that would probably be a wise choice."

Oakridge, like many of the older small towns in Texas, was built around a town square, complete with a fancy, white-painted bandstand at its center. Adam's office occupied the second floor of one of the ornate old buildings which ringed the small patch of park-like ground.

"Tell you what," Adam said, reaching for the telephone. "I'll check with Cory Bates. He handles most of the real estate around here."

As Adam talked with Mr. Bates, Laura used the opportunity to study him. She had known from the detective's report what Adam would look like—thirty-nine years old, six foot one inch tall, approximately one hundred and eighty pounds, dark brown hair, hazel eyes. But those were mere facts on paper. Nothing had prepared her for the sensual impact of the man himself. Statistics could not convey the masculine appeal of that lean, square-jawed face or the sensuality of that wide, chiseled mouth. And hazel was too bland a word to describe those slumbrous, deep-set eyes. No. Adam Kincaid wasn't at all the way she had pictured him in her mind.

He wasn't even her idea of what an attorney ought to look like. The three-piece charcoal suit fitted him to perfection and the crisp white shirt was stunning against his darkly tanned skin, but somehow the clothes seemed too tame for the man. He was broad at the shoulders and lean at the middle, and even though he was a big man he moved with the lanky, loose-limbed grace of a cowboy. Even his hands, she remembered, were hard with calluses.

But even more disturbing than Adam's appearance was

her reaction to him, this quivering awareness she felt whenever he looked at her, whenever he spoke in that deep, rumbling baritone. It had never occurred to her that she might be physically attracted to Adam Kincaid. Certainly it was the last thing she wanted.

If that look he gave her was anything to go by, the attraction was not one-sided. It was disturbing, but at least Adam didn't appear to be inclined to pursue the matter, and that was what counted. She would hate to think that he was the kind of man who would cheat on his wife.

"Well, you're in luck," Adam said as he hung up the phone. "Cory said that the old Blyden building, on the other side of the square, is for lease. It's housed Clarkes' Mercantile store for over eighty years, but Agnes and Luther Clarke both passed away last year. None of the heirs are interested in taking over the store and they've been unable to find a buyer, so they're going to liquidate the stock. They should be moved out in ten days to two weeks." Adam scrawled something on a notepad and handed it to her. "Here's Cory's phone number. His office is over on the other side of the square. He said he'd be glad to show you around tomorrow morning."

"Terrific. Maybe while I'm there he can help me find a house."

"Mmmmm. You may have a hard time there. Houses for rent are scarce as hens' teeth around here, and ones for sale even more so." Seeing Laura's disheartened look, Adam frowned thoughtfully. He was silent for a moment, then surprised them both by saying, "But, as it happens, I may be able to help you there. My grandparents' old place has been sitting vacant for a couple of years now and I've been toying with the idea of selling it. I inherited it along with a couple of hundred acres of land. I run a few head of cattle on the property, but the house is located on the far side and fenced off from the rest. I warn you, it's a big old-fashioned Victorian barn of a house, but if you think you might be interested I could take you out to look at it."

"Oh, I'm very interested. And I adore Victorian architecture."

"Fine. I have a few more appointments here, but I should be able to wind things up by about five. How about if I pick you up then?"

"That would be perfect."

As Laura rose Adam came around the desk and walked with her to the door. "By the way, if it turns out that you're interested in renting the space Cory shows you, bring the lease agreement by tomorrow and I'll look it over."

Laura was about to burst with sheer jubilation. It had worked. She now had a definite connection with Adam Kincaid. With patience and time, there was no reason why the rest of her plan shouldn't succeed. She looked up at him and smiled brilliantly. "Thanks. I will."

When they stepped into the outer office, a teenage boy jumped up from the chair by Carly Sue's desk, his face bright with anticipation.

"Mike!" Adam exclaimed in a pleased voice. "I didn't expect you so soon. How'd it go with Dr. Conrad?"

An ear-splitting grin stretched across the youth's face. "Great. He signed the release and said I could go back to football practice anytime."

"Terrific." Adam clapped him on the back and ruffled his black hair affectionately. With his arm around the boy's shoulder, he turned him toward Laura. "Mrs. Phillips, I'd like you to meet my son, Mike," he said proudly. When the young woman behind the desk cleared her throat and shot him a pointed look, he added with a grin, "And this is my secretary, Carly Sue Paxton. Mike, Carly Sue, this is Mrs. Phillips, a new client of mine. She's going to move to Oakridge and open a business here."

"I'm very pleased to meet you, Mrs. Phillips. I hope you'll like living in Oakridge," Carly Sue said in her friendliest voice.

Laura barely heard her.

She was standing stock-still, hardly able to breathe, staring transfixed at the boy who had mumbled a quick hello and was now shifting self-consciously from one foot to the other. Her heart was pounding so hard and so fast it was almost suffocating her. One thought, and one thought only, kept repeating itself in her mind.

My son. This is my son.

Chapter Two

Laura would have recognized him even without the introduction. He looked exactly the way Keith had looked fifteen years ago. Except for his eyes. Those he had gotten from her.

Emotions swamped her, clogging her throat and squeezing her chest, making her knees weak and her head spin. Her heartbeat thundered in her ears. For the first time in over fourteen years she was seeing her son. It had happened only once before. Then it had been a mere glimpse of a red, squalling face, a cap of black hair, of tiny fists flailing over the top of the blanket as the nurse took him out of the delivery room. Out of her life. And even that brief look had been blurred by tears.

"Are you all right, Mrs. Phillips?"

It took a few seconds for Adam's question to register. "What?" Laura asked blankly as she reluctantly dragged her eyes away from Mike and met his father's puzzled look. Then, with a jolt, she realized that she had been staring.

"Oh! Oh, yes, I'm fine." Desperately, she gathered her scattered wits and struggled to pull herself together. Her breathing was still shallow and her insides were quivering, but outwardly she managed to present a semblance of calm. "I'm sorry, my mind was wandering. Please excuse me."

Not quite meeting his eyes, Laura smiled nervously at Adam, then extended her hand to Carly Sue. "I'm very glad to meet you, Ms. Paxton." Irresistibly her eyes slid back to her son. "And you, too, Mike," she added softly.

Hooking his thumbs into the front pockets of his jeans, Mike studied his scruffy tennis shoes. His neck and the tops of his ears turned pink.

"Oh, please, call me Carly Sue," Adam's secretary insisted, breaking the awkward silence. "If you're going to live here, we'll be seeing each other often, I'm sure."

"Thank you. And I'm Laura."

"What kind of business are you planning to open, Laura?" Carly Sue asked eagerly, her eyes alight with curiosity.

"A dress shop." Laura's smile was self-deprecating. "In Houston they're called boutiques, but I always think of them as shops." She was trying hard to keep her eyes off Mike, but she was aware of him with every fiber in her body. Her nerves were humming like high-voltage wires.

"Hey, great! It's about time we women had a decent place to shop around here. I buy the basics locally—you know, jeans, T-shirts, that sort of thing—but when I want something stylish I have to drive to San Antonio."

Growing increasingly impatient with the feminine talk, Mike nudged his father's arm. "Uh, Dad. I gotta go or I'm gonna be late for practice, so could you sign the release? You know how the coach is. He won't let you come back after an injury unless both the doctor and the parent sign it."

Laura's head snapped around, her topaz eyes wide. "You've been injured?" she asked in a small, strained voice. The thought of any harm coming to him made her sick with fear.

"Naw, it wasn't much. Just a little sprain." Mike dismissed the matter with the prideful disdain of a very young male. "I could have played last week if the doc wasn't such a fuss-budget."

The urge to question him further was strong but Laura held it in check. At this point, she knew she couldn't afford to show too much concern.

"Here you go, son." Adam straightened from signing the slip of paper and handed it back to the boy. Grinning, he clapped his shoulder and gave him a light shove. "Now, go on. And tell the coach I said to work your tail off."

"No sweat. He does that anyway." Stuffing the paper in his hip pocket, Mike muttered a quick goodbye and headed for the door at a pace just short of a run. No sooner had it closed behind him than it opened again and he stuck his head back inside. His eyes sought Laura and one side of his mouth lifted in a lopsided, self-conscious grin. "Uh...it was nice meeting you, Mrs. Phillips."

Laura thought her heart would burst. "It was nice meeting you, too, Mike," she replied with a tremulous smile, barely getting the words out through her aching throat.

As his footsteps clumped down the stairs Laura swallowed hard and drew a deep breath. "That's quite a boy you have there, Mr. Kincaid," she said quietly.

"Yes. Yes, he is," Adam agreed, and when she glanced up at him Laura saw that he was staring at the closed door, his face filled with fatherly pride.

Joy and gladness, and a profound gratitude swelled within Laura, adding an additional burden to her overwrought emotions. She knew if she didn't get out of there, they were going to overwhelm her. She needed to be alone, to sort out her feelings, to absorb all that had happened.

Sending the room's other two occupants a bright smile, Laura began to edge toward the door. "Well, I really must be going. It was nice meeting you both. And I'll see you later, Mr. Kincaid.''

"Yes. At five.''

When she had gone Carly Sue cocked her head to one side and murmured thoughtfully, ''Now, that's what I call one classy lady. But I can't help but wonder why a woman like that would want to move to Oakridge and open a shop.''

For a moment Adam didn't reply. Then he pulled his gaze away from the closed door and looked at her. ''I've been wondering the same thing myself.''

"Well, whatever, it's our gain. And I intend to be her first customer.''

"I wouldn't count on it,'' Adam remarked sardonically as he turned and started for his office. ''It's probably just a whim. Five'll get you ten she'll grow tired of the whole thing and hightail it back to Houston before she even gets the place ready to open.''

"You're on, smarty,'' Carly Sue called out disrespectfully as he closed the door behind him.

After shrugging out of his coat, Adam walked back to his desk, determined to finish the work he had started earlier, but as he passed the windows he spied Laura cutting diagonally across the square toward the inn. He stopped and stood with his feet braced apart, hands loosely splayed on his hipbones, watching her. She walked with the fluid grace that seemed to typify all her movements. A gentle breeze tossed her honey-colored hair around her shoulders and molded the soft wool dress against her legs. Adam's eyes fell naturally to the gentle undulation of her hips, and he felt an immediate tightening in his loins. A curse, searing and explicit, hissed from his lips but his gaze never left her.

What was it about the woman that drew him? Because there was no denying it; he was fascinated. Fascinated, irritated, and damned uncomfortable. From the moment she walked in the door he'd had to struggle to keep his mind on business...and his eyes off her body. She was a lovely woman, certainly. Those delicate features set in a perfect oval face added up to a fragile, almost ethereal beauty that took a man's breath away. But there was more to it than that, he knew. It was the way she moved, the honeyed quality of her voice, her gentle manner, that inexplicable air of vulnerability about her. Laura Phillips was without doubt the most utterly feminine woman he had ever met. Utterly feminine and *very* sexy. It made a man want to protect her and ravish her all at the same time.

And those eyes. His expression brooding, Adam watched Laura cross the street and climb the three steps to the wide veranda that stretched across the front of the inn. *Every time I look into those warm brown eyes it feels as though my insides are melting.* Of course, he told himself ruefully, you've got a weakness for big, soulful, topaz eyes. Heaven knows, Mike has used his to advantage more than once.

A heavy sigh escaped Adam as Laura disappeared into the inn. It had been a long time since he'd been this attracted to a woman. Hell, who was he kidding? He'd *never* been this attracted to a woman. Not even Carol.

Pain flickered across his face at the thought of his wife. No. No, he couldn't let himself get involved with a woman like Laura Phillips. He didn't need that kind of trouble.

Slowly Adam's gaze wandered over the buildings that surrounded the square. There were a few brick fronts to be seen, but most, like the inn, were made of limestone. All were two-storied, old and ornate, built in a bygone era when a higher value was placed on beauty and craftsmanship. There was a steadiness here, a stability that he found comforting. The oak trees in the square had been there since before the first settlers arrived, and the pristine white bandstand, with its fancy Victorian gingerbread trim, had been built before the turn of the century. The town was quiet and unpretentious, the pace slow, the people friendly. And he loved it, every last brick and stone.

He had left it for a while but he had come back. Now

he had put down roots, found his niche, and, if not ecstat-
ically happy, he was content with his life. He would be a
fool to let a woman, *any* woman, disrupt it. Especially one
like Laura Phillips.

With a groan, Adam turned away from the window and
flopped down in his chair. Why on earth had he offered to
show her his grandparents' house? Until that moment he'd
had no real plans for selling it, but somehow, when she'd
mentioned needing a place to live, the words had just come
tumbling out.

Stupid ass! Being alone with Laura in that deserted house
was just asking for trouble. Selling it to her was even cra-
zier. The old homestead was on a corner of his property,
only about a mile beyond his own home on a dead-end
country lane, and there were no other neighbors around for
miles.

Grim-faced, Adam stared at the telephone on his desk.
*If you're smart, Kincaid, you'll call the woman and tell her
you've changed your mind.*

Laura's heart was still pounding madly when she unlocked the door to her room and stepped inside. As though
in a daze, she tossed her purse on the dresser, stepped out
of her shoes, and collapsed onto the bed. Lying on her back,
staring blindly at the plastered ceiling, she savored the
quivering excitement that suffused every cell in her body.

She had seen her son. Talked to him. Been close enough
to touch him.

The thought brought a fresh surge of emotions, so intense
Laura felt as though her heart would burst. Pressing her
palms against her midriff, she squeezed her eyes tightly
shut and fought to contain the sweet, joyous ache.

It was more than she had expected, more than she'd
dared even to hope for, meeting him so soon. But now that
she had, she was more determined than ever to stay. The
last-minute doubts she had experienced before entering

Adam Kincaid's office had vanished the instant she had come face to face with her son.

Before, he had been a faceless, shadowy figure that clutched at her heart, but now he was reality—form and substance, a recognizable individual. No longer would she search the face of every fourteen-year-old boy she saw and wonder...and die a little inside. Now she knew. And knowing, how could she possibly leave?

A smile curved Laura's mouth as she pictured his face, the irrepressible grin that formed a deep dimple in his left cheek that she knew he probably hated. It was obvious that the Kincaids had done a good job in raising Mike. He seemed healthy and happy and full of life, delightfully normal. And he was such a fine-looking boy, with his black hair and clean-cut features. When he was older he was going to be a very handsome man, indeed...just like his father.

Opening her eyes, Laura rose from the bed and slowly walked to one of the tall windows that overlooked the square, her stocking-clad feet making no sound as she crossed the faded oriental rug. She folded her arms over her midriff and absently massaged her elbows, a pensive look settling over her face as she gazed out through the old-fashioned lace curtains. For years she had pushed out of her mind all thought of the man who had fathered her son , but meeting Mike, seeing the uncanny resemblance, had opened the gate on the past. Memories, images, came flooding in and she was powerless to stop them.

Keith Hunter. He had been the epitome of every young girl's dreams: tall, dark, handsome, and utterly charming. He had been twenty that summer, a junior in college, and at sixteen she had thought him wonderfully mature and sophisticated.

She had been thrilled when he'd asked her out, but when she'd sought her parents' permission to date him, they had quickly burst her bubble of happiness.

"Absolutely not, young lady," her father had thundered. "I wouldn't let you go out with a boy your own age. I'm certainly not going to allow you to date some wild college boy.''

"But, Father," she'd pleaded, "we wouldn't be going out alone. Keith wants to take me to a party. It's going to be at Della Chapman's house."

"I know what kind of parties you young people have today. Drinking and drugs and sex. That's all your generation ever thinks about." He eyed her coldly, his face like granite. "No daughter of mine is going to get a chance to behave that way."

"But it won't be like that, I promise. And Della's parents will even be there to chaperone."

"The matter is closed, Laura." He gave his newspaper a snap and raised it in front of his face.

"Please, just—"

"You heard your father, Laura," her mother interjected in her calm, controlled voice. She didn't bother to look up from the sweater she was knitting. "The answer is no."

Laura knew there was no point in arguing further. Her parents were rigid, unbending people. They had made their decision. Hell would freeze over before they would change it. She stood there for a moment and stared at them, her eyes swimming with hurt and frustration. Then she burst into tears and ran from the room.

Neither of her parents followed her to offer consolation, nor did she expect them to. They were not demonstrative people. Not once could Laura remember them kissing her, or even touching her with affection. Nor could she recall seeing them display any tenderness or feeling for each other. Curled up in a tight ball of misery, she lay on her bed for hours, sobbing quietly and wondering how she was going to face Keith.

But to her surprise, Keith was understanding.

"Hey, babe, don't cry," he crooned when she sobbed out her story the next day. "It's not the end of the world. So your folks won't let us go out together. So what? Big deal. We just won't tell them."

Laura looked up at him and blinked, and scrubbed at her wet cheeks with the back of her hand. "You...you mean...meet secretly?" she gulped, hope and doubt warring within her. "You wouldn't mind?"

"Naw. Besides..." Keith cupped her chin in his palm and rubbed his thumb back and forth across her lips. His eyes glittered warmly as he gave her a slow, secret smile that sent delicious shivers down her spine. "...this way it'll be even more romantic."

Laura gazed up at him with shining eyes, sure that she had found her Prince Charming.

Looking up at the sky, Laura shook her head in disgust. It was hard to believe that she'd ever been that young and foolish. What Keith Hunter had been was a callow, selfish youth with a smooth line. And she had fallen for it. Oh, how she had fallen for it, Laura reflected bitterly. She had been so starved for love and affection, she had responded to his smooth words and clever blandishments like a flower opening its petals to the sun.

Looking back, she could see that the cold sterility of her upbringing had made it easy for Keith to seduce her. At sixteen her need for love had been a raw hunger that ate at her soul. She had eagerly believed his passionate avowals, reveled in his tender caresses. In love, and believing herself loved at last, she had been unable to deny him anything.

The physical intimacy had not been all that wonderful, but Laura had adored the touching, the closeness, the cuddling that went with it. She had wanted it never to end. Had been sure that it never would.

But it had. Suddenly. Cruelly.

She had been frightened when she began to suspect that she was pregnant, and that fright had grown worse when the doctor confirmed it, but she had also been absolutely confident that Keith would make it right. They would get married. It would be difficult, true, with both of them still in school and no job. But they would make it. After all, they were in love and they had each other.

The memory of her naiveté drew a disdainful snort from Laura. What a fool she'd been. What a young, blind fool. Less than twenty-four hours after she'd told him she was pregnant, Keith had left town. She had tried desperately to find out from his parents where he'd gone, but they refused to speak to her, and within a month they had gone also.

Laura had been left with shattered dreams, a broken heart, and the terrifying prospect of telling her parents of her condition.

The sudden loud jangle of the telephone made Laura jump, jerking her out of her painful reverie. She hurried to the bedside table to pick the receiver up.

"Hello."

"Laura? It's Diane. The suspense has been killing me all day and I couldn't wait another minute. So tell me quick, how did it go?"

Laura sank down on the side of the bed, smiling at the anxious note in her assistant's voice. It was an excellent indicator of the state of her friend's nerves. Calm, steady, frighteningly efficient Diane never got flustered, never lost her cool.

"I saw him, Diane," Laura whispered shakily, her eyes closed against the renewed rush of sheer joy that swelled in her chest. "I saw him."

"Who, Adam Kincaid?"

"No, my son." Laura's voice cracked on the last word as she said it aloud for the first time. "I saw my son."

There was a beat of silence, tense, unsure. "Oh, Laura," Diane murmured in a subdued, troubled voice. "So soon? And how? Do you mean from a distance? What?"

"No, I met him. Talked to him. It was after my meeting with his father. When we came out of his office, Mike was waiting in the reception room. Oh, Diane, you should see him," Laura went on in a rush. "He's everything you could ask for in a son."

"I'm sure he is," Diane said quietly. "But I'm sorry, Laura, I still think you're making a mistake. Why don't you come back home where you belong and forget this crazy scheme."

Sighing, Laura bent her head and absently rubbed her forehead with the tips of her fingers. It was an old argument, one they had been over many times. "No. No, I can't do that. Especially not now."

Diane muttered something under her breath. "I knew this would happen if you ever saw him! Dammit, Laura! You can't do this! It's—"

"I'm not doing anything wrong!" Laura countered, gripping the receiver fiercely. "I'm not going to try to take Mike away from the Kincaids. I'm not even going to let him, or them, know who I am. I just want to be here so that I can see him once in a while. Watch him grow up. Maybe, if I'm lucky, even get to know him." Laura's voice dropped to a whisper that quivered with emotion. "That's all. Surely you can understand that."

There was a long sigh at the other end of the line. "Yes, of course I can," Diane agreed softly, but there was a touch of sadness in the placating words. "It's just that things are never that simple. I don't want to see you hurt, Laura."

Laura smiled, some of the tenseness draining out of her. Diane, in addition to being her second in command, was her closest friend, and the only person, other than her husband, whom she had ever told about her past. She had been the first salesperson Laura had hired when she opened her original shop, ten years ago. Newly widowed at the time, Diane had been in her late thirties, with three strapping sons to feed and absolutely no job experience, and Laura had not had the heart to turn her down. It was a decision she had never regretted. Diane was personable, hard-working, and had a bent for organizing that made her invaluable.

Years ago, after exhausting themselves getting ready for a sale, they had shared a late night meal at a little Italian restaurant around the corner from the shop, and somehow, over lasagna and a bottle of Chianti, had found themselves exchanging life stories. The bond that was forged that night had proved to be a strong one.

"Don't worry, Diane, I'm not going to get hurt," Laura assured her gently. "No one will ever know who I am, and I promise you, I'm not expecting too much from this."

"Oh, Laura, that's just my point. What kind of life is that for you, always on the outside looking in, like a kid with her nose pressed against the candy store window?"

"Diane, please. I don't want to argue about this. My mind is made up."

"All right, all right, I'll hush," her friend conceded reluctantly, then could not resist adding, "But you know as well as I do that John would not have approved."

As she had intended, the words struck home, and for a moment Laura closed her eyes against the guilt and pain that pierced her. Diane was right; John would not have approved. Her husband had adored her and had seldom opposed her in anything, but he would have been appalled to know that she had used the detective's reports to locate Mike. He had only ordered the investigation in order to set her mind at ease, knowing that she still grieved over the loss of her child and longed to at least know his whereabouts and that he was happy and well cared for. John had given her every scrap of information the detective had uncovered, except for names and the town where they lived.

It wasn't until months after John was killed in a car crash, when she had finally recovered enough to go through his things, that she had found the detective's reports. It was then, as she had sat there reading them over and over, that the idea of moving to Oakridge had begun to form. For the past year she had struggled against temptation, guilt, and need pulling her in two directions. In the end need had won. She had been left alone, with no one to love, and the pull of that lost child had simply been too strong to resist.

And now that she had seen him, it was impossible.

After a moment of strained silence Laura replied, "I

know that, Diane, but it doesn't change anything. I'm staying."

There was determination in the softly spoken words that reflected an inner core of strength in Laura, the existence of which few people even suspected. Diane had recognized it a long time ago.

"Okay, boss," she said with a sigh. "You win. But at least tell me about your meeting with Mr. Kincaid. Is he anything like you thought he'd be?"

Laura stirred uneasily as she recalled the sensations that Adam Kincaid had aroused in her. "Yes, he's very nice, and he seems to be a very good father. At least, Mike seems crazy about him. He's agreed to take me on as a client, and this afternoon he's even going to show me a house he has for sale. And speaking of which, if I don't hang up and get a move on, I'm going to be late," she said, groping for an excuse to end the conversation. Strangely, she found that she didn't want to discuss Adam Kincaid with Diane.

"Okay, I'll let you go. But you be sure and keep me posted, you hear?"

"I will, don't worry. And Diane..." Laura paused, her face softening with affection. "Thanks for caring."

"Sure. That's what friends are for."

When she hung up the phone Laura just sat for several minutes, staring at it. Her reaction to Adam, to even the mere mention of his name, disturbed her. And annoyed her. She didn't want to be attracted to any man. Especially not a married one. *Most* especially not to this one.

A glance at her watch prodded Laura into action and she rose, unzipping her dress as she walked to the walnut armoire that served as a closet. It's just physical attraction, she told herself firmly. Some kind of weird "chemistry." As two mature adults, we should be able to ignore it. She hung up her dress and slipped it into the closet and pulled out a pair of oatmeal-colored raw silk slacks and a loose, string-knit brown top. It's probably just a temporary aberration anyway, she thought crossly. Once I meet Carol Kincaid and get to know her and Adam as a couple, I'm sure it will pass.

Laura fell in love with the house on sight. There was a kind of warmth about it, a coziness, that appealed to a deep-seated need in her. She could imagine it sheltering a large, close-knit family, the kind for which she had always longed, filled with laughter and love, smelling of fresh-baked bread and apple pies.

Old and stately, like a haughty dowager whose once great beauty was still apparent despite the passage of time, the house sat far back off the narrow lane in isolated splendor. The clapboard siding was painted a mellow sandalwood, the ornate gingerbread trim a soft, contrasting cream. The wraparound porch had an inviting Queen Anne cupola at one corner, with a conical metal roof that resembled a dunce cap. Looking at it, and the inviting wooden swings on both the front and side porches, made Laura think of lazy summer afternoons and lemonade. The double front doors were of intricately carved walnut and each held a large oval of frosted, etched glass. Four brick chimneys jutted from the steeply pitched roof which soared among the spreading branches of the surrounding oak trees. Around the base of the house a wide, weed-choked flowerbed held a variety of overgrown shrubs and plants, and along one side an untended rosebush struggled up a trellis. Though it was mid-September, a few scraggly blossoms made a crimson splash against the clapboard structure.

The yard was neatly mowed, but beyond the white-painted fence that surrounded it on three sides, the land was wild and untamed.

"Oh, Adam, it's lovely," Laura said as they climbed the four steps to the front porch. She stood to one side while he fitted the key into the ornate brass lock, her eyes shining. There were small signs of neglect: cobwebs, wasp nests, a layer of dirt and grime, but nothing that couldn't be easily set to right.

"Better wait until you've seen the inside before you make any snap decisions."

Stale air, dust, and trapped heat enveloped them when they stepped through the door. Laura gasped and fanned her hand in front of her face.

"I'll open some windows," Adam said, moving around her to disappear into the parlor.

Standing in the dim foyer, Laura gazed slowly around. An intricately carved Victorian halltree with copper hat hooks and a wavy, beveled mirror sat against one wall, and opposite it was a huge grandfather clock. Through the arched opening to her left, Laura saw a green velvet medallion-back settee, a rococo chair and a hand-painted double-globe lamp on a marble-topped table. The house had a feeling of grace and charm, but Laura also noted the faded wallpaper and the worn, heart-of-pine floors, the dullness of the wainscoting. Her eyes moved up the impressive stairway to the second floor landing, and on to the soaring ceiling above, which showed signs of needing paint. The place had been a jewel when it was built, but age and the past two years of emptiness had begun to take their toll, giving it an air of genteel shabbiness.

"It needs a little work, I'm afraid."

At the sound of Adam's voice Laura turned her head. He was standing at the arched entrance to the parlor, watching her, and in that instant when their eyes met she felt the same sharp pull of desire she had felt earlier, when he had picked her up. It had upset her then and it upset her now, but there didn't seem to be a thing she could do about it. Despite the upbraiding she had given herself during the four-mile drive from town, his nearness had caused her entire body to tingle with excitement.

Laura tore her eyes away from his and looked around again, struggling against the painful tightness in her chest. She was suddenly, alarmingly aware of how completely alone they were.

She cleared her throat, but when she spoke her voice held

a husky tremor. "Yes, a bit," she agreed. "But the results should be well worth it. If I'm not mistaken, all the wood-work, including the banister, is either mahogany or cherry. With some refinishing and new wallpaper the house could be beautiful."

Adam watched her intently. He had seen that brief flash of awareness in her eyes. And her instant withdrawal. There had even been a touch of fear in that look. She was at-tracted, but it was fairly obvious that Laura Phillips was no more interested in getting involved than he was. Terrific. That suited him right down to the ground.

"The kitchen and the bathrooms were renovated a couple of years ago, with a few modern conveniences added, and the wiring and plumbing are in good shape. Basically all it needs is a facelift."

As Laura looked around once again Adam's eyes traced over the graceful curve of her throat. He felt an urge to press his lips against that delicate skin. To taste her there. And other places. Irresistibly, his gaze dropped to the gentle swell of her breasts. Through the loose-knit brown top he caught a glimpse of ecru lace, and felt an immediate tight-ening in his lower body. *Oh, hell! I don't need this. I should have used my head and told her to forget it.*

Abruptly, Adam stalked into the foyer and grasped Laura's elbow, making her jump. "Come on," he said tersely. "I'll show you the rest of it."

As they moved from room to room they were both scru-pulously polite, their conversation neutral and businesslike. They were both careful never to look directly into the other's eyes, and except when Adam occasionally placed a guiding hand at her back or on her elbow, they kept a prudent distance between them. Even so, Laura could feel the very air around them pulsing with awareness. She knew that Adam could feel it, too.

They covered the downstairs, then the upstairs, finally ending up in the master bedroom. It was a corner room, with tall windows on both outside walls. The wallpaper was a pale blue floral and the pine floor was covered with an oriental rug in wine, cream, and blue. A massive walnut armoire, a marble-topped dresser, and a matching man's chest of drawers occupied two walls. Set catercornered between the windows was an enormous brass bed, covered with a cream, popcorn-stitch crocheted spread.

Broodingly, Adam watched Laura's agitated movements as she wandered around the room, touching the furnishings, the curtains, inspecting the view from the windows, looking at anything and everything but him. He knew that she was trying to keep the situation from getting out of hand, but dammit, her nervous flitting was just making things worse.

Laura came to a halt in the center of the room and looked around, trying desperately to ignore the fact that Adam was only a few feet away. The air was thick and heavy, and it had nothing to do with the closed-up stuffiness of the house.

It was getting late, and the setting sun filtering through the lace curtains lit the room with a hazy golden glow that gave it a romantic, surrealistic look. It made the polished brass bed gleam with a warm luster, and to her acute discomfort, Laura couldn't seem to keep her eyes off it. She glanced at Adam to see if he had noticed, and her heart gave a painful jerk when she saw that he was staring at her, a burning look in his eyes.

For a moment their eyes locked, and Laura felt a wild tingling run over her skin, as though every nerve ending in her body had sprung to attention. Sexual tension crackled between them. She swallowed hard, unable to speak, unable to move. She couldn't even breathe.

Panicked, Laura tore her gaze away and turned, grasping the footboard of the bed for support. The slick metal was cool against her palm. Outside a bird trilled its evening song and the cicadas set up a chorus of buzzing. All Laura heard was the heavy thudding of her heart pounding in her ears.

"Laura, look at me."

She jumped at the sound of his voice just behind her,

but she didn't turn around. Suddenly Adam's hand closed over hers, and slowly, but determinedly, he pried her fingers loose from the brass tubing and turned her around. Once again holding her captive with his burning gaze, he lifted both her hands and placed them against his chest. With infinite slowness, his hands glided down her arms, then slipped around her back and gathered her close.

"No, please," Laura pleaded as his head began its slow, inexorable descent, but the word came out as a breathless whisper, barely audible.

Adam's mouth hovered just a breath away from hers. "It's no use, Laura. I'm through fighting it."

A small, desperate sound rose up in her throat, but it was swallowed up by his gently devouring kiss. The touch of his lips against hers was electrifying. It made her heart pound and spread a tingling heat through her body that seemed to melt her bones. Helplessly, Laura's eyes fluttered shut, and as he drew her closer she sagged against him.

His body was hard and taut, incredibly arousing. His scent was intoxicating. Laura was trembling violently, on fire, her senses spinning, tumbling out of control. *This is wrong. You've got to stop. You've got to*.

Adam nibbled at her lower lip with savage tenderness and a shiver rippled through Laura. Her fingers curled into the material of his shirt, clutching it tightly. With a moan, her lips parted, yielding to his enticing demand.

Passion flared with her small surrender. As his tongue plunged into the moist warmth of her mouth, Adam urged Laura back against the footboard of the bed, pressing the length of his body against hers, running his hands feverishly over her, from waist, to hips, to thighs, and back up again to press against the soft sides of her breasts.

The cold brass pressing against her back brought a measure of sanity. Laura tore her mouth from his. "No!" When Adam would have reclaimed her lips, she turned her head aside and pushed at his chest with all her might. "No!"

Adam became perfectly still, then drew back slightly to

look at her, his hands still gripping her waist. His dark
brows drew together in a frown when he met her accusing
look, the anguish behind it. *What the hell?*

"What's the matter, Laura?"

Laura sucked in her breath at the bold question. "What's
the matter? You know perfectly well what's the matter! I'm
surprised you even have the nerve to ask." Her breast was
heaving with the force of her emotions, panic, anger, and
a deep sense of shame roiling within her.

"Don't play games, Laura. You wanted that as much as
I did. We've both been aware of the attraction between us
from the moment you stepped into my office, and you know
it."

"That is not the point!"

"Then suppose you tell me what is?" he shot back angrily.

"The point, Mr. Kincaid, is that I do *not*, under any
circumstances, become involved with married men."

"Ma—" Adam halted abruptly, his eyes going wide.
Then, as his face hardened, they narrowed. "For your information, Mrs. Phillips, I am no longer married," he said
in a low, dangerous voice. "My wife died almost two years
ago."

Chapter Three

In the thick silence that followed, Laura could only stare at him.

Adam isn't married!

Her instant reaction was relief. Then, as the full import of the situation hit her, relief changed to shocked dismay. *Dear Lord! My son has no mother!*

All this time she had pictured Mike with a set of loving parents—both a father and a mother to fuss over him and care for him, teach him the things he needed to know—and for the past two years he and his father had been alone. It was not what she wanted for her son, not what she had intended when she had given him up, and, though she knew it was irrational, for a moment Laura felt cheated, betrayed. But then she looked up and met Adam's angry gaze and thought of all that he and Mike had lost, and she was pierced with a deep sense of sorrow for both of them.

"I...I'm so sorry, I..." Laura blinked her eyes against

incipient tears and drew a steadying breath. "I didn't know."

Adam frowned at the suspicious moistness in Laura's eyes, his expression briefly puzzled. "No. You just assumed that I was married and not averse to a little fooling around." Disgusted, Adam turned away and walked to one of the windows. He stood staring out, his hands in his pockets. His back was rigid and she could see a muscle jumping in his jaw.

"Adam, please I—"

"If you've seen enough, we'd better go," he said curtly. "It will be dark soon." Without waiting for her, or even looking in her direction, Adam turned and walked out the door.

Numb, Laura listened to his quick, angry footsteps recede down the stairs. By the time she roused herself enough to follow, he had already left the house.

He was so angry. And she really didn't blame him. But it had never occurred to her that he was no longer married. It should have, she realized now. Instinct alone should have told her that Adam was not the kind of man to play around. Laura heaved a sigh of pure self-disgust. She couldn't believe she'd botched things so.

After closing and locking the windows, she stepped out onto the front porch and found that he was waiting in his pickup with the motor running.

The moment Laura slid in beside him and closed the door Adam reversed out of the drive and started back down the narrow lane toward the highway. He didn't speak, and after a quick glance at his set profile, Laura prudently decided on the same course. She turned her head and gazed out the side window.

The thick woods grew right up to the edge of the road on either side. There were no streetlights in the country, and without them it was as dark as the bottom of a well. The only sounds were the low purr of the engine and the pop of gravel beneath the tires.

There was just one other residence along the road, a sprawling ranch-style house that Adam had earlier identified as his, and as they drove by it Laura's gaze was drawn irresistibly. There were several lights on inside the house, and the tempo of her heartbeat increased as she wondered if Mike was there.

That brief meeting with him had not been nearly enough. She had fourteen years of yearning bottled up inside her. Laura doubted that she could ever get her fill of being around him, looking at him, listening to him talk, touching him. Oh, yes, she wanted very much to touch him. Her son. Her baby.

Laura swallowed hard to ease the tightness in her throat. Did the pain ever end? The memories ever fade? Hers hadn't. For fourteen years she had lived daily with the guilt and regret. The soul-deep feeling of loss. And not one day of those fourteen years had passed that she had not asked herself if she'd made the right decision.

But then, her choices hadn't been all that many. Her parents had given her exactly two.

"We'll send you to stay with my Aunt Lucy in Dallas," her father had decreed when he had sufficiently recovered from his initial burst of rage. The look he gave her was icy cold, filled with revulsion. "When the child is born, you'll give it up for adoption."

"Give it up!" Reflexively, Laura placed her hands over her lower abdomen, as though to shield the life that was growing there. His first reaction to her stammered confession had been to give her a slap that had sent her staggering backward to sprawl awkwardly on the couch. Frightened and sick at heart, she had huddled in the corner and listened while both parents hurled abuse at her. The blistering denouncements had left her pale and shaken, but now every last vestige of color drained from her face. "But...but I *can't!*"

"You can and you will. I'll not raise your bastard for you."

"Bu-but, this is my baby. Mine. I can't just—''

"It's a child of lust and we will not have it in this house!" her father burst out viciously. A purple vein throbbed in his temple as he glared down at her, his face livid. "You will give it up or you'll pack your bags and leave this house. Tonight."

Even now, the memory of that ultimatum made Laura shiver. At sixteen the thought of being totally on her own—penniless, homeless, and pregnant—had terrified her, and she had given in. With a sigh, Laura looked down at her fingers, tightly entwined in her lap. If she had only had the courage to leave, things would have been different.

But it was no use thinking about that. She hadn't had the courage. If she had, she wouldn't have spent the past fourteen years grieving, and wondering. And she certainly wouldn't be here now, riding down a dark country road, wondering how to placate this angry man.

As Adam swung the truck out onto the highway, Laura turned her head and looked at him. In the dim glow from the dashboard his face was barely discernible, but she could tell that he was still angry. Her breath came out in a long, silent expulsion of air. Why did there have to be this damnable attraction between them? she asked herself angrily, fighting down the panicky sensation in the pit of her stomach. It was ruining everything.

The four miles into Oakridge were covered quickly. When Adam brought the truck to a halt in front of the inn, neither he nor Laura moved for a moment, and the strained silence seemed to throb between them. Finally, casting him a cautious look, Laura said hesitantly, "I like the house, Adam."

His eyes met hers, but they were unreadable. "Do you?"

"Yes, very much. I'd like to buy it. And the furnishings, too, if you want to sell them." She made him an offer that she knew was generous and waited anxiously for his answer.

Adam studied her for several more seconds, then looked

away and stared straight ahead. "I haven't actually decided yet whether or not I want to sell it. I'll think over your offer and let you know."

"Well, now, I dunno 'bout that. The owners may foot the bill for a bit of repaintin', but I doubt they'll go for any fancy redecoratin'." Cory Bates scratched his balding head. Squinting his eyes, he looked around the interior of the store as though trying to visualize the changes she wanted. After a moment he gave up, a perplexed look on his face. The few strands of sandy hair on the top of his head were standing straight up.

"Then perhaps they would be willing to split the costs," Laura said, peering at the antique ceiling fans that whirred lazily overhead. She wasn't concerned. She had known she would probably have to absorb the cost of the alterations, but the businesswoman in her had made her ask. "Of course, you realize that I'm only talking about the redecorating costs. Any structural repairs are the owners' responsibility. I suspect that this place will need new wiring and plumbing." She waved her hand toward the storage room at the back. "And that antiquated restroom has to go."

Cory Bates cleared his throat and nervously hiked his pants up over his protruding belly. "Uh, yes, ma'am. I'll see what I can do."

Laura turned aside to hide the small smile that curved her mouth. Mr. Bates was beginning to worry that a prospective client was about to slip through his fingers. It had been obvious from the beginning that he thought she would be a pushover. Because of her outward appearance, it was a mistake many people made until they knew her better. Though far from hardnosed, Laura didn't let anyone push her around. Not any more.

Laura inspected the bare, narrow-plank flooring. It was so worn and dark with age, it was impossible to tell what kind of wood it was. It's just as well I'd planned to carpet, Laura thought idly, because refinishing was hopeless.

Running her hand along one of the ancient walnut and glass display cases, Laura asked, "Has this always been a mercantile store?"

"Yes, ma'am. Before Agnes and Luther took it over, forty years ago, it belonged to Luther's folks." He gazed around at the shelves lining the walls, which contained an amazing assortment of merchandise: thread, bolts of material, small appliances, dishes, linens, cleaning materials, tools, tractor tires, fertilizer, patent medicine, saddles, lipstick, perfume, and many things that Laura could not identify. "Yes, sirree, lots of folks around here are right sorry to see this place go, 'cause if you needed somethin', most likely Clarke's had it."

Laura gazed up at the ornately plastered ceiling. "What's upstairs?"

"Oh, that's just Mr. Lenton's office. He's a CPA. Won't bother you a bit."

"I see. Well, Mr. Bates, I like the location and the space is adequate. But before I commit myself, I'd like for you to speak to the owners about the changes I'll require. And in the meantime, I'll take a copy of the lease agreement to my attorney and have him look it over."

Laura bid Mr. Bates goodbye outside the store and started across the square for Adam's office. Ignoring the fluttering sensation in the pit of her stomach, she told herself there was no reason to be nervous. Adam had been cool and distant the night before when they parted, but he'd had plenty of time to get over his anger. And after all, the mistake she'd made hadn't really been so terrible. She'd had no way of knowing that he wasn't married.

Adam was standing beside Carly Sue's desk when Laura entered the outer office, and when their eyes met she felt again that disturbing jolt of awareness. She jerked her eyes away quickly and focused on his secretary, who was smiling brightly up at her.

"Hi, Laura. Did you find something you like?" At Laura's surprised look, Carly Sue laughed and waved her hand dismissively. "Shoot, everybody in town knows you spent the morning with Cory looking for a location for your shop. You can't keep anything a secret in Oakridge."

For an instant sheer terror gripped Laura. Oh, Lord, I hope you're wrong, she thought fervently.

She smiled, hoping they hadn't noticed the slip in her composure. "As a matter of fact, I think I've found just what I need."

"If you've got the lease agreement with you, come into my office and I'll take a look at it," Adam said. When she pulled the folded sheaf of paper from her purse, he stepped back and motioned for her to precede him.

Laura sat down in the same chair she had occupied the day before and waited expectantly, trying not to fidget. Adam perused the first page of the lease and glanced up at her. "So you settled on the Blyden building?"

"Yes. The location is perfect. It's a bit antiquated, but with a few repairs and remodeling it should work out just fine." Laura felt some of the tension drain out of her. Adam wasn't exactly exuding friendliness, but at least the icy anger was gone.

Instead of reading the rest of the lease, as she had expected, Adam tossed it on his desk and leaned back in his chair. Bracing an elbow on the chair arm, he propped his chin on his fist and studied her. "Do you want my advice?" he asked quietly.

"Yes, of course. That's why I'm here."

"All right. My advice to you is to forget the whole thing." He paused for his words to register, then added in a softer voice, "Go back to Houston, Laura. Forget this business about opening another shop."

She stared at him blankly. She wanted to believe that she had misunderstood him, but the look in his eyes told her otherwise. Panic began to nibble at her. "But...but...*why*? I know I can make a success of the store. It may not ever be as profitable as the ones in Houston, but that doesn't matter." She sat forward in the chair, a touch of desperation in her eyes. Unconsciously, she licked her lips as she marshaled her thoughts. "Look, maybe I'd better explain in more detail what I have planned. You see I—"

"Laura." Adam interrupted her softly, but firmly. "It's not the shop that concerns me. You're a successful businesswoman and I'm sure you know what you're doing."

"Then what's the problem?"

"The problem is, this is a small town and you're a big city lady. I doubt that you'd be happy here for long. You're used to a different lifestyle, a different pace, a different breed of people. Our little one-horse town would bore you silly in three months."

Laura lifted her chin and stared at him coolly. "Pardon me for saying so, but you don't know me well enough to make that kind of judgment, Mr. Kincaid."

His ironic smile chided gently. "Come on, Laura. Face facts. I mean, just look at you." He gestured toward the outfit she was wearing. The aztec-print challis shirt in gray, rust, and cream, teamed with a cream silk blouse and a short rust suede jacket, was casual, tasteful, and had that certain undeniable chic that was so easy to recognize and yet so difficult for the average woman to attain. "You stand out here like a hybrid rose in a patch of daisies."

He didn't want her there. He couldn't have said it more plainly if he'd written it out in foot-high block letters. Laura felt as though she'd been slapped, and she stared at him, her face growing pale. Hurt overwhelmed her for a moment, but then, slowly, pride and a building, consuming anger came to her rescue.

"It was your professional opinion I asked for, Mr. Kincaid. Your personal one I can do without." Rising, Laura snatched up the leased papers and stuffed them in her purse. "Since it's obvious that you don't want my business, I'll find another attorney." Head high, her back stiff, she marched to the door, then paused and looked back at him.

Her expression was as cold as ice, but her topaz eyes were shooting fire. "I trust you will send me a bill for all your sterling advice. Goodbye, Mr. Kincaid."

Just seconds after she had gone Carly Sue appeared in the doorway, her hands on her hips. "I swear, Adam Kincaid, sometimes I think you need your head examined."

Adam gave her a sardonic look. "Listening, were you?"

"Since you left the door open, I could hardly help but hear." She advanced into the room, her mouth compressed into a grim line. "What in the world is the matter with you, Adam? You couldn't have done a better job of driving her away if you'd used a whip and a chair." She shook her head, perplexed. "Laura Phillips is not only a very good client to have, she's a lovely, intelligent woman. You could do a lot worse for yourself, you know," she snapped, giving him a disgusted look.

Surprise widened Adam's eyes. Placing his palms flat against his temples, he groaned, "Oh, Carly Sue, not you, too. Isn't it enough that every matchmaking old busybody in this town is trying to pair me up with someone, without your helping them?"

"It's high time you started thinking about the future, Adam. You're not getting any younger, you know."

"Oh, thanks, I needed that."

"What you need is a wife. And Mike needs a mother," she declared bluntly. "It seems to me that Laura Phillips would fill the bill just fine." She paused and frowned. "Unless, of course, you're not attracted to her?"

Adam's snort of laughter was dry and mirthless. Oh, he was attracted to her all right. And it surprised hell out of him. After Carol, he hadn't expected to be attracted to another woman ever again. He hadn't wanted to be.

Not that he'd been celibate. There had been women. Meaningless, brief encounters. And always with women who, like himself, neither wanted nor gave more than a few moments' pleasure. Appeasement of a basic, biological need.

But with Laura it was different. She appealed to him on all levels: physical, mental, and emotional. And he didn't like it.

"I'm neither blind nor dead, Carly Sue. And a man would have to be one or the other not to be attracted to Mrs. Phillips," he answered candidly, giving her a lazy smile.

"Then what's the problem?"

"I just don't want to get involved."

"Oh, terrific." Carly Sue looked at the ceiling in supplication and spread her hands, palms upward. "Just great. Can you believe this? He meets a gorgeous, fascinating, warm, not to mention wealthy, widow, and *he* doesn't want to get involved. Of all the stupid, imbecile..."

Adam's lazy grin brought her tirade to an abrupt halt. Thoroughly disgusted, Carly Sue glared at him in wrathful fury for a moment, then turned on her heel and stalked out. Just before she jerked the door closed behind her, he heard her mimic nastily in a whining falsetto, "I don't want to get involved."

The taunt rang in his ears as the door shut with a decisive thud, and Adam's grin faded. Not when the chances of her sticking around are almost zero, he added silently to himself.

Laura stormed into the room and slammed the door behind her. She flung her purse onto a chair and kicked her shoes off, sending them crashing against the wall. "Damn that man!" Rigid with fury, she stood in the middle of the floor, her hands clenched at her side, her chest heaving. He had no right to do this to her. It wasn't any of his business whether or not she was happy here. Who the devil was he, to tell her what to do?

Mike's father, that's who.

Like air escaping a balloon, all the fight went out of Laura in a rush, and her shoulders slumped dejectedly.

Mike. How could she have forgotten that he was her

reason for being here? Now she'd ruined everything. Despair washed over her, and though she tried to fight back the incipient tears, it was no use. Laura's face crumpled, and with a cry, she flung herself down on the bed, burying her face against her crossed arms as the wracking sobs shook her.

Tears flowed in torrents from her eyes, and her shoulders heaved. She cried wretchedly, all the misery, all the loneliness, the longing deep in her soul overwhelming her. Her sobs were harsh and choppy and hurt her throat, but she couldn't seem to stop them. They tore from her endlessly, filling the room with sounds of anguish.

The sun was beginning to set when she finally quieted. Sniffling, she turned her head and stared through the gloom, blinking wet, spiky lashes. The forearm beneath her cheek was slick with tears and there was a damp circle on the candlewick bedspread.

Gradually the sniffles lessened into choppy sighs. Laura sat up and swiped at her eyes with the heels of her hands. Outside, the streetlights around the square flickered on, spilling a faint, eerie light through the lace curtains. Her nose was stopped up and her head was booming. Laura stood and dragged herself into the bathroom to search for some aspirin, but the sight of her red-rimmed eyes and ravaged face nearly made her start crying again. Stoically, she downed two tablets. After blowing her nose and wiping her eyes she snatched up a handful of tissues and left the room, turning out the light as she went.

In the rapidly darkening bedroom she sat down in one of the chairs and stared out the window at nothing. The street lamp across from the inn was making a buzzing noise, and she could hear a faint murmur of voices from the veranda below. Laura had never felt more alone in her life.

Had she been wrong to come here? Everyone but her seemed to think so: Diane, Adam...even John, had he lived, would have disapproved strongly, she knew. Laura drew a deep breath and released it on a long, shuddering sigh, and dabbed at her eyes with the wad of tissue. Was what she was doing really so terrible? Was it wrong to want to see her son? Be near him? It wasn't as though she were trying to take him away from his father. She knew she didn't have that right. Regardless of the circumstances, no matter how much she wished things had been different, she'd made her decision over fourteen years ago.

But surely it wasn't asking too much just to be here? To see him occasionally? It was such a small thing, and it wouldn't hurt anyone. Now that John was gone, she had no one. No one at all...except Mike.

She could not, and did not, count her parents. That bond, however weak, had been severed twelve years ago when they moved to the West Coast. A small hollow laugh escaped Laura. In the end it hadn't mattered that she had knuckled under to their demands, because they had never been able to forget her mistake, or forgive her. She had barely finished school and gotten a job when they announced their plan to retire and move to California. There hadn't been any question of her going with them.

They had been relieved when she married John and became "respectable," but beyond an obligatory call once or twice a year, she never heard from them.

Laura knew that her parents, most of all, would not approve of her being here. To them there were no shades of gray—only right and wrong, black and white, good and bad.

Laura rose and walked to the window. She opened the sash and shivered as gooseflesh sprang up on her arms. The air was cool with the gentle bite of autumn and smelled faintly of wood smoke and cedar. Laura gazed out at the square, with its venerable old oaks and its ornate bandstand. The traffic was sparse, and most of the shops were already closed and dark. On the other side of the square, lights from the town's only movie theatre burned brightly, but through the trees Laura couldn't make out the sign on the modest marquee. A car filled with noisy teenagers drove by, back-firing twice as it careened around the square. Before disappearing down a side street several of its occupants leaned out the windows and yelled taunts at a young couple strolling arm in arm down the sidewalk, but they merely laughed and yelled back good-naturedly.

Laura smiled. The town was exactly as she'd pictured it all those years. Exactly as she had hoped it would be: small, close-knit, and peaceful. She was fiercely glad that Mike had been raised in this environment, where people knew one another, cared about one another.

Was that why Adam wanted her to leave? Because she was an outsider? Hurt welled up inside Laura again as she thought of that scene in his office, but she quickly battered it down. She wasn't going to let Adam Kincaid or anyone else dictate her life. She wasn't a malleable, frightened sixteen-year-old girl anymore.

Laura slammed her balled fist against the window frame. She had as much right to be here as anyone. Her son was here, she liked it here, and by heaven, it was here she was going to stay.

Chapter Four

Ice clinked as the waitress tipped the pitcher and refilled Laura's glass with tea. "I hear tell things are going great guns over at that shop of yours," the woman commented casually.

Laura hastily swallowed the bit of food in her mouth and smiled up at her. "Yes. Yes, they are," she confirmed.

"Well, Ezra Simpson always was the best contractor around these parts." Maybelle wiped up a few drops of spilled tea from the Formica-topped table with a towel, then leaned an ample hip against the side of the booth. "He'll do a good job for you. You can count on that. May not be as fast as some I could name, but he'll do the job right, and he's as honest as the day is long."

Laura returned her sandwich to her plate and brushed the crumbs off her fingertips. She had eaten at the café often enough in the past two weeks to know that once started, the gregarious woman could go on indefinitely. "I'm very pleased with Ezra's work," she said carefully, knowing that every word that came out of her mouth would probably be repeated a dozen times before nightfall.

At first Laura had been surprised, even a little shocked, at the way everyone not only knew, but discussed, everyone else's business, but she was gradually coming to accept it. She had wanted the closeness and comforting tranquility of a small town, she reminded herself, and with that closeness came familiarity.

"'Course, it'll seem strange, not having Clarke's settin' over there like it has ever since anyone can remember," Maybelle said with a reminiscent sigh, glancing out the window at the brick-fronted building on the corner diagonally across from the café, where two men on ladders were removing the faded metal sign from above the door. "But of course, everybody's real eager for you to open your shop," she added hurriedly. "Leastways, the women are. I don't suppose you know yet when that'll be?"

"If everything goes right, in about a month or six weeks. At least, that's what I'm shooting for. I'd like to be open for the holidays, anyway."

"Well, that's just fine. I—"

Whatever comment Maybelle was about to make was cut off by the jangle of the bell above the door as it was pushed open to admit two men. One was tall and rangy, raw-boned, the other stocky, with a stomach that poured over his low-slung belt, but they both had the same weathered look, the same rolling gait that marked them as ranchers.

"Hey Maybelle. How about a little service over here, sweetheart," the tall one called out boisterously, slapping his big, work-worn hand on the counter as he slid onto a stool and hooked the heels of his run-down cowboy boots over the brass rail. "I need a cup of mud."

Maybelle gave Laura an apologetic smile and started back across the room. "Just keep your shirt on, Charlie. And you call my coffee mud again and I'll put a knot on your head you can wear a hat on."

"Aw, now, Maybelle, honey, you know I'm just funnin'.

Why, the only reason I even come in here is to drink yore coffee. It's the best in the state. Probably the best in the whole danged country.'' He winked and poked the other man in the ribs. ''Ain't it, Floyd?''

''The best,'' Floyd agreed with a silly grin.

''Huh!'' Maybelle retorted succinctly, sliding two cups of steaming coffee onto the counter before them.

Tuning out the good-natured bantering, Laura started to reach for her sandwich once again, when from the corner of her eye she saw the familiar green pickup drive by. Laura stared out the window, watching as Adam guided the truck around the square. When it disappeared from sight down one of the side streets, she slumped back against the padded seat of the booth. It had been two weeks since she'd stormed out of his office, and in that time she'd seen him only at a distance. Of Mike she'd seen nothing.

She wondered if Adam has been deliberately avoiding her. Since both his office and her shop were on the square, she had seen him coming and going several times, and she knew he'd seen her, yet he never came into the café when she was there, and she never saw him in the post office or the pharmacy or any of the shops.

The chicken salad sandwich no longer had any appeal and Laura pushed it away. Things weren't going the way she had planned at all. Who would have thought that in a town of only six thousand people it would be difficult to run into someone occasionally? *Who do you mean, Laura? Mike...or Adam?*

Pushing the disturbing thought aside, Laura placed a tip on the table, then picked up her check and scooted out of the booth.

''I tell you, Floyd, our boys are gonna whup the socks off 'um,'' the man named Charlie declared as she neared the cash register. ''Those kids on the junior varsity team are tough. In another couple of years, when they're playin' varsity, we'll probably take the state championship.''

"I dunno, Charlie. That Gonzales team is strong this year, and they've got a good quarterback."

"So do we. Tommy Johnson is fast and accurate, and with the Kincaid kid as his number one receiver we oughta really rack up the points tonight."

At the mention of her son Laura's head snapped around and she stared at the two men. Suddenly her heart began to pound.

"Well, I dunno—"

"Well, I do. You just be there tonight and you'll see."

"Shoot fire, Charlie! Course I'm gonna be there. My boy Pete plays linebacker. You know that."

Laura edged around the two men and made her way to the cash register, her expression thoughtful. When she handed her money and bill over to Maybelle she said, "I gather the local team is playing here tonight."

"Yeah, the junior varsity," the other woman confirmed. "Tomorrow night the big kids play."

Laura wasn't interested in the big boys, but she smiled. "Do you have to be a student to attend?"

"Heavens, no," Maybelle said quickly. "Why, half the town shows up for the games. The more the better. All you have to do is buy your ticket at the gate." She paused and tilted her head, giving Laura a curious look. "Why? You plannin' on going'?"

"I may," Laura said with a smile as she accepted her change.

An hour later she was in her car, headed toward the high school on the outskirts of town.

It was getting dark when Laura parked in the gravel lot beside the school. Maybelle had been right when she said that half the people in town attend the games. Cars were streaming into the lot at a steady rate. Assuming they knew where they were going, Laura followed the crowd that swarmed toward the misty glow of the stadium lights on the other side of the three-story red brick building. The autumn night was crisp and cool. The scents of gravel dust and heated vehicles hung in the thin air, and mingled with it was the ever present hint of cedar. Above, the sky was a cloudless, dusky blue.

Rounding the corner of the building, Laura saw that the Oakridge stadium was in reality merely a football field with a section of wooden bleachers on either side, conveniently located behind the school so that the players could use the gym locker rooms. At the back of the wooden bleachers were several concession stands, and Laura's nose twitched at the smell of frying meat, popcorn, and roasted peanuts. After purchasing a soft drink and a small sack of popcorn, Laura made her way around to the front of the bleachers.

The first person she saw was Adam.

He was standing by the players' bench in front of the stands, his back to her, talking to another man. He was wearing low-slung, faded jeans, a blue and red plaid flannel shirt, a brown suede vest, and worn cowboy boots. Beneath the bright stadium lights his dark brown hair had the sheen of a beaver pelt.

Laura stopped and stared at him, a fluttery sensation in the pit of her stomach. For a moment she forgot the crowd in the stands, blocked out the buzz of voices, the occasional burst of laughter, the people jostling past her. Her gaze was riveted to the broad-shouldered back.

As she watched, Adam half turned and scanned the crowd, and her heart began to beat at double time. Common sense told her he couldn't possibly have spotted her, but she quickly began to search the upper section of the bleachers for a seat. Before she could find one, the people in the stands suddenly erupted in a cheer and came to their feet. Laura turned and saw the players and their coach run out on the field.

In the padded green and white uniforms and helmets they all looked the same to Laura, and she was afraid for a moment that she wouldn't be able to pick Mike out from the rest. She squinted her eyes and craned her neck, trying to get a better look, but couldn't make out any distinguishing features. Then she saw Adam lean over a player with the number eighty-six on his jersey and whisper something in his ear, giving him an encouraging thump on the back. Laura's eyes fastened eagerly on the boy. When he took off his helmet and put it on the bench beside him, his black hair glinted like a raven's wing in the brilliant light, and a slow smile curved Laura's mouth.

The toss occurred without her being aware of it, and Mike was trotting out onto the field. She stood staring after him until she realized that Adam had started toward the bleachers. Swiftly, Laura climbed the steps to the top row and wedged herself onto the bench between two large women.

Laura's eyes fastened on Mike and never left him throughout the game. When the crowd cheered, she did, too, but the only plays she saw were the ones he executed, and at those times she was filled with pride. Whenever he was tackled she winced and watched anxiously, her heart in her throat, until he was once more on his feet.

Not wanting to bump into Adam, Laura remained in her seat during half time, and again when the game was over, until she saw him leave the stands. The Mustangs had won handily and the crowd was exuberant and noisy as they filed out. Trailing along behind them, Laura smiled at their high-spirited bantering.

She had just reached the ground and started back toward the parking lot when Adam stepped out from under the bleachers and into her path.

"Hello, Laura," he said as she pulled up short and stared at him warily.

Laura's heart was pumping like a wild thing but she managed a cautious "Hello, Adam."

He stood with his legs braced apart, hands in his pockets, and looked at her intently, his expression brooding and somber. "I was surprised when I saw you earlier," he said finally. "Somehow, I didn't think you'd be interested in football. Especially not junior high football."

The words brought an immediate stiffening of her spine, and her chin tilted a fraction higher. "Since I am now a part of this community, I felt I should help support the kids," Laura informed him defiantly. "Do you have any objection to that?"

Adam ducked his head and rocked back and forth on his heels, then looked up at her from under his brows. "You're really determined to stay, aren't you?"

"Yes, I am."

"I've seen Ezra and his crew over at Clarke's this past week, so I assume you signed the lease. I hope you had someone look it over for you. Cory's a good ole boy but he's not above slipping something by you if he can."

"Yes. I had my Houston attorney check it out for me."

An awkward silence followed, and Laura's nerves grew taut. Adam's masculine scent wafted to her on the cool night breeze, heady and exciting. She was disturbingly aware of his size, the breadth of his shoulders, the sprinkling of curly dark hair visible in the V opening of his shirt. Laura pulled her eyes away from the disturbing sight but then they came to rest on his lean waist and the faded tight jeans that outlined so blatantly the evidence of his masculinity.

A flush colored her cheeks and she quickly looked up—straight into his eyes. They were heavy-lidded, dark and mysterious.

"Laura, about—"

"Hey, Dad!" Mike yelled as he came running up. "Did you see that catch in the third quarter? Oh, hi, Mrs. Phillips," he added hastily as he came to a breathless stop in front of them.

Gulping for air, Mike whipped off his helmet and held it under his arm, braced against his side. His black hair was plastered to his head like a skull cap. The green and white uniform was streaked with dirt and grass stains. His skin was flushed and his eyes sparkled, and rivulets of sweat and grime trickled down his face. He was grubby, smelly, and obviously exhausted.

To Laura, he was beautiful.

Leather padding rattled as Adam clapped the boy on the shoulder. Pride and love shining out of his hazel eyes, he smiled down into Mike's eager face, and watching them, Laura felt a sweet ache beneath her breast-bone. "I saw," Adam replied in a tone that said much more than flowery praise. "You played great, son."

Mike's grin widened. "Thanks, Dad. The coach says if we keep playing like we did tonight, we've got a good chance of beating Lockhart, and they're tough."

Laura's eyes greedily drank in the sight of him. Mike and his father rehashed the high points of the game, and as she pretended to listen her chest swelled with a fierce maternal pride. He was a boy any parent could be proud of: nice looking, pleasant, happy and well adjusted. He was surprisingly muscular for his age, she thought as her eyes roamed over him. And tall. The three-inch heels she was wearing boosted her height to five feet nine, and he looked her eye to eye. Emotion swamped her. This was her son, the child she had yearned for all those years, and he was standing just inches away. Laura longed to reach out touch him, to hold him close against her heart...just once.

But of course she couldn't.

"You played very well, Mike," she said during a lull in the conversation. She smiled warmly. "Congratulations. I was very impressed."

"Thank you, ma'am," he replied shyly. He spared her a quick glance, then looked down. His already flushed face turned a deeper shade of red as he shifted restlessly from one foot to the other in a way that Laura found endearing.

"Hadn't you better head for the showers?" Adam asked, breaking into the embarrassed silence.

Mike snapped to attention at once. "Oh, yeah." He took two steps, then turned back. "By the way, I forgot to ask.

Would you take me and the guys out for pizza after we're dressed?''

A small smile curved Laura's mouth at the way Mike's voice cracked, alternating between a deep baritone and a high-pitched squeak.

"Sure," Adam said with a grin. "I guess I can spring for that."

Mike lingered a moment longer. "Uh...you gonna come in and talk to the coach, like you usually do?" he asked, casting an uncertain glance Laura's way.

"No, not tonight. I need to discuss something with Mrs. Phillips. When I get through I'll wait for you in the car. Just come on out when you're ready." Adam gave the boy a playful pinch in the arm and grinned. "Now, hit the showers, tiger."

Mike darted another odd look at Laura, then shrugged. "Okay. See you in a few minutes," he called as he took off at a trot toward the gym.

He's a nice boy,'' Laura said in a husky voice.

"Yeah. The best."

Pulling in a deep breath, Laura took a firm hold on her rioting emotions and smiled up at Adam politely. "Well, good night, Mr. Kincaid," she said as she began to edge away. "I really must be going, I—"

A hand on her arm stopped her. "Laura, I..." Adam hesitated, his features twisting in a wry grimace. "I'm sorry about the things I said to you. If you'll forgive me, I'd like to start over." He looked at her steadily, his eyes questioning and faintly apprehensive.

The heat from his hand seemed to brand Laura through the soft knit of her sweater, and she stared up at him, her heart thumping wildly. From the corner of her eye she saw Mike stop before the gymnasium door and stare suspiciously at them, but she was too stunned by Adam's nearness, too vibrantly, overwhelmingly aware of him, to wonder why. "I'd like that," she said nervously, unable to look away from his steady gaze.

The tense watchfulness left him and a slow smile spread across his face. "Good," he said in a soft voice that did strange things to her insides. The smile grew sheepish and his brows lifted as he asked hopefully, "I don't suppose you're still in the market for an attorney?"

The gentle massage of his hand at her elbow was driving Laura crazy and she gently eased her arm free and stepped away, smiling to soften the action. "As a matter of fact, I am. I haven't gotten around to contacting anyone else." *Because I didn't want anyone but you.* "Are you still interested?"

"I'm interested," he said quietly.

The light in his eyes told her he was interested in more than just being her attorney. Laura was both appalled and excited. This was not what she had come here for. It would be dangerous and incredibly stupid to get involved with Adam. It could lead nowhere. But still...if she could keep things on a purely business level...

"And if your offer on the house still stands," Adam continued before she could respond, "I'd like to take you up on it."

Laura's eyes opened wide. It was foolish to even consider it. But the temptation was strong. So very strong. She wanted that lovely old house. She wanted to be near Mike. And, she admitted with brutal self honesty, she wanted to be near Adam, too. *It won't work, Laura, you know that. You've got to tell him that you've changed your mind.* She smiled weakly at Adam and opened her mouth to tell him, but to her dismay, what came out was "Yes. Yes, that would be wonderful."

"Good. If you'd like, I'll draw up the papers in the morning, and you can drop by, say around ten, and we'll go over them."

"Fine. I'll see you then. Good night, Adam." Laura glanced toward the gym, but Mike was nowhere in sight. With a last smile for Adam, she turned and started to walk away, but he fell in step beside her.

"I'll walk you to your car," he said, cupping her elbow in his hand.

His touch was light and undemanding, but Laura was intensely aware of the grip of those lean strong fingers. A searing warmth spread across her skin from the point of contact and she felt a shiver ripple through her. Laura prayed silently that Adam hadn't felt it, too.

He chatted amiably as he led her through the darkness, telling her about the games Mike and his team had already played, the ones they would play before the season was over, what he thought their chances were. Laura made non-committal comments at the appropriate places, but her mind wasn't really on the conversation. She was intensely aware of the heat from Adam's body as he walked along beside her, the deep timbre of his voice, the darkness of the cedar-scented night...and the quivering deep inside her.

There were only a few cars left in the lot and no-one else was in sight when they reached her car. Laura fumbled in her purse for her keys, finally extracting them only to have even more difficulty fitting the proper one into the lock. When at last she managed to get the door open she turned back to Adam and smiled nervously. "Well, good night. I'll, uh...I'll see you tomorrow morning."

Adam didn't respond. In the weak light spilling out of the car she could see that his intent gaze was fixed on her mouth, and her heart began to thump painfully. Slowly his gaze lifted and their eyes locked. Keys rattled in Laura's trembling fingers and she clutched the edge of the car door for support. He was going to kiss her. And she wanted him to. Everything about Adam appealed to her, called to her, touched her mind and her heart. He drew from her physical responses that were new and frightening...and utterly delicious. She yearned desperately to give in to them. But she couldn't. She couldn't.

Longing and despair mingled in Laura's eyes as she met Adam's passionate gaze. She couldn't move, couldn't breathe. He braced an arm against the car and his head began a slow descent, and for an instant Laura felt her body sway helplessly toward him. *You can't let this happen, Laura. You're playing with fire.*

A silent moan filled her head, but Laura could not ignore the truth. Painfully, she turned aside and slid into the car. Somehow she managed to get the key in the ignition and start the engine. From the corner of her eye she saw Adam standing beside the car, a shadowy figure, still and rigid. Waiting. Rolling the window down part way, Laura darted a glance in his direction, not quite meeting his eyes. "Good night, Adam."

There was silence for a moment, then his quietly whispered "Good night, Laura" floated to her.

Adam watched her drive away, not moving until the taillights on her car disappeared around a corner. Why had she pulled away like that? She had wanted him to kiss her; he'd stake his life on it. And what was the fear he'd glimpsed in her eyes? Adam turned and walked across the lot to his car, a frown creasing his brow.

He slid in behind the wheel and settled down to wait. Turning sideways, one knee crooked on the seat, he looped an arm around the headrest, draped the other over the steering wheel, and stared out at the darkness. He hadn't intended to talk to Laura, but when he'd turned and seen her standing there before the game started, all his good intentions had flown out the window. It irritated him that he was so attracted to the woman, but it was useless to deny it. Or fight it.

And he certainly didn't understand it. Laura Phillips wasn't anything at all like Carol.

A small, sad smile pulled at the corners of Adam's mouth. Carol. Sweet, comfortable, tomboyish Carol. He'd known her all his life and they'd been sweethearts since high school. Their marriage had been solid and had brought him happiness and contentment, especially after they adopted Mike.

Adam sighed heavily and leaned his head back against

the window. He had loved Carol deeply, and yet, not in all the years he had known her had she aroused in him the passion, the restless yearning he felt for Laura Phillips. The woman hadn't been out of his mind since she'd walked into his office two weeks ago.

Adam's balled fist lightly rapped against the seat back. Did he dare let himself become involved with her? She was a city woman. Despite her enthusiasm and obvious intentions, there was a good probability that she would soon become bored with their quiet little town and move back to Houston. It was one thing to indulge in a harmless fling with a lovely, lonely widow, but he had a gut feeling that whatever developed between him and Laura would be anything but casual. He also knew that he could never be happy in a place like Houston.

He and Carol had learned that lesson together, early in their marriage. Adam shook his head in disgust as he recalled their youthful enthusiasm. Fresh out of college and eager to shake the dust of a little town off their feet, he and Carol had headed for Dallas. They were going to take on the world, be big-city sophisticates, live the good life. It had taken only one year for them both to realize that they hated it.

If he had any sense he'd stay the hell away from Laura Phillips, he told himself sternly.

The door to the gym opened, and Adam watched Mike and his three friends pour out of the building and head for the car, shoving and heckling one another good-naturedly. Grim-faced, he straightened up and flicked on the engine.

Unfortunately, it seemed he didn't have a lick of sense.

Chapter Five

Carly Sue was clearly delighted to see Laura the next
morning when she arrived. After greeting her like a long-
lost friend, she ushered her in to see Adam, giving him a
hard stare and muttering that he was to behave himself this
time, before returning to her own office.

Just to be sure he did, she reappeared five minutes later
bearing a tray with two cups of steaming coffee, and
beamed her approval when she found them both engrossed
in the legal contract she had obviously typed just that morning.

For several minutes after Carly Sue had tiptoed out, the
only sound in the room was the occasional rustle of paper
as Laura turned the pages.

"Well, what do you think? Do the terms of sale meet
with your approval?"

Laura looked up and smiled across the desk at Adam.
"Yes, this seems fine, but"—she flipped back two pages
of the document—"for your own protection, I think you

should include a clause that gives you first right of purchase on the furnishings, should I decide to sell any of them. After all, they belonged to your grandparents.''

''That's all right. I trust you,'' Adam returned warmly.

Guilt pierced Laura and she felt the smile freeze on her face, then slowly melt. *You wouldn't say that if you knew who I was,* she thought sadly. *Why I'm here.* She looked back at the document in her hand and pretended to read while trying to banish the wayward thought. *It's not as though you're trying to cheat him or take something away from him.*

''You're welcome to have your Houston attorney look it over,'' Adam said after a moment.

''No, no. That won't be necessary. This is fairly straightforward. I'll contact my assistant today and arrange for a transfer of funds. If it's agreeable with you, we can sign the papers on Monday.''

''That'll be fine.'' Adam rapped the edges of the contracts against the desk, then put them to one side. Leaning back in his chair, he smiled. ''So, how's the renovation going?''

''Just great. Mr. Simpson is doing a very nice job. I'm—'' Laura halted and tipped her head to one side, lifting her brows and catching the edge of her lower lip between her teeth. The look in her eyes was both eager and uncertain. ''Would...would you like to see it?'' she asked hesitantly.

''You mean now?''

At her nod, Adam rose and came around the desk. ''Sure. I'd love to. Let's go.''

When they entered the reception room he seemed surprised to find Carly Sue sitting behind her desk.

''What are you still doing here?''

''Oh, I had some things I wanted to catch up on,'' Carly Sue said with a casual wave of her hand, but her avid gaze was bouncing back and forth between Adam and Laura.

The look Adam gave her was openly skeptical, but he

didn't comment on her devotion to her job. "Laura and I are going over to take a look at her shop. Lock up for me when you leave, will you?" Giving her no chance to answer, he quickly ushered Laura out the door.

A rich chuckle vibrated from his throat as they descended the stairs. "Carly Sue doesn't even work on Saturdays. The only reason she came in this morning was to type up that contract." Amusement twinkled in his hazel eyes when he glanced down at Laura, and he leaned close and murmured out of the side of his mouth, "She was just hanging around to make sure I wasn't rude to you again."

Laura laughed, too, but when they started across the square she looked up at him curiously. "So, why were you? Rude, I mean?"

One corner of Adam's mouth kicked up in a wry grimace. When they reached the other side of the square, he cupped her elbow and led her across the street. She thought he wasn't going to answer, but when she unlocked the door to the shop he held it open for her, and as she ducked in past him he said softly, "Maybe someday I'll tell you."

She shot him another curious look, but he wandered away from her, hands in his pockets, to survey the gutted interior of the shop.

The shelves lining the walls had been torn out, exposing gouged, dingy plaster. In places there were gaping holes where the interior walls had been knocked out to install new wiring and plumbing, and toward the back of the store the studs were already in place for the new dressing rooms. Except for one long antique display case, all the counters and furnishings had been removed, and where they had been, the floor was checkered with light, rectangular patches. There were ladders, sawhorses, and scaffolding everywhere. Dust hung in the air and the floor was littered with crumbled plaster, sawdust, scraps of wood, old paint buckets, cigarette butts, cellophane wrappings, empty soft drink cans, and Styrofoam cups that bore the dregs of cold coffee. The stench of raw wood, old plaster, and plumber's compound was overpowering.

Adam kicked aside a splattered dropcloth and turned to Laura, his expression bemused. "*When* did you say you planned to open?"

She laughed. "I know it looks awful now, but the plumber and electrician are almost through, and in a few days these dressing rooms will be framed in," she said, tugging him by the arm to the back of the store to view the new addition. "Once the replastering is done, it will just be a matter of painting and papering, and laying carpet and new flooring in the back. Then I can have the fixtures installed and start stocking."

"Oh, is that all?" Adam said, smiling at her enthusiasm.

Ignoring the teasing note in his voice, Laura walked to the middle of the floor and began to turn slowly, gesturing with her hand. "Over there will be the very casual clothes, over there the moderate daytime wear, shoes there, lingerie there. In the winter that area will be for coats and sweaters, and in the summer, swimsuits. Back in that corner will be a small selection of formal wear. "And this," she said, moving over to the long walnut and curved glass display case and running her hand along its smooth surface, "this is all I salvaged out of the original store. I plan to use it for accessories. You know, scarves, jewelry, that sort of thing."

"If you say so," Adam said doubtfully, looking around at the mess. "But I gotta tell you, I've seen pictures of bombed-out buildings that looked better than this."

"Come on, Adam, where's your imagination? I guarantee you in a few weeks you won't recognize the place."

Adam walked toward her slowly, a thoughtful, half smile curving his mouth, his eyes intent. He halted just inches from her, and when he spoke his voice was low and husky. "You're really eager to get started, aren't you?"

Laura's chest tightened as she met his warm, probing look. Suddenly she was aware of how alone they were, of the absolute quiet in the litter-strewn shop. Since she had walked into his office that morning, Adam's attitude had been friendly and businesslike, and she had relaxed and responded in kind, but now, in the space of just a few seconds, that had changed. "Yes. Of course I am," she replied nervously. "Did you think I wasn't?"

He continued to study her for a moment, then lifted one shoulder in a negligent shrug that told her nothing. Laura frowned, but before she could question him further his eyes made another sweep of their surroundings. "How did you ever get started in this business?" His gaze came back to her upturned face, then dropped to roam appreciatively over her red silk blouse and tapered, front-pleated navy slacks, lingering for a disturbing instant on the jutting fullness of her breasts and gentle flare of her hips. Laura's heart pounded erratically, causing the delicate material covering it to flutter. "You look so fragile, to say nothing of being young, to be the owner of a successful business."

The warmth in his eyes, his nearness, the deep timbre of his voice flooded her senses, and it took a moment for his question to register. "I, uh...I had help from my husband in the beginning." She paused and smiled, memories of the steady, dependable man she had married momentarily overriding the disturbing sensations coursing through her. "John, I'm afraid, had a tendency to spoil me shamefully. When he realized that I was serious about wanting to open my own shop, he provided the financial backing for the first one. It was so successful that the next year I was able to open a second. In the nine years I've been in business I've acquired seven shops." She gestured vaguely with her hand. "This will be number eight."

He continued to watch her, saying nothing, and after a moment Laura shifted restlessly. "Well, if you're ready," she began, turning toward the door, but before she could take a step he put his hand on her arm and stopped her.

"Laura," he said softly, bringing her eyes darting up to

his face. "I've been invited to a party tonight. I'd like for you to go with me."

The warmth of his hand burned her flesh through the thin silk of her blouse and set off a storm of tremors. She stared at him, her eyes round, her heart pounding. It was tempting. She wanted very much to say yes—longed to say yes—but knew in her head, if not her heart, that it wasn't the smart thing to do.

"I'm...sorry, Adam, I really can't," she said with a regretful shake of her head. "I—"

"Laura," he insisted quietly, cutting off her refusal. "If you want to make a success of your store, you need to meet some of the local people. The party tonight is to celebrate George and Thelma Watley's twenty-fifth wedding anniversary. The Watleys are one of the most prominent families in the county, and the people you'll meet there will all be potential customers."

Laura hesitated as the temptation grew stronger. He was right. She did need to get out, make friends, get to know the people who would be her customers, she rationalized. It would be good for business. Good for her, personally. She gnawed her inner lip and looked at Adam, felt the attraction that zinged between them. But if she went with him she would be opening the door to a relationship that simply couldn't be, that was doomed before it ever started. It would be foolish, stupid. Dangerous. She knew she shouldn't. She really shouldn't, but...

Laura met the waiting intensity in his eyes and glanced away skittishly, then looked back. Finally, drawing a deep breath, she gave him a wavering smile and said, "All right. I'll go."

That evening, Laura dithered for over an hour, trying to decide what to wear. Once she had settled on the simple blue sheath with long fitted sleeves, another hour was wasted in a one-sided debate over whether the gold or the sapphire earrings went best with it. In the end, she wore pearl studs.

The reason she was going to so much trouble, Laura told herself as she fussed with her hair, pulling the honey-colored tresses back at her temples with combs, was to impress the local ladies and drum up interest in her store. It had nothing whatever to do with Adam.

As she had a hundred times since leaving him that morning, Laura cursed herself for a fool. What on earth was she doing? She had no business going out with Adam Kincaid. Not for any reason.

Laura applied perfume to her wrists and the pulse points on her neck with a shaking hand. Somehow she was going to have to discourage him.

When she made the decision to come to Oakridge she hadn't counted on this attraction that had sprung up between them. It was disturbing—and it was ruining her carefully thought out plan. Dammit! She wanted to be his friend, not his lover!

But even as the words shouted through her mind Laura knew it wasn't precisely true. She would like to be both... maybe even more. But it just wasn't possible.

She felt guilty enough about her deception as it was. If she allowed the relationship between them to develop into anything beyond friendship, she would have to tell him the truth.

The thought caused a spasm of fear to clutch in her stomach, and Laura moaned and closed her eyes. She could just imagine it. *"Oh, by the way, Adam, before things get serious between us, I feel I should tell you that I'm Mike's natural mother."*

A delicate shudder rippled through her as she pictured what his reaction would be. No. She didn't dare risk telling him. If Adam ever learned the truth, he would be furiously angry, probably even hate her. Certainly he would never trust her or want her near his son.

And that is why you're here, don't forget, she admonished her reflection in the mirror. Not to wallow in this heart-pounding, breath-stealing attraction you feel for Mike's father. You're not a love-starved teenager anymore. You're a grown woman. You should have better control over your emotions, for heaven's sake.

With a low sound of disgust, Laura turned away from the mirror and stomped to the armoire to search for the strappy high-heeled sandals that matched her dress. She didn't understand why she responded to Adam the way she did. Not in fifteen years, not since Keith had turned his back on her, had she felt this soul-stirring passion. In all honesty she hadn't really felt it then. At sixteen she had merely been desperate for love, enthralled by the idea that it was at last being offered her.

After Keith's desertion she'd been determined that never again would anyone play her for a fool, and had shunned all masculine advances. Until John. Typically, he had wooed her with quiet determination, until finally, in a desperate attempt to discourage him, she had told him the whole story. But, to her surprise, John had understood and sympathized, and had grieved with her for her loss and her pain...and for that she had loved him...quietly, contentedly.

With the sandals dangling from two fingers, Laura stomped across to the bed and sat down, slipping her feet into the dainty shoes. It was ridiculous, at her age, to be experiencing these disturbing, exhilarating feelings, she told herself firmly. She had to nip them in the bud, now, before things got out of hand.

The knock on the door made her jump. She glanced at her watch and frowned. She had meant to be dressed and waiting for Adam in the lobby when he arrived, but she was obviously running late. Scooping up her small clutch bag and lacy shawl, she stood and squared her shoulders. Remember, Laura, she reminded herself, keep it light, keep it casual.

Her resolve lasted all of the five seconds it took to cross the room and open the door.

There was nothing casual about the impact the man standing in the hallway had on her senses. Dressed in a dark gray suit, white silk shirt and gray and green striped tie, Adam took her breath away. She stared at him in hushed appreciation, her hand trembling on the doorknob, feeling the sweet, sharp tug of desire, and not knowing what to do about it.

Neither did Adam, apparently. His eyes were dark and smoldering as they swept over her, from the top of her head to her strappy sandals, and back again. They stopped for a moment on her mouth, then dropped to the throbbing pulse visible in the hollow at the base of her throat. After an electrifying moment his gaze lifted to meet hers, and he murmured softly, "Hello, Laura."

"Hello."

"You look very lovely tonight," he said in that same low tone.

"Thank you," she managed, though the words were hardly more than a cracked whisper. Trembling, she forced herself to look away from those sexy hazel eyes and opened her bag to check that she had her key. Though her legs felt like rubber sticks, she stepped out into the hall and pulled the door shut behind her.

When Adam's hand settled against the small of her back as they walked toward the stairs, Laura felt her heart kick into high gear, her blood begin to surge hotly through her veins...and she knew she was in trouble.

The Watleys' house was just a few blocks away. During the short ride they managed to make stilted small talk, but beneath it there was a coiled tension, a sizzling awareness that ate at Laura's nerves until she thought she would scream. She was immensely relieved when Adam pulled onto a street lined with cars and found a parking space.

The huge old red brick house sat in the middle of the block, far back off the street on a roomy, tree-studded lot.

Flanking it, there were generous side yards, and tall, neatly trimmed boxwood hedges to separate it from its neighbors.

The minute they stepped in the door there was a shout from the living room, and a short rotund man began working his way through the crowd toward them. Laura looked around as they awaited his arrival.

There was laughter, music, conversation. The same ingredients as in the dozens of parties she had attended in Houston, yet she sensed a difference. The laughter was genuine, the music easy, the conversation more relaxed. These people were here to enjoy, not to see and be seen. They had known one another for years and there was no need for pretense. Watching, Laura knew a sharp sense of longing to be one of them, and wondered if she would ever belong.

"Adam! You ole sonofagun, it's about time you got here," the stout little man declared as he cuffed Adam on the arm and shook his hand. "The punch bowl has already been emptied once."

"Evening, George." Adam grinned as he returned the enthusiastic handshake. Looping his free arm lightly around Laura's waist he drew her nearer. "Laura, this sawed-off runt is George Watley. George, this is Laura Phillips, a new resident of Oakridge and a client of mine."

"Hello, Mr. Watley. And happy anniversary."

"Why, thank you. And make it George, please," he said, pumping her hand with only slightly less enthusiasm than he had Adam's. "And you're the lady who's opening a dress shop in the old mercantile store, aren't you?"

Laura smiled. "Yes. Yes, I am."

"Well, come on in here and let me introduce you around," he said, commandeering her arm and leading her into the crowded living room. "My wife, Thelma, will be tickled pink to meet you."

People were everywhere—clustered in corners, roaming through the generous rooms, spilling out into the entrance hall, and seated on the stairs. As George guided her through the crowd Laura's senses were assaulted with the mingled scents of perfume, tobacco, soap, and aftershave. There were a few familiar faces—Carly Sue and her husband, Mrs. Fogherty from the post office, Mr. Denton, the bank president—but most were strangers. Laura caught the interested looks and sidelong glances that followed them.

George was headed for the two women standing in front of the fireplace. One was small and birdlike, with soft pampered skin and a cap of neat dark hair. The other was tall and raw-boned, her iron-gray hair pulled back in a severe bun, her face strong and full of character. As they neared the two women they both looked up, and George announced proudly, "Thelma, honey, this is Laura Phillips, the lady who's opening up that new dress shop you've been so curious about. Laura, this is my wife, Thelma, and this is Harriet Beacher."

"Why, my dear, I'm just delighted to meet you." The birdlike woman smiled and extended her hand. "And I'm so pleased you're opening your shop. I can't tell you what a pain it is to have to drive all the way into San Antonio or Austin for nice clothes."

At that moment Adam walked up, carrying two glasses of champagne. He handed one to Laura and, to her surprise, leaned over and kissed the tall woman on the cheek. "Hi, Aunt Harriet," he said with a teasing grin. "How's my best girl?"

"Don't bother turning your charm on me, young man. I'm the same as I was three hours ago when you dropped by for coffee," she snapped bluntly, giving him a piercing look. "And just why didn't you tell me that you knew Mrs. Phillips?"

"You didn't ask me," Adam answered guilelessly.

Her look went from piercing to pure exasperation. "You always were an impertinent devil, Adam Kincaid. Just like your father. Heaven alone knows why I'm so fond of you."

Harriet turned to Laura, her direct gaze searching, assessing. Laura, uncomfortably aware that she was being thoroughly and efficiently sized up, resisted the urge to squirm. Evidently the older woman decided that she passed muster, for after a moment she gave a satisfied nod and her stern face softened ever so slightly, a hint of a smile tilting the corners of her mouth. "I'm Adam's aunt. Welcome to Oakridge." She eyed Laura narrowly once again. "Something about you is very familiar. Have we met before?"

Panic flared within Laura. For an instant her breath caught and the pupils of her eyes expanded until there was only a thin ring of topaz around the outer edge. No. No, she can't have connected me with Mike, she told herself logically, struggling for calm, battling down the burst of fear. Except for his eyes, he doesn't resemble me at all. Retrieving her composure, Laura smiled politely. "No. No, I don't think so," she replied.

"Funny," the older woman murmured thoughtfully. "I could almost swear—"

"Never mind, dear." Thelma Watley interrupted Harriet's musing and grasped Laura's arm. "I'm sure it will occur to you sooner or later. But right now I must take Laura around and introduce her to the other guests. Please excuse us."

Though Laura told herself she had nothing to fear, she breathed a sigh of relief as she allowed her hostess to lead her away.

Thelma made sure that Laura met everyone, and during the next few hours, as she smiled and made small talk, her apprehension began to slowly fade. Several times her eyes sought out Harriet Beacher, but the older woman was always chatting happily with one person or another. It was obvious that the matter of Laura's familiarity no longer interested her. She never even glanced in her direction.

The only one watching her was Adam.

Though he occasionally wandered off in search of refreshments, or to speak to someone across the room, most of the time he stayed by her side. Whether near or far, she felt his eyes on her constantly. Adam seldom touched her, made no overt moves, no intimate, suggestive comments, yet she was intensely aware of his presence. It was almost as though they were the only two people in the room.

She laughed and talked, listened politely to the other guests' conversation, partook of the buffet table, and joined in the toasts to the anniversary couple, but it was all surface activity, strangely remote and automatic. Her mind was filled with Adam.

Over and over, her eyes were drawn in helpless fascination to the crease that came and went in his left cheek whenever he talked. The deep rumble of his voice sent tingles down her spine and his woodsy aftershave made her slightly lightheaded. The way his dark hair curled slightly over his ears and the back of his collar, the silky look of it, had her fingers itching to twine through it, to test its texture and thickness. The hard strength of his big body, the deceptive indolence of his movements, made her heart quicken, her pulse pound.

It was disturbing and exciting, and Laura was very much afraid that Adam was aware of her feelings, and shared them. It was there in his eyes whenever he looked at her.

By the time they finally bid their host and hostess good night, the tension that had been building between them since she had opened her door, hours earlier, had reached a fever pitch. As they walked side by side down the dark drive toward the street, Laura's skin tingled with excitement and fear. Her heart beat with a slow, heavy thud that shook her chest.

At the pickup they paused, and Laura waited for Adam to unlock her door. Instead his hand tightened on her elbow and he turned her toward him. She looked up, her eyes going wide as his free hand grasped her other arm and he pulled her near. They were standing beneath a huge, spreading oak that grew next to the curb, and in the faint moonlight filtering through its branches she could see the burning look in his half-shuttered eyes, the taut, intent expression on his face, and her breath caught.

Seconds ticked by in silence. Laughter and faint strains of music floated from the house. Overhead autumn leaves rustled dryly. And still their eyes clung. *Do something. Stop it now, before it's too late*, Laura's conscience prodded, but she couldn't look away, couldn't move. Couldn't speak.

But their eyes were speaking for them, revealing the longing, the urgent need that raged in both of them. A fine tremor shook Adam's hand when he raised it to gently caress her cheek.

"Laura." Her name whispered from his lips, reluctant, yet heavy with yearning, stirring something deep in her soul. With infinite slowness, he pulled her closer. Laura shivered and stared at him desperately, and when the tips of her breasts brushed his chest she moaned and closed her eyes, savoring the exquisite sensation. They remained that way for a moment longer, barely touching, and when Laura raised her lids she found Adam watching her still, his eyes almost black with passion.

Slowly, slowly, his hands left her arms to slide around her, one spreading across her back, the other over her hips, drawing her ever nearer, until the full globes of her breasts were flattened against his chest. A throbbing heat flared in her lower body as she absorbed the feel of his rigid virility against her soft abdomen.

Laura's head tipped back, her eyes slumbrous and heavy-lidded. Her hands rested against his chest, and unconsciously her fingers began to flex, digging into the warm, hard muscles beneath his shirt.

Adam sucked in his breath, and she felt him shudder. He buried his face in the fragrant cloud of hair at her neck as his arms tightened reflexively, crushing her to him.

"I've been watching you all night, imagining how it would feel to hold you like this. Did you know?"

"Yes," she whispered hoarsely, sliding her arms around his back and pressing her body to his.

"You were wondering, too, weren't you, Laura?"

"I..."

"Weren't you?"

"I..." She paused, biting her lower lip, her eyes tightly closed, but the lie wouldn't come. "Yes. Yes, I wondered," she admitted weakly.

"Then don't pull back. Don't fight me, Laura." He trailed a string of hot kisses up the side of her neck, then his teeth nipped her lobe. "Lord, you feel so good, smell so good. Since that first day, when I kissed you in the old farmhouse, I've been tormented by the memory of your softness, how you felt in my arms, the sweetness of your lips." He raised his head and looked at her. "I want to kiss you again, Laura," he whispered roughly.

Laura stared up at him, unable to speak, and unconsciously, she ran her tongue over her parted lips.

An urgent sound rumbled up from Adam's chest. Her heart pounding, Laura watched his head begin its slow descent, and as his mouth drew near to hers her eyelids fluttered shut once more.

The kiss was aggressive, desperate. Pent-up longings surged to the surface and they clung to one another in almost frantic need. Laura didn't pull back from the rough caress, but welcomed it, reveling in the explosion of passion she had never felt before, had never expected to feel. She was like a child let loose in a candy store, greedily tasting new delights, savoring each exquisite sensation.

At her soft moan of pleasure, Adam lifted his head. His chest rose and fell heavily. A regretful frown drew his brows together at the sight of her swollen lips, and he dipped his head to brush his mouth across hers in a featherlight touch.

"I'm sorry. I didn't mean to hurt you," he said against her lips.

"You didn't." Adam kissed her again. It was the gentlest of caresses. Tender. Tormenting. Laura's lips parted, and their moist breath mingled. His tongue touched the corner of her mouth, then bathed its curving outline. Laura turned her head, blindly seeking complete possession, but he evaded her. Lightly, delicately, his teeth nipped her lower lip, then he drew it into his mouth and sucked gently. Laura groaned. "Adam, please."

"Please what?" His tongue glided over the soft skin of her inner lip.

"Oh, Adam." Her hands clutched at the hard muscles of his back. "Kiss me, Adam. Now," she demanded weakly, her voice breaking on a desperate little sob.

It was as though she had tripped the switch that released the floodgates. Adam's response was instantaneous and overwhelming. His arms tightened around her almost painfully, and with a low growl, his lips captured hers once again.

There was hunger and need, a longing that called to her, demanded an equal response. Laura gave it unhesitatingly. Her mouth opened willingly, accepting the thrusting invasion of his tongue. Her hands withdrew from his back, glided up over his chest and shoulders to twine through the silk-soft hair at his nape.

Then Adam backed her up against the truck. Without breaking the soul-stirring kiss, he slowly pressed the full weight of his body to hers. She could feel his hardness, his warmth, searing her through their clothes. His hands moved to her waist and inched up her ribcage to press against the sides of her breasts, while he slowly undulated his hips against her. Laura's gasp was lost in his mouth. Her fingers clutched his hair as she felt the fiery tingle in the tips of her breasts, between her thighs.

A burst of laughter broke them apart. Adam's head jerked around, and over his shoulder he saw that the Watleys' front door was open and another group of guests was departing. With a muttered curse, he grasped Laura's elbow, jerked the passenger door open, and quickly assisted her into the truck.

Dazed, Laura watched him stride stiffly around to the other side and slide in behind the wheel. They were several blocks from the Watleys' home before she recovered her senses, and the enormity of what she had done hit her. Recalling her uninhibited response, Laura cringed inwardly in agonized embarrassment. Dear heaven! How could she have behaved that way? And what must Adam think of her?

Gnawing worriedly at her lower lip, she studied his set profile, but in the dim light from the dash she could not make out his expression. As though sensing her scrutiny, he glanced her way and a strange little half smile softened the austere lines of his face.

"What are you doing way over there," he said in a low, husky voice that sent a tingle racing over Laura's skin. He reached out and cupped his hand around the back of her neck and tugged her toward him. "Why don't you scoot over here by me."

Laura resisted, pressing herself against the door, and it was then that she noticed that they had left the town behind. Her eyes opened wide in alarm. "Where are we going?" she demanded, the note of panic in her voice clearly discernible as her head swiveled sharply toward him.

"To the farmhouse" was Adam's calm reply. Laura's gasp and the following silence drew his gaze, and he frowned as he noted her gaping expression. "I know it's not ideal, honey, but our choices aren't all that great. Dink Pettigrew is working the night shift at the inn, and if we go there it'll be all over town before morning. And my place won't do because of Mike."

Laura stared at him, her shock quickly turning to anger. "I don't want to go to the farm or anywhere else with you," she snapped. "Just take me back to the inn. This minute."

Adam brought the pickup to a halt at the side of the highway and turned to face her. His expression was cold, his eyes narrowed. "Somehow, that's not the impression I got just a few minutes ago," he said quietly.

Embarrassed color flooded Laura's cheeks, and she was profoundly grateful for the darkness. "Well, you were wrong," she declared shakily, not quite able to meet his eyes.

"Don't give me that. You were more than willing. What is this? Some kind of game? Do you enjoy playing the tease? Or is it the fact that I'm just a small-town lawyer that's bothering you?" He was furiously angry, his voice growing colder and more clipped with every word. "Is that is? Aren't I rich enough for you? Successful enough?"

"No! Of course not!" Laura cried, genuinely shocked. "Look, just because I don't want to jump into bed with you doesn't mean—"

"Oh, but you did want to, Mrs. Phillips," he goaded nastily. "You wanted to very much. You still do. Playing the stud for a frustrated widow isn't all that appealing to me, but I'm willing to make an exception in your case."

Laura almost choked on her rage. "You egotistical bastard. What makes you think you're God's gift to women? And how typical for a small-minded, neanderthal hick to think that a woman can't function without a man. Well, let me tell you something, mister, I don't need you or any other man. For anything." She gave him one last glare, then turned away and grabbed the door handle. Before she could get it open Adam's hand clamped over hers. His eyes stabbed into her, his arm stretched across her breasts pinning her to the seat.

"Where do you think you're going?" he growled.

"If you won't take me back to town I'll walk. Now, let me go."

"Don't be ridiculous. Just calm down and I'll take you back." They stared at each other in hostile silence for several seconds. When he was satisfied that she wouldn't bolt again, he straightened and put the truck in gear. Gravel sprayed in the air as he made a screeching U turn. Not one word was spoken between them until they reached the inn.

Laura was out of the truck before he brought it to a

complete stop. "Good night, Mr. Kincaid," she snapped, slamming the door behind her.

She rushed up the steps, but before she reached the top one, he had pulled away in a squeal of tires, leaving the smell of burned rubber hanging in the air.

Chapter Six

Laura sipped the black coffee cautiously. With her elbows propped on the table, she cradled the cup with both hands, letting the aromatic steam waft across her face. Her eyeballs ached and her head felt like a block of wood. Disconsolately she conceded that last night's crying jag, and the hours of self-recrimination that had followed, had solved nothing.

She took another sip of coffee, then returned the cup to its saucer, keeping her forefinger crooked through the handle. Her other hand lay on the table, and she idly traced the squiggly pattern in the Formica with her fingernail. Depression sat on her shoulders like a lead yoke. Nothing seemed to be working out right. Every time her relationship with Adam progressed a step, something happened to push it back two.

On the other side of the café a group of ranchers were gathered around a table for their regular morning coffee session. As usual, in between hurrahing Maybelle, they were swapping tall tales and discussing everything from the price of grain to the situation in the Middle East. Lost in her morose thoughts, Laura tuned out the raucous palaver and stared out the window, wondering what she should do, if she had ruined any chance she'd had of getting to know Mike...and Adam.

The bell above the door jangled. Disinterestedly, Laura looked up...and froze. Adam, looking large and intimidating, was just closing the door behind him.

Panicked, Laura's eyes darted around for an avenue of escape, but there was none. Adam stood squarely in front of the door, hands on his hips, his eyes making a searching sweep of the small café. She slid lower in her seat and ducked her head, hoping he wouldn't notice her, but peeking through the veil of hair that had swung forward over her cheek she saw that he was already striding in her direction.

Stubbornly, she refused to look up when he stopped beside the booth where she sat.

"Good morning, Laura," he said quietly, after a moment of strained silence.

Her face cool and remote, Laura raised her head and looked out the window.

"May I join you?"

"No."

A stained, gray Stetson plopped onto the vinyl seat opposite her. Adam slid into the booth after it. Laura's head snapped around, sending her hair swinging out in a rippling, honey-colored curtain. Outrage flashed from her eyes and tightened her expression. "How dare..." She stopped and darted a look around, then continued in a low, furious hiss, "I said no, you can't sit here. Now, go away."

"Laura, we have to talk."

"I think you said quite enough last night. I'm not interested in hearing any more of your insults."

She reached for her purse and started to slide out of the

booth, but he stopped her cold with a quiet "I'm sorry, Laura."

She looked at him warily, not certain she'd heard him right. He was dressed in jeans, a plaid shirt, and a faded denim jacket. He looked rugged and appealing, and totally male, and she was held mesmerized by the earnest look of entreaty in his eyes. With a stiff little nod, she placed her purse back on the seat, folded her hands before her on the paper placemat, and waited for him to speak.

His gaze lowered to the salt shaker he was absently rotating. "Last night I behaved badly, and you had every right to be angry. I came on too strong, then when you said no, I reacted like the bastard you called me."

He looked up to find that Laura's face remained set, her posture rigid. After her temper had cooled the night before, she had admitted to herself that she was as much to blame for what had happened as Adam. She had done nothing to discourage him, had, in fact, welcomed his kisses, had returned them eagerly. She could understand his anger, up to a point, but the hurtful things he'd said still rankled.

"I've got a helluva temper and...well, I guess I'm sensitive about some things, and I shot off my mouth when I shouldn't have," he continued. "But I'm hoping that you'll forgive me again, and give me another chance."

Laura turned her head and stared out the window, then cut her eyes back to him resentfully. "I'm not a sex-starved widow desperately searching for a lover," she said, hurt quivering in her voice.

"I know that." Adam reached out and pried her hands apart. Holding both of them in his, he smiled at her warmly, his eyes coaxing. "I didn't mean any of the things I said, Laura. I was angry and hurt and frustrated, and I was striking back, but I knew, even as I said them, that they weren't true."

From the corner of her eye Laura saw that Maybelle was watching them with interest, and she tried to pull her hands from his grasp. "Adam," she admonished a bit desperately when he refused to release her. "We'll be the topic of the latest gossip if you don't let go."

Adam chuckled wickedly and shook his head. "It's too late to worry about that, honey. In this town, if you're seen with the same person twice you're as good as engaged. By now we're already an item."

"You're not serious."

"'Fraid so."

At her dismayed expression his fingers tightened and his thumbs stroked back and forth across the tender skin on the backs of her hands. "So you see, you have to forgive me." He cocked his head to one side and gave her a coaxing, teasing look. "You will forgive me, won't you, Laura?"

"Yes. Yes, of course," she said with obvious agitation, and this time she did pull her hands free. "But—"

Adam's brows rose. "But...?"

"But"—Laura squirmed, not wanting to sound presumptuous, hating what she was about to say, yet knowing she had to—"but that's all. We both forget what happened last night. We...we remain friends, but nothing more." She shook her head emphatically and tried to ignore Adam's growing scowl. "I don't want to get involved with you, Adam."

"Why not? You're single. I'm single. We're attracted to each other. Why fight it?"

"Because...I...just don't think it would be wise," she answered feebly.

"Why?" Adam fired right back. "Because of our business relationship? We're both mature adults. We should be able to keep the two things separate." He halted, his eyes narrowing on her. "Or was there some truth in what I said last night? Does the fact that you could probably buy and sell me twice over bother you?"

"No! It's not that at all!"

"Then what's the problem?"

Laura gazed at him helplessly. *The problem is me. That*

I could very easily fall in love with you. That I'm your son's natural mother. And that if you ever found out you'd probably hate me, and I don't think I could stand that. Finally she swallowed around the constriction in her throat and stammered out, "I...I'm just not ready for a serious relationship yet."

Adam relaxed somewhat. One corner of his mouth quirked up in a lopsided, self-derisive smile. "Neither was I, in the beginning," he confessed. "But I've discovered that's not something you can control." He leaned forward, his voice becoming low and rough with urgency. "We've got something pretty special going for us, Laura. You can't just throw it away. I won't *let* you throw it away."

"But—"

"No buts. I won't rush you, for now. At least...not too much. But make up your mind to it, if you stay here you're going to have to give this relationship a chance, because I'm not going to go away."

Dismay and elation flooded Laura in equal measure. She didn't know whether to laugh or cry. Or both. He was giving her no choice, really, and illogically, foolishly, deep in her heart she was glad. Fingering the edge of the paper placemat, she met his level, demanding gaze, unable to think of a single thing to say.

"Here's your breakfast, such as it is." A plate containing a poached egg and a single piece of toast was plopped down in front of Laura, making her jump. She looked up to find Maybelle standing beside the booth, eyeing her speculatively. After pouring more coffee into Laura's cup, she turned to Adam and placed her free hand on her generous hip. "How about you, Adam? You want some breakfast"—she glanced at Laura and looked back at him with a sly smile— "or are you just visitin'?"

Adam grinned wickedly. "Just visitin', Maybelle. But I will join Laura in a cup of coffee."

The smug look on the woman's face as she turned and bustled back to the counter for another cup made Laura groan silently. By noon half the people in town would know that they were more than just business acquaintances.

After Maybelle had served his coffee and moved away, Adam leaned back and smiled. "I guess you'll have Ezra fix up the house after he's finished with the store, won't you?"

Laura accepted the change of subject gratefully. "No. I want to do it myself," she said as she peeled the top from a tiny plastic jelly container. "I plan to move in immediately and make the improvements a little at a time. You said yourself all it needs is a little cosmetic work." She spread the grape jelly on a triangle of toast and smiled at Adam's astounded look. "Contrary to what you may think, I am perfectly capable of stripping woodwork and hanging wallpaper."

"You know, I believe you are," he said finally, looking strangely pleased. "Tell you what, I'll help you in the afternoons whenever I can, and on weekends. That way you'll get through sooner."

Laura's smile faded and a look of caution entered her eyes. Though it was tempting, in more ways than one, she knew it wasn't wise, but when she opened her mouth to tell him so, Adam cut her off with "Mike will help, too, if you're worried about being alone with me."

The forkful of egg halted halfway to her mouth. "Mi..." She stopped to clear her throat. "Mike? He...uh...he won't mind? I mean, there are probably lots of things he'd rather do than help me fix up an old house." Her heart was hammering at the mere prospect but she struggled to keep her expression calm.

"True. But I make sure that Mike's play time is balanced with an equal amount of chores and responsibilities. Besides, he knows that around here we help out our neighbors when we can."

Laura's emotions were in chaos. It was what she wanted, what she'd moved there for: to get to know Mike, for him to get to know her, to establish a bond between them. What she hadn't planned on was becoming romantically involved with his father. And she knew if she said yes she would be accepting more than just his offer of help. They both knew it.

She sipped her coffee, stalling for time, torn between guilt and longing. Did she dare let their relationship develop, as Adam obviously intended it to? He wanted more than mere friendship; he'd been honest with her about that. *The trouble is,* her conscience smote her, *you haven't been honest with him.*

But she *couldn't* be honest with him. Not yet. Maybe later, she told herself with a kind of frantic hopefulness, if they came to really care for each other, she could tell him then. If not, if the attraction fizzled, there would be no need to confess.

It was sheer rationalization, and Laura knew it, but as she looked across the table at Adam's ruggedly appealing face, as she thought about the son she so desperately wanted to know, the temptation became too strong to resist. Laura took a deep breath, hesitated, then said quietly, "Well, if you're sure you don't mind, I could use your help."

Niggling doubts continued to plague Laura, but during the following week she was so busy that for the most part she was able to push them aside. Monday, after concluding the purchase of the house, she spent the remainder of the day with Ezra Simpson, inspecting the progress in the shop and discussing the work schedule. The next day she checked out of the inn and drove back to Houston. There she met with her attorney and her banker, and spent two days with Diane, tying up loose ends and going over last-minute details. Friday morning she packed up the remainder of the things she wanted to take with her, closed up her apartment, and drove back to Oakridge, tingling with excitement and hope, and just a bit of apprehension.

It was dark when Laura arrived at the house, and she

was pleased to see that Adam, as he had promised, had sent someone over to clean and air it out. For the next several hours Laura trudged back and forth between the car and the house, unloading her things and putting them away. It was after midnight before she unearthed the linen and made up the brass bed in the master bedroom. After a hot shower she crawled between the crisp sheets and collapsed in exhausted slumber, a pleased smile curving her mouth in anticipation of the next day.

Laura was peeking out the parlor window for the tenth time in as many minutes when the pickup pulled into the drive shortly after breakfast. She released the lace curtain to rush to the front door and stepped out onto the porch before Adam brought the truck to a halt.

A light frost coated the lawn. The rising sun cast long splinters of sunshine through the trees, making the icy crystals glitter like diamonds. Laura smiled and waved to Adam, but when Mike climbed out of the cab her eyes latched on to him hungrily. Emotion welled within her as she watched him saunter to the back of the truck. In the chill morning air his breath puffed out in small, billowy clouds. His legs looked long and gangly in the tight-fitting jeans, his hands and sneaker-clad feet large. The wind ruffled his black hair and molded his sweatshirt against his lean but powerful torso. Already his shoulders and chest were impressively wide. It seemed miraculous to Laura that the red-faced baby she had once glimpsed had developed into this big, strapping boy.

Coming around from the other side, Adam joined him, but before they could lower the tailgate the Irish setter dancing around in the back of the truck leaped over the side. The dog streaked around the yard, a blur of mahogany red, leaving a circular line of tracks in the frost, barking and kicking up grass and dead leaves in an excess of energy and sheer high spirits.

Mike laughed. "Here, girl, here, Molly," he called.

The dog raced over to him at only slightly reduced speed and cavorted eagerly at his feet. When Mike dropped to one knee and fondled her head, she licked his face, her whole body wiggling in ecstasy, her plumed tail whipping the air.

Deeply touched by the sight of the boy and his dog, Laura watched them with misty eyes.

"Here, Mike. Give me a hand with this," Adam instructed, pulling two tool boxes from the bed of the truck and giving one to the boy when he rose.

A friendly smile curved Adam's mouth as he and Mike climbed the porch steps, but the look in his eyes was warm and intimate, sending a tingle racing over Laura's skin. She was ready for work, dressed in tight, faded jeans and an oversized flannel shirt whose tail flapped around her thighs, and when his eyes swept over her she could see by his expression that he approved. "Good morning," he said pleasantly. "How was your first night in your new home?"

"Fine." She glanced at Mike, but he quickly looked away. He stood stiffly beside his father, holding the tool box in one hand, the other absently scratching the Irish setter's head. A wavering smile pulled at Laura's mouth when her gaze swung back to Adam. "I...I really do appreciate this."

"Think nothing of it. We're glad to help. Aren't we, son?"

She received the merest glance from Mike. "Yes, ma'am," he said in an expressionless voice.

"Son, why don't you go get the drop cloths and the ladder while I take these things into the house," Adam said.

"Okay." Mike handed the tool box to his father and loped back down the steps. Laura had the uneasy feeling that he was glad for the excuse to get away from her.

Laura led the way inside and held the door open for Adam, but when she closed it and started for the living room, he put both boxes on the floor and grabbed her wrist, swinging her around in front of him. "Wait a minute," he said softly. Cupping her chin in his hand, he brought her startled face up and captured her parted lips with his.

It was the softest of kisses, yet it slammed through Laura with a force that rocked her all the way to her toes. Lips rubbed, tongues touched, moist breaths mingled, and Laura felt her breasts swell, her feminine core flower and throb.

When Adam pulled back he gazed deep into her eyes. "Hi," he said in a husky voice.

"Hi."

"I missed you."

"I...I missed you, too," she managed in a breathy whisper.

The second kiss was heated, more demanding, as strong arms wrapped her in a passionate embrace that didn't end until the heavy tread of Mike's footsteps crossing the porch warned them of his imminent arrival.

Flustered, Laura pulled away. Avoiding Adam's amused eyes, she rushed to the door to hold it open while Mike maneuvered the ladder into the hall. Molly came trotting in on his heels, her tongue lolling out of the side of her mouth, tail wagging.

Adam frowned when the dog began an immediate investigation of the new surroundings. "Maybe you'd better leave Molly outside, Mike," he suggested. "Mrs. Phillips may not like animals in her house."

"Oh, no, that's all right—" she began, but Mike was already stalking toward the door.

He jerked it open and uttered a sharp command. Molly whined once in protest, but when her master repeated the order she slunk dejectedly out.

"Really, Mike, I don't mind if she stays," Laura insisted worriedly when she saw his set expression.

He gave her a cool look. "It doesn't matter." He turned away to pick up the ladder and then carried it into the living room.

Laura stared after him, feeling sad and troubled. She would have let him bring a full-grown lion into the house, if that was what he wanted. With a dejected sigh, she trailed along behind him.

They started in the living room. After covering the furniture with cloths, they began stripping the faded wallpaper from the walls. By the time they stopped for lunch they had progressed through the entry hall and were working on the dining room. Through it all, Mike was silent and distant.

Over sandwiches and soft drinks, consumed around the old oak table in the kitchen, Laura tried several times to draw him out, but all her friendly overtures were met with monosyllabic replies, delivered with a stiff formality that bordered on rudeness. The moment Mike swallowed the last bite of his sandwich he asked to be excused, and when he disappeared through the door, Laura turned worried eyes on Adam.

"I don't think he likes me," she said sadly, the admission bringing with it immeasurable pain.

"No, no, it's not that, honey." Adam gave her hand a consoling squeeze. "Like most fourteen-year-old boys, he's just feeling awkward and self-conscious. He'll get over it."

She tried to smile but all she could manage was a pitiful twitch of her lips. She gathered the dishes and carried them to the sink, turning on the hot water and adding a squirt of liquid detergent. Keeping her back to Adam, she fought back tears and the terrible feeling of despair that was burgeoning inside her.

Adam's arms circled her waist from behind, crossing over her midriff, his fingers shaping her ribs while his hands pressed against the undersides of her breasts. "Hey, don't worry," he murmured. His breath was warm and moist in her ear as his lips nibbled the velvety swirls. "He'll loosen up soon."

The smell of lemony soap rose from the sink. Outside, Molly was barking at a squirrel in the pecan tree, and from the dining room came the scrape of metal as Mike repositioned the ladder. With a sigh, Laura relaxed back against the hard wall of Adam's chest and closed her eyes, savoring the comfort of his arms about her. "I hope you're right," she said longingly.

Adam turned her around and, mindless of her soapy hands, looped her arms around his neck. Lacing his fingers together at the small of her back, he smiled down while his warm hazel eyes roamed her face. Their lower bodies were locked together, and he rocked his hips gently against her, smiling wider as her eyes grew large and a flush spread up her neck and face all to the way to her hairline. "If it were any other male but my son occupying so much of your thoughts, I'd be jealous, but at least now I know how to get your attention," he said, chuckling wickedly as her flush deepened.

"I...I feel it's important that Mike and I get along," she stammered, ignoring the last part of his statement. "If you and I are going to...to..."

"Oh, we're going to, honey," Adam declared suggestively as his head descended. "We're definitely going to."

Their lips met warmly in a soft caress that grew steadily firmer as passion built. Laura did not pull away from the hungry demand but welcomed it. She needed to be held, to be desired, to be reassured that he cared for her. Her emotions felt bruised, her spirits flagging, and she burrowed close, wrapping her arms around him, seeking a balm for her aching heart from this man she was coming to care for so deeply.

Adam's hands roamed over her, exploring the slenderness of her waist, her narrow back, the delicate shoulder blades. Slipping beneath the loose-fitting flannel shirt, his fingers worked erotically up and down the shallow trench that marked her spine, and she shivered helplessly and pressed closer.

His tongue swirled over the delicate skin of her inner lip, tested the slightly serrated edge of her teeth, then dipped into the sweet warmth beyond. Their tongues entwined lovingly, tasting each other's essence, and for a time, the world and all the problems they faced fell away.

Long moments later, when their clinging lips parted both were breathing hard. Passion still swirled in Adam's hazel eyes when he studied her swollen lips, her half-shuttered glazed eyes, and with a wavering sigh, he lowered his forehead against hers and closed his eyes. "Oh, lady. You take my breath away."

He straightened and framed her face in his hands, his thumbs caressing her cheekbones. His eyes were warm, slightly teasing, and very tender. "Now," he began decisively, "I want you to stop worrying about Mike, Just be patient and give him time, and everything will work out. You'll see."

Laura smiled wanly and nodded. She wanted to believe him, but it was hard.

It grew even harder as the day wore on. Mike worked unstintingly, but he remained frigidly polite and distant, speaking to her only when she asked a direct question and never looking at her if he could avoid it. By the time they quit for the day Laura had given up trying to break the ice.

"We'll leave the tools here and be back tomorrow, after church," Adam said as they walked toward the front door, dodging around ladders, trim knives, scrapers, and plastic bags crammed with the shredded wallpaper. The worst of the mess had been disposed of, but the floor was still littered with torn scraps. A fine, powdery residue covered everything, and dust motes hung in the air.

"Are you sure I can't talk you into staying for dinner?" Laura asked hopefully. She cast a worried glance at Mike. Despite his attitude, she was hoping they would stay.

"Sorry. I'd like to, but Aunt Harriet is expecting us." Adam paused with his hand on the doorknob and smiled coaxingly. "Why don't you come with us? I'm sure she'd be delighted to have you."

Any temptation Laura might have felt to take him up on his offer was quickly squelched by the look of burning anger that flashed in Mike's brown eyes. Regretfully, she shook her head. "Thanks, but no. I think I'm going to have a quick bite, followed by a long hot soak and an early night.''

''Okay, see you tomorrow,'' Adam said as they stepped out onto the porch into the gathering dusk. Mike loped down the steps and called to his dog, but Adam lagged a few feet behind. When the boy started down the walk, he halted and said, ''Go on and get in the truck, Mike. I'll be right back, I forgot something.''

Laura moved aside as Adam stepped into the foyer and closed the door behind him. ''What did you forget?''

''This.'' He hooked a hand around her neck to pull her near, tilted her head up with his free hand, and pressed a hard kiss on her parted lips.

When he released her, her heart was thudding. Adam flicked the end of her nose and grinned. ''That was to hold me until tomorrow,'' he whispered, and then he turned and was gone.

Dreamily, Laura stood in the open doorway and watched him stride down the walk, swing around the front of the truck, and slide in on the driver's side. But when her gaze switched to the sullen boy beside him a deep sadness entered her eyes. Forlornly, she slumped against the jamb and watched him as Adam reversed the truck out of the drive, and wondered at her own naive dreams.

She had planned so carefully, had such high hopes. It had never once occurred to her that Mike would reject her out of hand.

Chapter Seven

Laura emptied the packets of cocoa mix into three mugs and filled them with hot water from the kettle. As she began to stir the first one the door behind her swung open, and she looked over her shoulder in time to see Mike stiffen and jerk to a halt at the sight of her.

"Sorry. I didn't know you were in here," he said flatly.

"That's all right. Come on in."

Reluctantly he complied, giving her a wide berth as he headed for the sink. "I just wanted a drink of water."

"How about some hot chocolate?" Laura offered with a smile, quickly adding marshmallows to the three mugs and placing them on a tray. "I was just about to bring it in."

"No, thanks." Without even looking at her offering, he pulled a paper cup from the dispenser by the sink and filled it from the tap.

Laura watched him drink the water down, toss the cup into the trash can, then turn and start back for the door.

Before he reached it she asked softly, "Mike, what's wrong?"

He paused only briefly and slanted her a cold look over his shoulder. "Nothing," he said, and pushed through the door into the hall.

Laura gazed at the swinging panel. When it finally came to a halt she turned back to the three mugs of cocoa. Steam wafted in curling tendrils from the foamy brown surface of the liquid, bringing with it the scent of warm chocolate. Fighting back tears, Laura picked up one mug and poured the cocoa down the sink.

She rinsed out the cup and placed it in the drain rack. With both hands, she gripped the edge of the sink and stared out the window above it at the dazzling October sunshine. Her lips were pressed tightly together. Her eyes were anguished. Two weeks. Two weeks, and nothing had changed. Weekends and most evenings after football practice, providing Mike didn't have any homework, he and Adam came over and they sanded floors and stripped woodwork, but he didn't relent in his attitude toward her. Not an inch.

Day by day, as she and Adam drew closer, her relationship with Mike grew more strained.

Why? What had she done that made him dislike her so? Laura's mind groped for an answer, her grip on the sink unconsciously tightening until her knuckles were white, but, as always, it eluded her.

Maybe she was expecting too much too soon. Maybe, as Adam said, she simply needed to give him more time. Don't push, Laura, she told herself firmly. Just be patient. He'll accept you eventually. He *has* to.

Resolutely, Laura picked up the two mugs and shouldered her way through the door.

They worked diligently for two more hours, until Adam finally called a halt. Tossing down the sandpaper he had been using on the banister, he announced, "All right, gang, that's it for today. I think it's time we rewarded ourselves with an afternoon off. Whaddya you say we go fishing?''

"All of us?" Mike asked dubiously, with a sidelong glance at Laura.

"Sure. We'll take a Thermos of coffee and laze on the riverbank in the sun. If we catch enough, we'll have fried fish and hushpuppies for dinner.''

The look on Mike's face made Laura hesitant, but Adam would not take no for an answer, and within minutes, she found herself in the kitchen preparing a pot of coffee.

Her large Thermos was in the very back of a lower cabinet, and she had to practically crawl inside to reach it. Just as she was backing out, warm hands settled on her bottom and fondled intimately. Laura let out a startled shriek, straightened, and whirled around.

"Adam, really!" she gasped as she met his salacious grin. "I'm surprised at you.''

"Sorry. I just couldn't resist when I saw that delectable little tush stuck up in the air like that.''

Laura eyed him askance. His tone and the bold, lascivious glint in his eyes were anything but repentant. She tilted her chin and tried her best to look stern, but it was difficult when he was so darned sexy and appealing, standing there in his tight jeans and baggy sweatshirt, giving her that wolfish grin.

"Well, you just keep your hands to yourself," she sniffed in mock indignation. "What if Mike had walked in?"

"So what if he had?" Adam reached out and encircled her waist with both arms and pulled her close. Laura's heart thumped madly as his warm, caressing gaze roamed her face. "Don't you think by now he knows why I spend every spare minute over here playing handyman?''

"You mean you're not just being neighborly?"

"Hardly." The word came out on a low, deliciously wicked chuckle that sent a thrill of anticipation feathering up Laura's spine, and when his head began its descent she closed her eyes and lifted willing lips to his.

Warm and moist and oh so sensuous, their mouths met, rubbed, aroused. Slowly, they drew out the tactile pleasure, malleable lips fused and open, each breathing the other's essence, savoring what was now, anticipating what was to come.

Adam's tongue bathed her lips, then slipped between them and touched the tip of hers, withdrew, and touched again. Laura moaned and threaded her fingers into the silky hair at his nape to urge him closer as her own tongue met the teasing challenge.

Passions built and the kiss grew deeper, more intense, until finally they were forced to draw apart and gulp for air. "Oh, Laura, Laura," he murmured as he strung a line of nibbling kisses down the side of her neck. "I want you. Lord, how I want you." His voice was thick and heavy with need, his breath moist and warm against her skin.

Laura clung to him weakly, her neck arched back, eyes closed, her fingers flexing rhythmically against the tense muscles in his shoulders as she whispered softly, "Adam. Adam."

Adam's hands roamed over her hips and waist, slid up over her ribs to the sides of her breasts. With soft pressure, the heels of his hands rotated against the swelling fullness, lifting, squeezing. Nuzzling aside the loose shirt, he pressed hot kisses on the firm, rounded flesh that strained above her bra.

The delicious shiver that rippled through Laura acted like a trigger, and he straightened abruptly and captured her lips once again in a hard, demanding kiss. With a growl, he turned and leaned back against the counter, bringing her to stand between his spread thighs. His large hands cupped her buttocks, moving her hips in a sensual rhythm against his aroused body.

A sound, a harsh intake of breath followed by a short moan of distress, penetrated the ardent haze that surrounded them. They drew apart, slowly at first, but when Laura glanced over her shoulder and saw Mike, she jerked out of Adam's arms. Mike stood frozen in the doorway, his extended hand still pushing against the door. His face was anguished.

The absolute horror in his eyes tore at Laura's heart, and she took a step toward him, one hand reaching out to him. "Mike, dear, don't be upset. Let us—"

"No!" He screamed the word, glaring at her with hate-filled eyes that were rapidly filling with tears. Shaking his head slowly, he began to back away. "Just stay away from me! Just stay away!"

And then he bolted.

The door swung madly as they stood there, too stunned to move, listening to his running footsteps recede down the central hall. When the front door banged back against the wall, Laura winced and turned frantic eyes to Adam.

She placed her hands on his arm. "Oh, Adam," she wailed beseechingly. "You've got to do something!"

He sighed wearily and ran his hand through his hair. "What do you suggest?"

"Go to him. Talk to him. Make him understand."

He gave her a sardonic look, a half smile twisting one corner of his mouth. "Oh, I think he understands, all right. He just doesn't like it."

"Adam, *please*. I can't stand to see him so unhappy. Go to him, please. For my sake."

Her distress was obvious, and as he looked down into her pleading eyes, Adam's grim expression softened. His hand cupped her cheek tenderly and he gave her a warm, reassuring smile. "Okay, I'll go." Bending, he brushed a kiss across her trembling mouth. "But don't worry. Everything will work out."

For a long time after he had gone, Laura stood in the silent kitchen, her arms hugged across her midriff. Guilt overwhelmed her. It was a heavy ache in her chest that wouldn't go away. For several minutes she closed her eyes and breathed deeply, but it didn't help. Over and over, she kept hearing the pain in Mike's voice, seeing the shock and anguish on his face.

Finally the sound of the coffee maker gurgling to a stop broke into the heavy silence, and she turned and snapped it off. With leadened steps, she pushed through the door and walked down the hall into the parlor. The floor was littered with tools, newspapers, paint cans, sandpaper, steel wool, rags. The sharp smell of varnish remover hung in the air. The furniture was draped with sheets, and when Laura uncovered the chair beside the fireplace, dust and bits of trash billowed.

She sat down in the chair and leaned her head back against its high, ornate back. Everything had seemed so simple when she'd made her plans; she would make friends with Adam Kincaid, and through him, get to know her son. Laura shook her head and gave a short laugh. Which just goes to show how the best-laid plans can go awry, she thought glumly. She was falling in love with Adam and losing ground daily with Mike.

Both situations were disastrous, yet there didn't seem to be a thing she could do about either. Except wait, and hope.

She rolled her head against the chair back and stared sadly out the window. Why, she wondered, did loving always hurt so much.

It was almost nine that evening when Adam called. He sounded tired as he explained that it had taken several hours to locate Mike, and several more for their discussion. About what had transpired between them, he relayed very little, except to say that they had talked it out and everything was fine now, and they would be over tomorrow after church, as usual.

Laura was a bundle of nerves when their truck pulled into the drive shortly after noon the next day. Nervously, she left the window where she had been keeping watch and hurried to the door, but had to pause to run her damp palms down the sides of her jeans before opening it.

Her eyes went instantly to Mike, then skittered to Adam. He gave her a warm, reassuring smile.

"Hi. If you're still speaking to the Kincaid men, we'd like to come in. Mike has something he wants to say to you."

"Of course," she said quickly, stepping back to hold the door wide. As she closed it behind them she silently cursed herself for being so jittery. She had meant to be composed and casual, but despite her best effort there was a quaver in her voice and her smile felt fixed and wooden.

For a moment no one moved or said a word, and the awkward silence grew. Laura folded her arms across her midriff to keep from twisting her hands together. Mike stood as stiff as a statue, his face an expressionless mask, until his father nudged his arm and gave him a pointed look.

"I'm sorry," he said in a flat voice that held not a hint of emotion. His brown eyes were cold and focused on a point just beyond Laura's left shoulder. "I shouldn't have run out like I did."

But your feelings haven't changed, have they, was the thought that immediately crossed Laura's mind. A soul-deep sadness pierced her as she realized that, regardless of what Adam thought, Mike was just giving lip service; he wasn't in the least sorry for either his attitude or his actions.

She wanted to cry. Instead, she smiled sadly and said, "That's all right, Mike. I understand."

Adam rubbed his hands together. "Well, now that we've got that out of the way, let's go on that fishing trip we planned yesterday." Surprised, Laura started to protest but he stopped her with an upraised hand. "No. I won't take no for an answer. We all need a break. The stream that cuts through my land is within easy walking distance of here and chock-full of fish just begging to be caught. Mike and I brought a can of worms, the poles, and a hamper of food, so you just do whatever you have to do to get ready, and let's be on our way.''

After the scene the day before, Laura was reluctant to accompany them, but Adam waved aside all her protests. A short time later, as they climbed through the fence at the back of her property and started down the narrow path that angled through the woods, she was glad she had allowed herself to be persuaded.

They walked single file down the trail, with Mike in the lead and Molly scampering ahead, busily investigating everything. Occasionally the dog would tear off into the woods, barking excitedly at some small animal or bird, then come trotting back when the foe was routed, looking pleased with herself.

The light frosts of October had tinted the leaves gold and red. It was one of those perfect autumn days, the sky a vivid, cloudless blue, the air crisp and clean, redolent with the scents of dried leaves and cool earth and warm sunshine. As they hiked along the winding path Laura breathed deeply, savoring the nip of fall in the air. Except for the snap of twigs and the rustle of leaves underfoot, it was quiet and serene, and she smiled as she gazed around, a feeling of contentment beginning to seep into her. In the short time she had lived there, she had come to love the rugged countryside.

The land was hilly, swelling gently in places, and in others rising and dipping in deep folds, like a ruffle on a woman's skirt. There were a few open pastures but most of the hillsides around Oakridge were thick with forests. There were gnarled oaks, the branches of which reached out like grotesque arms, tall, dark green, symmetrical cedars, feathery mesquites, and along the creeks and rivers, majestic native pecan trees. It was dry, rocky country, and there was a toughness about it, a unique beauty that appealed to Laura.

They had walked only about a quarter of a mile when,

behind her, Adam muttered an annoyed "Oh, hell" and came to a halt.

"What's wrong?" Laura asked as both she and Mike stopped and looked back. Adam was standing in the middle of the path, the picnic hamper at his feet, looking thoroughly disgusted.

"I forgot the net. I'll have to go back for it. Mike, you take Laura on to the creek and I'll catch up with you." When Laura started to retrieve the hamper he waved her on. "No, leave that. I'll get it when I come back."

As Adam disappeared around a curve in the path, Laura turned cautiously back to Mike. "I can wait here for Adam, if you'd rather go on by yourself," she offered.

"Naw, that's okay." He gave a one-shouldered shrug. "It's just a little farther, anyway."

When he turned and resumed walking, Laura stared after him, stunned. He didn't seem to mind in the least, being left alone with her! It wasn't what she had expected at all.

A few yards down the path he stopped and looked back. "You coming or not?" he demanded.

A hopeful, hesitant smile tugged at Laura's lips, and then, with a start, she pulled herself together and took off after him, her heart lightening apace with her hurrying footsteps.

Within minutes Laura heard the gurgle of water. The path made a sharp bend around a boulder, angled down an incline, then suddenly they were free of the trees and standing on the bank of the creek. It was only about twenty feet wide but clear and fast running, the water tumbling over and rushing around the small boulders that littered the stream bed, creating foaming little white caps. It was not very deep where they stood. For several feet out from the bank Laura could see the bottom, where small rounded pebbles lay like scattered jewels, smoothed to a satiny luster by the unending flow of water.

"The best place to fish is down there," Mike said, pointing downstream to where the creek widened and made a sharp bend, creating a pool against the far bank. The water was obviously deeper there, more placid. The glassy surface barely shimmered with movement.

Moving a few feet farther upstream, Mike braced his foot on a boulder in the water's edge. "We can cross here."

Laura dubiously eyed the string of unevenly spaced boulders spanning the creek. They were bigger than most, their top surfaces well clear of the water, but she wasn't too keen on hopping across them.

"Come on, it's easy," Mike said, smiling encouragement as he leaped agilely from one rock to the next. Molly bounded after him joyfully, her tail fanning the air.

The land on the other side of the creek was several feet higher, and the bank angled up sharply, exposing a large pocket of soft clay, which the recent rains had made slick and gooey. Mike jumped from the last boulder onto the narrow strip of level ground at the bottom of the bank and leaned the three poles against the incline. Grinning, he held out his hand and called across to Laura, "Come on, I'll help you."

The grin was impossible to resist. Screwing up her courage, Laura took a deep breath and hopped out onto the first boulder. With each jump she had to flail her arms wildly to keep her balance, but finally she made it to the last one.

"Here, take my hand," Mike offered as she prepared to make the final leap, and Laura accepted gratefully. The tug he gave her hand brought her sailing over the water easily, but the instant she touched ground Mike's foot shot out, catching her across the shins, and with a startled shriek, she went sprawling, face first, into the clay bank.

For a moment, Laura was too stunned to move. She had managed to turn her head to one side but half of her face, her hands, and her upper torso were embedded in the sticky goo. Slowly, carefully, uttering little moaning sounds of distress, Laura began to extricate herself. There were small slurping, sucking sounds as she lifted her head and pulled first one, then the other hand free. Awkwardly, she pushed herself out of the bank and turned slowly.

The glutinous mess covered her. It clung to the side of her face and hair, squished between her fingers, and oozed down the front of her shirt. Using the back of her hand she wiped away the glob of clay that clung to her cheek and gazed at Mike with sad, reproachful eyes.

"Why, Mike? Why?" she asked in a voice that quavered with hurt.

He didn't pretend to misunderstand. His face grew stiff with defiant anger and his jaw hardened. "You'll never take my mother's place," he hissed. "Not with me, and not with my Dad, so you may as well stop trying! Dad and I were getting along just fine before you came along. We don't need you! And we don't want you!"

"Oh, Mike. I'm not trying to take your mother's place. No one can do that. I wouldn't want to. Don't you see—"

"Dad loved my mother very much," he ground out fiercely, cutting off her explanation. "He'll always love her. Never you."

He was shaking with barely suppressed fury, his nostrils flared and white, his eyes burning, and as she gazed at him Laura felt a crushing sense of defeat. "Oh, Mike, I—"

"Laura? Laura, good grief, what happened?" Adam's shout cut her off, and she and Mike turned in time to see him drop his load on the opposite bank and hurry cross the creek, bounding from one boulder to the next with barely a pause. He leaped onto the narrow bank beside them and stared incredulously at Laura.

"All right, what the hell happened?" Sensing the tension between the three humans, Molly eyed them worriedly and whined.

Under his father's black scowl Mike shifted uneasily. As he glanced at Laura she could see the apprehension in his eyes. "I...well..."

"It was all my fault," Laura said quickly, drawing a startled look from Mike. "I simply lost my footing and fell flat on my face." She gave a weak laugh and swiped at the wet clay sliding slowly down her breasts. "Just call me Grace."

Adam was not completely mollified. Still glaring at Mike, he demanded, "What were you even doing on this side of the creek? I told you to take her to our favorite fishing spot, over on the other side, opposite the pool."

"I—"

"Don't blame Mike, Adam," Laura interceded again. "I was the one who wanted to come over here." She wasn't going to let Mike get into trouble over the incident. He couldn't help feeling as he did, and if she hadn't barged into their lives it wouldn't have happened.

"And now," she continued before Adam could speak, "if you don't mind, I think I'll go home and get out of these clothes before this stuff hardens."

With Adam leading the way, they recrossed the creek. This time Laura was not in the least cautious; a dunking no longer concerned her.

"Come on, I'll take you home," Adam said when she reached the opposite bank.

"Oh, no. No, please," she protested, pulling her arm free of his hold. "I want you to stay here with Mike. You promised him a fishing trip, and I think he deserves one. You both do."

"Laura, I can't just let you go home alone, like that."

"No, honestly, Adam, it's what I prefer." She gave a distasteful grimace and pulled her sticky shirt away from her body with her forefinger and thumb. "I'm going to have to soak in the tub and shampoo my hair, then scrub all this goo out of my clothes, and that will take all afternoon. You and Mike just go ahead and enjoy yourselves. You probably need some time alone together anyway, after spending so much at my place."

"Well...if you're sure that's what you want..."

"It is," she said quickly. "I'll see you both later."

The moment her back was turned she bit down on her

lower lip and blinked hard, trying to hold back the threatening tears, but it was no use. By the time she rounded the first curve, they were streaming down her cheeks unchecked. As Laura stumbled blindly along the narrow path, the irony of the whole thing pierced her with a bittersweet sadness. On the one hand, she was deeply grateful that Carol Kincaid had inspired that kind of love and loyalty in her son. It was exactly the kind of relationship she had wanted him to have with the woman who raised him. Laura couldn't begrudge either of them that. But oh, it hurt—how it hurt—that he felt such loathing for her.

By the time she had reached the house, Laura had come to a decision. She would have to stop seeing Adam.

It wouldn't be easy to cut him from her life. Already, just thinking about it, she felt the pain of loss. But she had to do it. Because if she didn't, Mike would be the one to suffer.

Stupidly, she had come here with such high hopes, wanting only to see him, to secretly cherish and love him, and all she had done was make him miserable.

Listlessly, her tears spent, Laura entered the house through the back door. In the utility room she stripped out of her muddy clothes and put them to soak in the washer, then climbed the stairs. The moment she entered the bathroom she caught a glimpse of her mud-caked, ravaged face in the mirror. Quickly, she turned away and busied herself with filling the tub.

It doesn't matter, she told herself stoutly, as she eased down into the hot bathwater. She had come here looking for her son, not a lover. Anyway, she had known from the beginning that it could never be. Adam could never be hers. She'd been a fool to let things develop this far. There was nothing to do but end it. Now, before things became serious between them. *It's too late. You're already in love with him,* a tiny voice protested, but Laura resolutely ignored it...and the ache in her chest.

For a moment Laura considered just packing up and

leaving—but only for a moment. She may never have Adam, or have a close relationship with her son, but at least if she stayed she could see them occasionally. And maybe, when Mike realized that she posed no threat, his hostility would fade.

When Adam and Mike arrived late that afternoon, she was ready for them. Dressed in her gown and robe, she was sitting at the kitchen table drinking coffee when she saw them emerge from the woods and climb through the back fence. Molly scooted under on her belly and trotted behind them.

Before they reached the house, Laura stepped out on the back porch. Adam's brows rose when he saw her attire. "Not dressed yet? Don't tell me it took this long to scrub off the muck."

"No. I just don't feel like getting dressed."

"Well, you'd better get a move on, woman. We've got fish to fry." He turned to Mike and grinned. "Show her, son."

Mike dutifully held up the stringer of fish, but he didn't look at Laura.

"So you have," she said, smiling wanly as she stepped to the edge of the porch and looked at their catch. "But I'm afraid you'll have to have your fish fry without me. I'm not feeling well."

A frown replaced Adam's smile as his face clouded with concern, and he was instantly up the steps and at her side. "You're ill?"

"No, it's just a headache. Nothing serious." Laura started to back away, but Adam cupped her chin and looked into her eyes. She knew that they were red-rimmed and bloodshot, the lids puffy, but she hoped that he wouldn't guess the cause.

"You do look a bit peaked. You should take some aspirin and go to bed."

"Yes. Yes, I will." Adam's eyes dropped to her mouth

and when he started to lower his head, Laura hastily backed away. "Well...uh, you two enjoy your fish. Good night."

Adam's eyes narrowed as he watched her edge toward the door. "Good night, Laura," he said softly. "I'll call you tomorrow morning."

Laura escaped into the house, but hurried through the kitchen and down the hall to the parlor. Peeking through the window, she watched Adam and Mike stow their gear in the back of the truck and climb in. For a moment after he had started the engine, Adam just sat there, staring at the house with a puzzled frown, but finally he put the truck in reverse and backed down the drive.

Laura stayed at the window a long time after the truck's red taillights had disappeared down the road.

Chapter Eight

At the first sound of Laura's voice Adam's spirits lifted, only to plummet when he realized that he had gotten the recording again. With an oath, he slammed the phone receiver back into its cradle.

What the hell is going on? He drummed his fingers on the desk top and scowled darkly. He had neither seen nor talked to Laura since the morning after the fishing trip. Whenever he'd called, he'd gotten that damned recording, and when he'd dropped by, the house was in darkness and there was no answer when he rang the bell or knocked. A couple of times he'd had the feeling that Laura was there, but just simply not answering the door. He hadn't wanted to believe it, because that would mean that she was avoiding him, but now he was beginning to wonder.

It was definitely strange that in a town this small he had not been able to catch so much as a glimpse of her in over a week.

She was putting in a lot of hours at the shop, he knew,

but he hesitated to confront her there. Besides the fact that she was busy, he didn't want to provide any more grist for the gossip mill.

Of course, Adam acknowledged silently, he probably wouldn't be so concerned if it hadn't been for their last conversation. Every word, every nuance of that brittle little encounter was indelibly etched in his mind, and as he played it back, Adam's scowl deepened.

When he had turned into her drive that morning, she had been on the verge of leaving.

"Good morning, hon," he'd called as he climbed from the truck and walked toward her. "I came by to see if you were okay. I tried calling a few minutes ago and got your answering machine. I was worried that maybe you were still not feeling well."

As he drew near, Laura opened the driver's door on the Continental and stood in the wedge of space between it and the car. Adam received the impression that she was deliberately trying to put a barrier between them. "I was in a hurry this morning, so I just didn't bother answering the phone. I'm sorry if I worried you."

Her hand was gripping the top edge of the door, and Adam put his over it and gently rubbed her knuckles. He smiled and lifted one brow. "You feeling okay this morning?"

"Yes. Just fine, thank you."

A look of puzzlement flickered over his face at her stilted tone, but he continued his gentle massage of her hand. "Good. In that case, Mike and I will report for duty tonight as usual. In another week or so we should have all the woodwork stripped and sanded and ready for refinishing."

"Uh...actually," Laura began hesitantly, pulling her hand free. "I was going to talk to you about that today. I've decided to hire Ezra to finish the job. He'll be through at the shop today or tomorrow, and after that I'll be busy getting it ready to open. I'll probably be working most evenings and weekends, so I really won't have much time to devote to the house.''

"Look, it's no problem. Mike and I can still do the work for you," Adam said, frowning slightly. "We don't mind."

"No, no, I couldn't let you do that," Laura protested. "You've both done more than enough for me already. In fact, I wish you'd let me pay you, at least for your time."

"*Pay* us?" Adam's expression held a mixture of anger and astonishment. "Good Lord, Laura! You don't seriously think I'd take money from you, do you?''

"Well, uh...no. I...guess that wasn't such a good idea. Look, Adam, I really must go." Before he could respond she tossed her purse onto the car seat and slid in behind the wheel, pulling the door shut behind her. She gave him a polite smile as she turned the key in the ignition. "Thank you for all you've done for me, Adam. And since I probably won't be seeing him anytime soon, would you thank Mike for me?"

He had been too astonished to do anything but nod mutely, and when she had put the car in reverse, he'd had no choice but to go back to his truck and move it out of her way.

What had he felt? Anger? Hurt? Bewilderment? Yes, certainly. But most of all he'd been afraid. Afraid of the remoteness in her voice, of that look of wariness and near panic in her eyes, of the invisible barriers he could sense she had thrown up between them. And nothing that had happened since had banished that fear.

Swiveling his chair around, Adam stared out the window in the direction of her shop, even though he knew he couldn't see it through the trees. If she was avoiding him, and it was beginning to seem more and more that she was, then why? What had he done? His eyes narrowed on the brilliant foliage of the oaks in the square as he backtracked in his mind for a clue.

Mike's tantrum had worried her, but she had accepted his apology graciously. Certainly she had been fine when they had set out on their fishing trip. Even after her accident she had not seemed unduly upset. Although—now that he thought about it—her casual manner had seemed a bit forced. And afterward, when he and Mike had stopped by, she had been withdrawn.

Adam's face grew thoughtful, his eyes narrowing even more. Had something happened at the creek between Laura and Mike?

Suddenly Adam bolted out of his chair and started for the door. Whatever the reason, he was damned well going to find out.

The light tapping on the door drew Laura's attention away from the stock she was tagging, and she looked up to see Harriet Beacher peering through the glass panel. When the woman beckoned to her, Laura put down the tag gun and went to the door.

"Harriet. How nice to see you."

"Hello, Laura. I know you're busy and I hate to disturb you, but could I speak with you for a moment?"

"Of course. Come in."

When Laura turned from closing the door she found Harriet standing in the middle of the floor, her rapt gaze slowly taking in the changes.

"Heavens! It's hard to believe that this is the same place! My dear, you have done a simply wonderful job. It's beautiful."

"Thank you," Laura said with a smile as she joined the older woman in her perusal.

As in all her stores, the decor was soft, understated elegance. A sea of plush, misty-green carpet had replaced the worn floors. The color was repeated in the floral wallpaper of dusty rose, green, and cream which covered the upper two thirds of the interior walls. Laura had kept the antique fans and the ornately plastered ceiling. The former were now painted a rich cream, as was the wainscoting and woodwork.

Plants were everywhere: draping ferns, graceful ficus trees, trailing ivies. The old walnut-and-curved-glass display case now formed a counter along one wall and was filled with silk scarves, lacy shawls, belts, gloves, earrings, bracelets, and assorted baubles. Against the wall behind it was a stack of antique, glass-fronted bookcases, which housed a fragrant assortment of cosmetics, perfumes, scented soaps, and sachets.

A Victorian settee and matching lady's chair in a deep green velvet sat to the left of the door, facing a marble-topped tea table. On the table, in a ruby-glass bowl, was an arrangement of pink and rose silk flowers, and next to it, an open china canister of potpourri, its subtle floral fragrance mingling pleasingly with the other feminine scents that filled the shop.

The freestanding brass clothes racks and the matching ones along the walls were, as yet, only partially filled, but the array of colors and sumptuous materials displayed were eye-catching.

Elegant little tables were scattered throughout the store, their tops cluttered with cut-glass ring holders, gold filigree boxes, hand-painted dresser sets, bisque figurines, china music boxes. In one corner an enormous walnut halltree was festooned with a plethora of beads and gold chains. Beside it, plumes of pampas grass sprouted from a copper umbrella stand. The tasteful decor, the obvious quality of the merchandise, the small items of whimsey, all discreetly whispered—*class*.

Harriet Beacher took it all in, and when she turned back to Laura her stern face was filled with admiration. "The ladies in town are going to be delighted, I assure you. When do you plan to open?"

"Saturday. The ad will be in the paper today, and the flyers are going out tomorrow."

"Well, good, good," Harriet said briskly. "Actually, I came by to see if you'd be interested in hiring a friend of mine to help out in the shop."

"Why, yes, I'm very interested. I've hired a woman named Irma Hopson, but I'll be needing at least one more clerk."

"Irma was a good choice," Harriet pronounced, nodding in approval. "And I think you'll like my friend, too. Her name is Racine Thayer, and a harder-working woman you'll never find. Her husband was thrown from a horse last year and he's disabled, so she really needs a job."

"I'd love to meet her. Why don't you tell her to drop by here tomorrow morning and we'll get acquainted."

"I'll do that," Harriet said, looking pleased with herself. Her business settled, she looked around the shop once again and said, "Would you mind if I took a look around, since I'm here?"

"No, go right ahead. Just call me if you have any questions." As Harriet wandered toward the back of the shop Laura returned to the rack of clothes she had been pricing and picked up the tagging gun. She had affixed only about a half dozen tags when the front door was pushed open.

"I'm sorry, we're not open ye—" she began, only to stop abruptly when she turned and saw who had entered. "A-Adam. You surprised me. What are you doing here?"

"I came to ask you to lunch."

As he walked slowly toward her, his eyes fixed on her face, Laura's chest tightened painfully. *Oh, dear Lord, he looks so good. And I've missed him so much.*

It had been ten days since she had seen him, ten long days of hard work and exhaustion, loneliness and heartache. She had told herself that it was really Mike that she missed, that Adam was no more to her than just a casual friend. But it wasn't true. It wasn't true at all. She was hungry for the sight of him.

In the feminine surroundings he looked so big and bold and utterly male, and as she stared at him Laura felt her senses stir and quiver with vibrant awareness.

He stopped beside the rack where she was working. Tearing her eyes away, Laura picked up the sleeve of a lilac silk blouse and concentrated fiercely on preventing her hands from shaking as she clipped a tag through the seam. He was standing so close she could feel the warmth that radiated from him, smell his woodsy aftershave and the clean, slightly musky male scent she had come to recognize as his alone. Longing and despair shivered through her.

"I'm sorry, Adam, I really can't. I have too much to do and just don't have the time," she said, flashing him a stiff smile, then quickly averting her gaze as she picked up another sleeve.

"You have to eat sometime," he persisted.

"I, uh...I brought a sandwich from home."

"I see." He was watching her like a hawk, his eyes narrow and unblinking, his face inscrutable. "How about dinner, then? Or did you bring a sandwich for that, too?"

The dripping sarcasm in his voice brought a flush to her cheeks, but she pretended not to notice it. "Well, actually, I do have a small refrigerator and hot plate in the back," she said with a self-conscious laugh. "I'll probably make do with a cup of instant soup."

When she went to move away, Adam stopped her with a hand on her arm. "What's wrong, Laura?"

"Wrong?" she repeated with feigned innocence, giving a shaky little laugh. "Why, nothing."

"Did something happen between you and Mike that day at the creek?" he pressed relentlessly.

"No! No, of course not!"

"Then why have you been avoiding me?"

"I-I haven't. It's just that I'm terribly busy right now. Getting ready for the opening and..." —she made a vague gesture with her hand, then let it drop and finished lamely— "...and all."

Adam looked at her in grim silence, then abruptly released her arm and stepped back. "All right, Laura. Since you're so busy, I won't take up any more of your time." He turned and stalked to the door, his back rigid as steel. When he had jerked it open, he paused to look back at her and said coldly, "When you can work me into your schedule, let me know."

Fighting back tears, her throat aching, Laura stood frozen and, through the front windows, watched him cross the street and cut across the square. She had hurt him, and in doing so, had hurt herself.

But there was no other way. They had no future together. Even if Mike were not antagonistic toward her, it still could never be. She couldn't tell him the truth about who she was, nor could she lie and say she didn't care for him. He would see through that instantly. Her only choice was to ease him from her life as gently as she could. Wistfully, Laura's eyes clung to Adam's receding form. The proud set of his shoulders tugged at her heartstrings, and her chin quivered as she recalled the anger and confusion and hurt that had been in his eyes.

She bit down on her lower lip and closed her eyes against the pain. *Oh, why couldn't I have met Adam under different circumstances? Why, out of all the men in the world, did he have to be Mike's father?*

"Does he know?"

The softly voiced question made Laura jump. She spun around, and looked at Harriet with wide, startled eyes. She had forgotten the woman was there. "Wh—what?"

"I said, does Adam know?"

"Know what?" Laura asked, blinking in confusion.

"That you're Mike's natural mother," Harriet said quietly, and as the words hit her, Laura felt as though every cell in her body had suddenly exploded.

Aghast, her face as pale as parchment, she stared at Harriet, unable to speak, unable to breathe. The world seemed to spin around her, and she clutched the brass clothes rack for support. "How—" She stopped and swallowed hard, but her voice still came out in a cracked whisper. "How did you know?"

Compassion softened Harriet's stern face as she saw the stark fear that Laura could not hide. "I didn't, until now.

At least...I wasn't certain," she said softly, and Laura gasped as she realized that she had given herself away. "It's the eyes. When we first met I knew there was something familiar about you, but I couldn't put my finger on it. Then finally it hit me; except for Mike, I've never seen eyes quite that shade of brown, or quite that clear. Also, the shape is the same."

At Laura's little moan of distress, Harriet's stern look returned. "I take it that you haven't told him."

"No...no, I...I didn't see any need. You see, it was never my intention to disrupt Mike's life. I...I just wanted to know him. To see him occasionally." Under Harriet's level stare, she hastened to add, "I never expected to become involved with his father. I swear it."

"Well, whether you did or didn't, you are involved with him, and my advice to you, my dear, is to tell him. And the sooner the better."

Laura raised a shaking hand to her mouth and slowly shook her head. Her eyes were wide and frightened. "I can't. I just...can't. Besides, as long as things are not serious between us, there's no need."

"Things are *already* serious between you, and you're a fool if you think otherwise," Harriet stated caustically as she headed for the door. "Anyone looking at the two of you together can see that. So tell him. You'll regret it if you don't."

"Harriet," Laura called to her as she started to step out the door, and the older woman paused and looked back. "Are you...are you going to tell him?" she asked in a soft, quavering voice.

Harriet sighed and shook her head slowly. "No. No, I won't tell him. I'll leave that up to you. But just remember, if you don't, and Adam ever finds out, he'll be furious. So think about it."

Laura did think about it. For days she thought of little else. While she interviewed and hired Racine Thayer the next morning, while she and the two women struggled through the gargantuan task of getting the store ready for opening, at night while she roamed the big empty house, she thought about telling him—or not telling him—and felt battered by conflicting emotions.

The problem was, no matter which way Adam found out, he would be furious. And though Laura knew he had every right to be, that didn't make it any easier to face. Just thinking about it made her feel sick.

So she just went on, day by day, trying to convince herself that it wasn't necessary to confess to Adam, that everything would work out, that whatever they had felt for each other would fade away to nothing. Eventually.

Occasionally Laura caught glimpses of Adam's green pickup around town, but he never came anywhere near her. In the evenings there was usually a warm glow of light spilling from the windows of his house when she drove by on her way home, and the sight of it made her ache with loneliness and longing. She wondered if Adam missed her, as she missed him. She wondered if Mike was happy now. She wondered if she would ever be.

Instead of lessening, Laura's misery grew. By the end of the week her need to see both Adam and Mike was so great it ate at her like a gnawing hunger, and when Racine chattered away all Friday afternoon about her son Paul, who played on the junior varsity team, and her plans to attend the game, the last of Laura's resistance crumbled.

She would leave before the game ended, she vowed to herself that evening as she joined the stream of people heading for the stands. And she would sit far to one side, in a crowd. That way Adam wouldn't see her.

When Laura took her seat she began to search for Adam's dark head. She scanned the players' bench and the lower rows intently, but there was no sign of him, and when the team came running out on the field, she gave up her search, her eyes fastening instantly on number eighty-six. She was standing with the rest of the crowd, giving them a rousing welcome, when from the corner of her eye she saw a man making his way down the row toward her.

"Excuse me. Excuse me, please. Excuse me," Adam said repeatedly as he squeezed past the row's other occupants, stepping sideways over their feet.

Laura's heart lurched at the sight of him. Panicked for a moment, she considered scooting out in the other direction, but the look Adam flashed her warned her not to, and dazedly she sank back onto the bench, her heart pounding ninety to nothing with excitement and dread.

Adam smiled crookedly at the man seated next to her and said, "Hi ya, Gus. How about moving down some." He nodded toward Laura and winked. "I think you've got my seat, ole buddy."

As Laura's face turned pink Gus and everyone around him laughed and obligingly shifted to make room, allowing Adam to squeeze in beside her.

When he was seated he turned and looked at her. There was anger and determination, and something else Laura could not identify in that steady gaze, and as she met it, she felt a frisson run up her spine. "Taking a night off, are you?"

"I...yes."

"Good." He looked at her for several more seconds, then picked up her hand and firmly laced their fingers together. "I'm glad you're here," he said quietly, then turned his attention to the play on the field.

Laura sat there, stunned. There was nothing she could do or say, not with all these people around. Not unless she wanted to create a scene. Her insides were fluttering crazily and it was suddenly difficult to breathe. She was intensely conscious of the hard warmth of his thigh pressing against hers, the callused palm against her soft one. *This is crazy, Laura. You can't just sit here, holding the man's hand, with half the town looking on. You are supposed to be easing him out of your life, remember. Tell him you've got to go, pull your hand free, and get up and walk out.*

But she didn't. All during the first half, she sat beside him, greedily savoring his closeness, his warmth, the feel of him against her. When Adam stood up to cheer he dragged her up with him, and when he sat down he propped their clasped hands on his thigh, but he never released her. And she didn't try to pull free—not until half time, when the crowd began to thin out as people went in search of refreshments at the concession stands behind the bleachers.

"Uh...Adam, I really should be going. I only intended to stay for a few minutes." She pulled on his hand and made a move to stand up, but Adam tugged her down.

"No."

Startled, she gaped at him, her eyes wide. "No? What do you mean, no?"

"I mean you're here with me now, and here you're going to stay. The opening is tomorrow. You wouldn't be here if everything wasn't ready. So just relax and enjoy the game."

"Oh, but—"

"Don't push it, Laura," he warned in an ominously low voice. He was staring straight ahead, watching the band march around the field, but his profile was set and harsh. "I don't have much patience left where you're concerned."

Laura started to protest, but one sharp look from those hazel eyes and she subsided. She had never seen Adam in this strange mood, but intuitively, she knew not to cross him. In silence they watched the band's performance, and during the second half Laura pretended an interest in the game, but she hadn't the vaguest idea what was going on. She even forgot to watch Mike.

But when the game was over and they left the stands, Mike was standing to one side, craning his neck as he searched the crowd. His face lit up when he spied Adam's dark head, and he plunged through the stream of people, only to come to a faltering halt when he drew near them and saw Laura. By the time they reached his side his face had grown stony.

124 THE HEART'S YEARNING

"Hi, son. Great game," Adam said with a grin, giving him a congratulatory cuff on the arm.

Mike stared at Adam and Laura's joined hands, then lifted his eyes to Laura. What she saw there made her heart sink. "Thanks," he replied tonelessly, shifting his sullen gaze to his father.

Adam had seen the look Mike had turned on Laura, and when she tried to pull her hand free he tightened his hold. The suspicion that had nagged at him for almost two weeks was beginning to look more and more like fact. Adam cursed silently as his sharp gaze sliced back and forth between Mike's tight-lipped expression and Laura's dispirited one, and his jaw hardened. If it's Mike's resentment that's keeping us apart, he thought grimly, I'll damned well put a stop to it. Now.

"You made some really great plays, son. Laura and I were proud of you," he said, his eyes narrowing as he watched Mike's lips tightened at the deliberate pairing. "But you'd better hightail it to the showers if you want to make it to the pizza parlor before it closes."

Mike's eyes darted to Laura, then back to his father. "We're still going?"

"Yes." Adam paused, then added quietly, "Laura and I are starved."

Anger flared briefly in Mike's eyes, then they frosted over. "I've changed my mind. I don't want to go," he said, staring sulkily at the ground. "I'm not hungry."

"Fine. Then you can watch us eat."

"But—"

"We're going, Mike. Now, get your rear in gear." Adam's voice was sharp, decisive, and brooked no argument.

"Perhaps it would be best if—" Laura began, but Adam cut her off.

"You're going, Laura."

Rebellion simmered behind Mike's tight face and his chest heaved as he struggled to contain the protests that were churning inside him. His mouth working, his nostrils flared and white, he glared at his father, but Adam's commanding stare never wavered. Finally, with one last fulminating look at Laura, the boy turned on his heel and stalked away.

"Tell your buddies they're welcome to come along, too," Adam called after him, but Mike neither replied nor looked back.

"Adam, I really don't think this is a good idea," Laura said a bit desperately as she watched Mike disappear into the gym.

Adam met her pleading look with barely concealed impatience. "I know what I'm doing, Laura, so don't fight me on this. It's time we had a long talk. There are several things we need to set straight, but we'll have to do it later, after I've taken Mike home." His eyes bore into her, daring her to protest, and as she met his steady, determined gaze, Laura felt a quivering weakness attack her.

He's right, she thought, finally accepting what had been inevitable from the beginning. The time for the truth had come.

Chapter Nine

The dinner was a disaster—every bit as miserable as Laura had known it would be.

Mike sat through it in tight-lipped silence, slouched down on his spine in a rebellious sprawl on the opposite side of the booth from Adam and Laura. Refusing to eat a bite, he drummed his fingers incessantly on the table and fixed his sullen stare on the tips of his tennis shoes, which were hanging over the end of the bench seat. Every attempt to draw him into conversation was met with a shrug or a curt, monosyllabic reply. Upset by his hostility, and worried over the coming discussion with Adam, Laura was barely able to finish one slice of the gooey pizza.

Adam ate with gusto, but she could tell that Mike's behavior was exacerbating his already uncertain temper. By the time they had finished and he had paid the check, his face was as stiff and forbidding as his son's.

At Laura's insistence Adam returned her to the school

parking lot so that she could pick up her car, but he let her know that the evening was far from over.

"I'll be over as soon as I drop Mike off at home," he told her as he assisted her into the Continental. "So wait for me."

During the drive home the reflection of his headlights winked in her rearview mirror until they reached his house. Even then, true to his word, he stopped only long enough to let Mike out. By the time Laura got her front door unlocked, he was pulling into her driveway. As Adam climbed from the truck and walked purposefully up the steps, she stood by the open door, watching him, waiting, her whole body trembling with dread.

He stepped inside and walked past her straight into the living room without saying a word. Feeling like a condemned prisoner, Laura closed the door and slowly followed.

Ezra Simpson and his crew had made short work of the remaining renovation. The ornately carved ceiling was freshly painted and the walls sported new paper in dusty rose floral on a cream background. A new, deep-pile oriental rug now rested on the gleaming heart-of-pine floor. The woodwork glowed, the freshly laundered lace curtains hung in creamy folds at the windows, the antique furniture, stripped of its dusty shrouds, looked richly elegant in the revitalized surroundings. But Adam didn't seem to notice.

When she entered the room he was standing in front of the fireplace, his back to her, but before she had taken three steps he swung around and launched his attack. "It's Mike, isn't it? He's the reason you've been avoiding me. Something happened between you two that day we went fishing, didn't it?"

Automatically, Laura's head began to move from side to side, but when she opened her mouth Adam cut off her denial with an upraised hand. "No, don't lie to me, Laura," he interjected quickly. "I know something happened because you've been distant and cool ever since that day. Now I want to know what it was."

"Does it matter, Adam?" Laura said on a weary sigh. "The point is, Mike doesn't like me."

"So why didn't you come to me and tell me what the problem was?"

"To what end?" Laura shot him a harried glance and waved her hand in a hopeless gesture. "You can't *make* Mike like me. We have no control over our feelings, or anyone else's."

"Maybe not. But I can damn sure control how he behaves toward you," Adam declared angrily.

Laura sighed, her shoulders slumping. She sank down onto the sofa and cupped her forehead with her hand. "What good would that do?" she asked wearily. "It wouldn't change anything. Mike still wouldn't approve of our relationship."

"*Approve!* He's a fourteen-year-old boy, for Pete's sake! We don't need his approval!"

I do, she cried silently, looking up at him with wide, troubled eyes. *I do.* And even more, she needed Adam's, but Laura was desperately afraid that she was going to end up with neither. Filled with an aching sadness, she shook her head slowly, and in a despairing little voice, said, "Oh, Adam, don't you see? I couldn't stand knowing that I was the cause of friction between you and Mike. I just couldn't."

"Laura, listen to me," Adam pleaded with rough urgency. "It's not you that Mike resents. At this point, he would feel the same about any woman I showed an interest in. Mike was very close to his mother, and he's having a hard time coming to grips with the idea that I could care deeply for another woman."

Joy splintered through Laura as she read the silent message in Adam's steady, hazel-eyed stare, but she clasped her hands tightly together in her lap and forcibly reminded herself of all that he didn't know.

"We were a close family," Adam continued. "Closer than most, and my wife and I lavished Mike with love and attention because...well...because he was so special to us." Adam had been pacing restlessly back and forth in front of Laura, but he stopped, and as he looked down at her his mouth curved into a strange, reminiscent little smile. "You see, Mike is adopted," he said softly, then shook his head as if to clear it, and gave a surprised little snort. "Sometimes I forget that. From the moment I first held him in my arms I've thought of him as my son, my flesh and blood."

Then he blinked rapidly, banishing the faraway expression from his eyes. "Anyway, the point is, because we were so close, it's probably going to take Mike a while to get over his resentment, but he will eventually."

Laura was thrilled that he had confided in her, and that his commitment to her son was so complete, but it changed nothing. "And what if he doesn't?" she asked, gazing sadly back at him.

"Dammit, Laura!" Adam exploded, raking his fingers through his hair in sheer exasperation. "I love my son, but I *will not* allow him to dictate my life!"

"Oh, Adam. It won't work, don't you see that?" *Coward,* she berated herself silently. For even as the words left her mouth Laura knew that, cravenly, a part of her was still hoping he would give up, and she wouldn't have to tell him the truth.

"No, I don't see that," Adam fired back at her. He was standing stock still now, in front of her, his hands clenched tightly at his sides. His face looked as though it were carved of stone. "But then that's not the reason you're backing off, is it? At least not entirely. From the very beginning you've resisted the attraction between us. I want to know why."

Laura stared at him with wide, frightened eyes, her heart pounding. *Tell him. Now is the time. Tell him!* She drew a shaky breath and wet her lips. "A–Adam, I...there is something—"

"Is there another man? Someone back in Houston you care for?"

"No."

"Are you bored here?"

"No."

"Are you worried that you'll grow bored here?"

She shook her head.

"Is it me? Am I too old for you?"

"No!"

"Too tall? Too short? Too dull? What?"

"No! No! No!" Her sharp denials interspersed with the rapid-fire questions that spat from him, and with each one her voice rose steadily to an almost hysterical pitch.

In the electrified silence that followed she could only stare back at Adam in anguish, and slowly shake her head. "I...I'm...I'm..." The confession trembled on her tongue, but as she met his demanding gaze, as her eyes traced over the rugged male features that had become so very dear to her, she simply could not force the damning words out. Disgusted with herself, she pressed her lips together and looked away, then just as quickly looked back. "Oh, why can't you just accept that it can't be?" she demanded, guilt and frustration making her voice sharp. "Why do you keep pushing?"

"Why?" Both Adam's voice and face were incredulous. "I would think that's obvious." He waited a moment, watching her intently, but when Laura merely stared back at him, her face blank with confusion, he added in an infinitely softer voice, "Because I'm falling in love with you."

Laura sucked in her breath and went perfectly still. Her topaz eyes grew wide, and unconsciously filled with longing. "Oh, Adam," she whispered in an aching little voice. "Adam."

Joy, and a terrible, soul-deep agony filled her. How could fate be so cruel, she wondered wretchedly, to tantalize her with the kind of love and happiness she had always longed for, in the form of a man she could never have? It wasn't fair.

As she sat there in silent torment Adam leaned down, grasped her upper arms and gently drew her to her feet. His rugged face softened and a tender look entered his deep-set eyes as he studied her pale face. "Didn't you know?" he asked with a touch of amazement, and when Laura mutely shook her head, a quirking smile lifted one corner of his mouth. "Where did you think all this was leading? Did you really think I would go to this much trouble, spend this much time with you, just to get you into my bed?" He shook his head, giving her a mildly chastising look and cupped one side of her face with his big hand. The rough pad of his thumb swept back and forth over the hollow beneath her cheekbone while his caressing gaze touched on her quivering mouth, the misty softness of her troubled topaz eyes.

"Honey, one-night-stands, or even casual affairs, are easy to come by. I won't lie to you, Laura. Since Carol died there have been women. I'm a man, with a normal man's needs. But there was never any emotion involved on either side, and I certainly never exposed Mike to any of them." His deep baritone softened and lowered, the sensuous rumble stroking over her like dark velvet. "But with you it's different. It has been since the moment you walked into my office. Oh, I admit that the physical attraction is there. There are nights when I can't sleep for thinking about what it would be like to make love to you, to explore every inch of you, to bury myself in your soft warmth."

His words sent a shiver racing through her, and feeling it, Adam's eyes flared hotly. As his head began its slow descent his voice came out in a husky whisper. "But I find I want more than just physical satisfaction from you, Laura. Much more." He brushed her parted lips with his own, lightly, tantalizingly. "And you want the same things, don't you?" He caught her lower lip between his teeth and nipped gently, then bathed it with the tip of his tongue. "Don't you?"

A tiny sound issued from Laura's throat, somewhere between a moan and a sigh. Adam's mouth brushed hers again. And again. Back and forth, back and forth, the warm moist caress continued, nearly driving her mad. She forgot Mike. She forgot the past. She forgot all the reasons why she should send him away. There was only the here and now, and the sweet mingling of love and passion that was impossible to resist.

Laura's hands slid up over Adam's chest and shoulders and locked behind his neck, and with an urgent little cry she pressed closer, her mouth blindly seeking the full possession of his.

But Adam was determined. "You want what we can have together, don't you, Laura?" he whispered against her seeking lips. "Don't you?"

"Yes," she gasped desperately. "Yes!"

With a low growl of satisfaction, Adam wrapped his arms around her and took her mouth with a fierce possessiveness that stole her breath away and demolished what remained of her puny defenses.

They clung to each other as the ardent kiss went on and on and passion spiraled. Tongues met, rubbed, withdrew, and met again. Adam's hands roamed her back and hips, pressing her tightly to him. Laura's fingers twined in his hair, testing its silkiness, learning the shape of his head.

Slowly Adam undulated his hips against her, and she moaned as heat rocketed through her veins to settle at the throbbing core of her femininity. The small sound brought an answering groan from Adam. He tore his mouth from hers and clasped her to him fiercely, pressing her face to his chest and laying his cheek against the top of her head. They held each other tightly, both gasping for air, their hearts thundering in unison.

"Let me love you, Laura," he rasped. "Don't throw away what we have. What we could have."

His warm breath filtered through her hair and tingled across her scalp, and Laura shivered. Guilt and pain battled with desperate need. She pressed her cheek against his warm chest and squeezed her eyes shut, her face contorting in anguish. *This is wrong. You should send him away. End it while there is still time.* Over and over, she repeated the words in her mind, trying to summon the courage to deny him. To deny them both.

But time had run out, and she knew it. She could no more deny what was happening between them, what was about to happen, than she could stop the world from turning. It felt so wonderful, so right, to be wrapped in Adam's arms. And she loved him so.

At her continued silence Adam grasped her shoulders and stepped back, frowning. "Laura, what—" he began, but when she lifted her head and he saw the love and longing shimmering in her eyes, his breath caught, and his own eyes grew wide.

Tenderly, his hands trembling ever so slightly, he cupped her face between his palms. "Oh, Laura, Laura," he whispered as he bent and touched his mouth to hers. His kiss was warm and soft and loving, and so utterly, sweetly sensual, Laura felt it all the way to her toes.

When at last their clinging lips parted, Adam drew back and looked at her, his eyes burning hotly over her flushed cheeks and kiss-swollen mouth. Then, without a word, he swept her up in his arms and strode from the room.

As he began his purposeful climb up the stairs, Laura looped her arms around his neck and rested her head on his shoulder. In some distant corner of her mind she knew that she should stop him. It would only complicate matters more.

But she simply could not. She had never known love like this before. All of her life she had dreamed of it, yearned for it, but she had never expected to find it. And now that she had, she could not let it go. Not yet.

What she had felt for Keith had been merely a mirage.

Thirsting, she had conjured up a dream, a shimmering fantasy, but it had had no substance, and when she had tried to hold onto it, it had vanished. Her love for John had been a gentle, abiding thing, born of respect and gratitude for his innate goodness, but it had not stirred her soul nor shackled her heart. Not like Adam had.

When he entered her bedroom, Adam flipped the switch beside the door, and a dim glow of light spilled from the lamp on the dresser. Adam set Laura down beside the bed and once more enfolded her in his arms, his mouth melding with hers in a slow, searing kiss that set her blood to pounding.

Unerringly, his hands found the back zipper on her skirt and eased it down. When the button on the waistband was released the garment dropped to the floor with a soft plop. His hands moved restlessly, lovingly over her back and hips, gliding over the satiny surface of her slip, stroking her slender curves, molding her soft, feminine body to his unyielding masculine length.

Laura could feel his heart thudding beneath her hand and the hardness of his arousal straining against her abdomen, and she pressed closer, glorying in the heady passion that was consuming them both. Frantically, she slid her arms around him and pulled his shirt free of his jeans, then, thrusting her hands beneath it, ran her palms over his sleekly muscled back.

Adam jerked, and shuddered violently, and tearing his mouth from hers, he clasped her tightly to him, pressing his cheek against the fragrant hair at her temple. "Oh, God, yes, sweetheart! Touch me. I love the feel of your hands on me!"

Laura was trembling all over. "I...I...like to touch you."

Adam worked a hand between them and began a deft assault on the buttons of her blouse. As they popped free, one by one, the backs of his knuckles lovingly grazed over her collarbone, the warm swells above her bra, the silkiness of her midriff. Then the blouse was eased over her shoulders and fluttered downward to join her skirt. Her slip went next, and in moments, her bra followed.

Easing back, Adam looked at her, his eyes flaring hotly as he took in the uptilted perfection of her creamy breasts. Slowly, as though in a trance, he cupped his palms beneath them and tested their weight, brushing his thumbs across their rosy tips until they were peaked and hard.

"Oh, Adam," Laura whispered, half in protest, half in pure ecstasy, but his fascinated gaze never left her. He squeezed, lifted, pressed the pearly globes together. Bending, he buried his face in the lush flesh, and Laura gasped and shuddered, her fingers clutching at his shoulders as his tongue dipped provocatively into the warm cleavage.

Laura was lost in a world of new and thrilling sensations, engulfed in the vibrant richness of mingled passion and love. Heady, delicious feelings she had never experienced before, had never even dreamed of, assailed her, making her heart swell, her pulses pound, her senses swim.

She was barely conscious of Adam lifting her in his arms and laying her gently on the bed, of him removing her shoes and panty hose and the lacy lilac panties that were the final, fragile barrier.

Laura lay trembling, her skin flushed and hot, her heart pounding erratically as she watched him shed his clothes. Helplessly, her eyes roamed over his broad shoulders, his deep muscled chest with its thick pelt of hair, the flat hard belly. Her feminine core quickened with a hot moist throbbing when she encountered the narrow hips and his proud, erect manhood.

As he stripped, Adam had been carrying on his own silent, devouring inspection, and when their eyes suddenly locked, a hot current of desire scorched the air between them. With a low growl, he kicked aside the pile of discarded clothes. And then he was there beside her.

Hooking one hair-roughened leg over hers, Adam raised up on his elbow and looked down at her. Laura quivered under his passionate gaze, breathlessly aware of his naked flesh searing into hers from ankle to hip. Then a smile curved his mouth, and bracing his free hand against the mattress on the other side of her shoulder, with agonizing slowness, inch by tormenting inch, he lowered his torso.

"Oh, Adam," Laura gasped, when the sensitive tips of her breasts pushed up through the mat of silky hair and encountered the warm, hard muscles of his chest. When he rubbed sensuously against her she gasped again and closed her eyes against the hot rush of erotic sensations coursing through her,

"This was meant to be, sweetheart," Adam murmured hoarsely against her lips. "We belong together." Slowly he rocked his open mouth against hers. Their warm breath mingled, their hearts thudded, their bodies throbbed. Fevered seconds ticked by in heady anticipation, then Adam's tongue slid into her mouth, thrusting deep. Slowly, erotically, he withdrew, thrust again, withdrew. Over and over, until they were both mindless with desire.

Laura writhed beneath him, her body craving, reaching for some unknown, never experienced pinnacle of pleasure that she somehow, instinctively, knew existed. The deep yearning clamored through her, demanding fulfillment.

Leaning to one side, Adam cupped her breast in his palm. "You're so beautiful. Even more beautiful than I dreamed you'd be." Laura's back arched as his thumb grazed over her nipple, bringing it to aching tautness. He laved it with his hot tongue, then treated the other to the same loving attention. "Your breasts are so full and firm. Your nipples so sweet and pink," he whispered a second before he took one into his mouth.

"Oh, Adam. Adam." Laura was delirious, glorying in voluptuous pleasure. She had never known loving like this. Not even her wildest fantasies had come close to the beauty of it. Adam's every touch, every look, every word made her heart sing, her body clamor for fulfillment. Filled to overflowing with love, she knew an urgent need to give him equal pleasure. Gliding her hands over his chest, she twined her fingers through the crisp hairs and tugged gently. Ever so lightly, her nails scored the tiny nipples nestled there.

Adam's body jerked at the first maddeningly delicate touch, then a low growl of pleasure rumbled up from his chest as her exploring hands slid downward over his quivering belly. The growl became a groan, and shudders wracked him as her warm fingers lovingly, intimately, enfolded his velvet hardness.

"I want you, Laura," he whispered raggedly in her ear. "I want to be inside you. Now." He raised up and looked deep into her eyes. In answer to his silent question, Laura cupped his face with her hands and smiled—a beguiling, beckoning smile as old as Eve, that told him all he needed to know.

Adam levered himself up until he was poised between her soft thighs. His hot, burning gaze locked with hers, he merged their bodies with a smooth, powerful stroke. He pressed deep, filling her, sheathing himself in her heavenly warmth, smiling as he watched Laura's eyes widen and glaze with ecstasy.

"You're mine," he rasped.

Then they were moving together as one. Clinging. Stroking. Lost in the sheer beauty and exquisite pleasure of loving.

Rapture held them enthralled, and at first their pace was deliciously slow, deliciously sensual, but as passion built urgency dictated their rhythm. Steadily, their bodies grew taut with sweet, sweet agony, and together they climbed higher and higher, straining for the summit.

When they reached it, Laura clutched Adam's back, and with his hoarse cry sounding in her ear, she moaned his name—over, and over, and over—as together they seemed to sail over the edge of the world.

Moments later they returned to earth on a cloud of languor, clinging to each other, their bodies slick with perspiration, their breathing labored. A soft smile curved Laura's mouth as she stroked the damp tendrils of hair at Adam's nape. Never had she felt so contented, so utterly replete.

When Adam rolled to his side and drew Laura to him she went willingly, snuggling her face against his shoulder with a contented sigh. Her smile deepened when she felt the soft rasp of his beard stubble as he absently rubbed his chin back and forth against her temple.

"That was beyond anything I've ever experienced," he said quietly after a moment, and when Laura leaned her head back to look at him, her heart did a somersault. Tenderness and love shone out of his eyes like a beacon. It warmed her all over, and filled her with a happiness she had never known. Tears brimmed in her eyes, and with a shaking hand, she reached up and touched his face with the tips of her fingers.

"I know, love," she whispered brokenly. "I know." Not trusting herself to say more, she kissed him softly and snuggled her head back in the curve of his shoulder, blinking away the tears that gathered in her eyes.

It was foolish to feel so happy, she knew. If anything, her situation was even more precarious now. But she couldn't help it. The loving they had just shared had been so awesomely beautiful, so perfect, nothing could dim her joy. Soon—very soon—she was going to have to tell Adam the truth. She knew that. No longer did she have the luxury of a choice. But not now. Not tonight.

Laura awoke with a start to find the room in darkness. Memory flooded her instantly, and with a smile she reached for Adam, but her hand encountered only a warm sheet.

"I'm here." Adam's voice came to her through the darkness, banishing her disappointment, and in the next instant the mattress dipped as he sat down on the bed beside her. Moonlight filtering through the curtains cast his face in soft-edged shadows, and as he leaned over her, she saw his mouth curve up in a smile, the white flash of his teeth. He kissed her long and hard, pressing her back into the pillow, and when he raised his head he feathered her jaw with the backs of his knuckles.

"I hate to leave you, sweetheart, but I must," he whispered regretfully. "I can't stay out all night, not with Mike at home waiting."

Stunned dismay rippled through Laura. She had forgotten all about Mike. "No. No, of course you can't," she agreed quickly, grateful that the darkness hid her guilty flush.

"Sweetheart, you..." Adam hesitated, and suddenly Laura was gripped with a feeling of unease. Then she again saw the flash of his teeth as a self-conscious smile tilted his mouth. "I know it's a little late to think about it, but...well...you are safe, aren't you?"

"Safe?"

"From pregnancy."

Shock rocketed through Laura. "B—but you said...I mean...Mike..."

Adam's gentle laugh cut off her incoherent stammering. "Honey, it was my wife who couldn't have children, not me."

"Oh," Laura managed weakly, staring at him through the darkness, horror-struck.

"Oh, indeed," Adam repeated in a softly chiding voice. "And all this time I assumed that, because your marriage was childless, you couldn't have any children, while you assumed...Oh, hell." He raked his hand through his hair, then gave her a long intent look. "Well, the odds are you haven't conceived, but we can't continue to take chances."

"N–no," Laura agreed shakily. Her heart was thumping in her chest. Was he trying to tell her he wasn't going to see her anymore?

His hand came up and cupped her chin and he smiled down into her striken face. "If you want me to, I'll protect you. Or you can do it. It makes no difference to me. But one of us has to, because there is no way in hell I'm going to stay away from you. Not after tonight."

Chapter Ten

The front door had no sooner clicked shut behind Adam than doubts tumbled down on Laura like an avalanche. *Pregnant.* The word reverberated sickeningly through her brain. A quick mental calculation told her that it was highly unlikely, but even so, she felt wretched.

"Oh, Laura, you fool," she muttered disconsolately, as she trudged back up the stairs. In the bedroom she shed her robe and returned to the rumpled bed. It still held Adam's scent, and as she snuggled her face into the pillow, tears stung her eyes. *Fool, fool, fool! How could you have been so unbelievably stupid? To risk making the same mistake all over again? You're thirty-one now, for heaven's sake, not sixteen. Idiot!*

The harsh self-flagellation went on and on. It was the early hours of the morning before Laura finally dropped off to sleep again, only to toss fitfully in the big brass bed, tormented by dreams of Adam and Mike lashing out at her furiously, then coldly walking away. When she awoke the next morning she tried to tell herself that she was being foolish, but her doubts persisted. The mistake she had made with Keith had torn her heart to shreds and altered the course of her life, but she had learned from it. At least...she had always thought so. Now she wondered if perhaps she had once again allowed her need for love to blind her.

But even if Adam does love you, how long do you think it can last? Laura asked herself bleakly, as she parked her car in the alley behind the shop and unlocked the back door. Once he learns the truth he'll probably never speak to you again. *And I wouldn't blame him in the least.*

Irma and Racine arrived a few minutes later, too excited about the grand opening to notice anything amiss with their boss.

Laura had chosen to wear an exquisitely simple blue Halston dress, matching sling pumps, and a single strand of pearls. Her honey-colored hair was pulled back at the temples with combs and billowed loosely about her shoulders. She smelled deliciously of Joy, and looked every inch the composed, elegant, tastefully attired proprietress of a chic establishment.

With brisk efficiency that belied her agitation, Laura dealt with the last-minute preparations, gave Racine and Irma their instructions, and at promptly ten o'clock officially opened the doors for business. For hours she graciously greeted the steady stream of ladies, served them refreshments, assisted with their selections, accepted their profuse compliments on the merchandise and the store's new look, answered a thousand questions, smiled, laughed, talked, and listened to long, rambling stories.

And through it all she worried; where did they go from here?

It was late in the afternoon, about an hour before closing time, and Laura was pouring a cup of spiced tea for a matronly, size twenty woman who was covetously eyeing a size ten suede jumpsuit, when she looked up and saw Adam. Their eyes locked, and as she watched him approach the cup she was holding clattered noisily. *Oh, Lord, he looks so wonderful, and I love him so,* she though despairingly. *How will I bear it if I have to give him up?*

With a distracted smile, Laura quickly pressed the cup of tea into the woman's hands. "There you are, Mrs. Campbell. I hope you enjoy it, and please feel free to browse."

Adam was the only man in the store, and as he cut a swath through the chattering women he drew several covert, and some not so covert, glances.

"Hello, sweetheart," he said when he reached Laura's side, and to her astonishment, he bent and kissed her full on the mouth. Straightening, he smiled warmly into her eyes. "How's it going?"

"F—fine," she managed in a breathy whisper, painfully aware that they were the cynosure of every other pair of eyes in the store. Flustered, she fiddled needlessly with the tray of petits fours, straightened the napkins, and checked the level in the tea server, but when she finally looked up and met Adam's determinedly possessive, slightly challenging gaze her heart began to pound. *He had done that on purpose!*

"I figured as much. Carly Sue came back from her lunch hour loaded down with packages and gushing with praise."

"I...I'm glad." Laura shivered as he ran his fingertips over the back of her hand. A hurried look around told her that the intimate little gesture, and her reaction, had been noted by several of her customers, and Laura groaned silently.

Smiling, Adam leaned closer. His eyes grew warm and his voice dropped to a low, husky pitch. "How about I take you out to dinner to celebrate your successful opening? We could drive over to Austin. Go someplace special."

"You took me to dinner last night," she said uneasily. "Besides, I don't think Mike would enjoy it."

"Mike's not invited. Anyway, he's going to a double-feature movie tonight with a bunch of his buddies."

"I see. Well, thank you, Adam, but I really can't. By the

time I get through here I'll be too exhausted for anything more strenuous than a long soak in a hot tub.''

''Okay, then I'll cook dinner for you.'' He smiled and touched the end of her nose with his forefinger. ''While you soak.'' Before Laura could protest, he leaned down and kissed her once again, then turned and started for the door. Over his shoulder he called, ''I'll see you at your place about seven.''

The knowing smiles cast her way sent a tide of scalding color surging up Laura's neck and face, all the way to her hairline.

Scant minutes after Laura entered her house, Adam arrived, carrying a large sack of groceries. The moment he stepped inside he shifted it to one side, hooked an arm around her waist and pulled her to him for a long, lingering kiss.

Laura's heart pounded madly. Beneath the open sheepskin-lined jacket he was wearing faded jeans and a red plaid flannel shirt, and her hands clutched the soft material reflexively. When their clinging lips finally parted they were both dazed and breathing hard. ''Hi,'' Adam said in a low, husky voice as he rubbed the tip of her nose with his.

''Hi,'' Laura managed weakly. They gazed at each other in silence, awareness throbbing between them. She was acutely conscious of his lean, muscled body, fitted tightly to hers from ankle to breast, the thunder of his heart beneath her hand, the disturbed cadence of his breathing. Against her nylon-clad legs, she could feel the rough denim of his jeans, and his wide, Western-style belt buckle pressed against her abdomen. The intimacy of the embrace stirred memories of the night before. With very little effort Laura could recall the feel of naked skin to naked skin, the flex and ripple of his muscles beneath her hands, the delicious rasp of his body hair against her smoothness.

Adam sucked in his breath at the look of dreamy passion on her face, and his eyes grew dark and smoldering.

"Lady," he growled with sensual menace, "if you want to be fed anytime soon, you'd better get up those stairs and out of my sight." Very determinedly, he turned her around and gave her a nudge in the right direction. As she drifted up the stairs in a sensual haze, he called, "Dinner will be ready in about a half-hour, so don't fall asleep."

Laura was already lowering her body into the big, claw-footed tub before she remembered that she had intended to tax Adam about his behavior in the shop. Oh, well, it would be better to wait until after they had eaten anyway, she told herself as she leaned back and rested her head on the rolled rim, sighing softly as the violet scented water lapped at her chin. A rejuvenating soak and a full stomach would help her cope.

When she emerged from the tub twenty minutes later, Laura patted herself dry, dusted with violet scented talc and slipped a wickedly sensual, deep blue velvet caftan over her nakedness. Gathered from an off-the-shoulder, peasant neckline, the garment fell to her ankles in soft folds. The lush material draped her breasts and flowed gently against her body as she moved, giving tantalizing hints of her rounded hips, the long smooth curve of her thighs. Full, belled sleeves covered her arms, leaving only her creamy neck and shoulders bare.

After slipping her feet into a pair of blue satin mules, Laura brushed her hair vigorously until it fell about her shoulders in a cloud of honey-colored silk. Foregoing her usual makeup, she smoothed a soft rose gloss on her lips, then turned and headed for the door.

When she entered the kitchen, Adam was just taking the steaks from the broiler. "Just in time," he tossed over his shoulder as he transferred them to waiting plates. Then he turned and looked at her, and the welcoming smile on his face quickly faded, and a hot, sensual look of masculine appreciation took its place. As his eyes slid over her from head to foot, Laura felt her body quicken, her breasts grow heavy.

Adam's long lazy stride ate up the distance between them. With slow, deliberate movements, he set the plates on the table, straightened, and framed her face between his palms. "You look sensational," he murmured.

Then he kissed her. Hotly. Deeply. Laura's hands gripped the sides of his waist as a quivering weakness spread through her, and her legs grew wobbly. When at last he raised his head, Adam smiled. "That was to hold me until later." He dropped another quick kiss on her mouth, then reached around her and drew out her chair.

After a few moments hunger quieted the sensual excitement that was rocketing through Laura, and she tucked into the simple meal of steak, baked potato, and salad with relish. Throughout dinner, and later, as they cleaned up the kitchen and stacked the dishes in the dishwasher, they talked companionably about the opening.   But when they carried their coffee into the parlor, Laura broached the subject that had been on her mind for hours.

"Why did you do it, Adam?" she asked, as she settled into the corner of the sofa.

"Do what?"

"Kiss me in front of everyone like that. Now everyone knows about us."

"So? What's wrong with that?"

"I don't particularly like being the subject of gossip, that's what's wrong."

"Why? Because it makes it that much harder to break off a relationship if everyone knows about it?"

"No!" Laura denied instantly, but a guilty flush heated her body. It hadn't been a conscious thought, but now that he had put it into words, she recognized how near the truth his accusation was. At least...that was part of it.

A coldness entered Adam's eyes, and his voice grew clipped. "Good. Because I'm not going to let you back out now. You've been waffling ever since we met but, dammit, Laura, whether or not you want to admit it, we made a commitment to each other last night. A commitment to at least explore our feelings, to give what we have a chance to grow.''

While she was upstairs, Adam had built a cheery fire in the fireplace, and Laura stared somberly at the dancing flames as she sipped her coffee. Common sense and her conscience told her to either tell him the truth or break it off, but she could do neither. No matter how she argued with herself, no matter the right or wrong of the matter, she simply could not give him up. Not just yet.

Placing her hand on his arm, Laura looked at him pleadingly. ''I know that, darling, and I agree, but...it's just that I think we should be, well, discreet.''

''You mean keep our relationship hidden? Dammit, Laura! I will not *sneak* around to be with you just to keep the local biddies from talking!''

''But Adam, if everyone is talking about us, think how uncomfortable it will make Mike. How much it will hurt him.''

Adam jerked up off the sofa and stalked to the fireplace. Hunkering down, he snatched a poker from the stand and jabbed viciously at the burning logs, sending a shower of sparks up the chimney. When he had the blaze roaring, he replaced the poker but remained where he was, staring into the flames. Finally he turned his head and looked at her over his shoulder, and in a voice that was tight with anger, said, ''Not even for the sake of my son will I carry on some secretive, backstreet affair.''

A painful tightness squeezed Laura's chest. She knew that somehow she had to make Adam change his mind. The secret she was keeping from him caused her enough guilt. She couldn't add to it by making Mike miserable. Laura placed her coffee cup on the marble-topped table beside the sofa and rose. She went to Adam and placed her hand on his shoulder. ''Then do it for me.''

''No.''

''Adam, please,'' she pleaded. ''I don't want to hurt him or come between the two of you.''

Adam stood and grasped her shoulders hard. "Laura, listen to me. I love my son, but I will not allow him to dictate my life. In a few years he'll be grown and gone, with a life of his own. What am I supposed to do? Put mine on hold until then? Sacrifice my chance at happiness, just because of his misplaced adolescent jealousy? Well, I won't do it. So don't ask me."

"But, Adam—"

"The answer is no," Adam insisted, cutting off her protest. "We are going to see each other openly, and Mike will just have to accept it."

"And what if I don't agree?" Laura snapped, as guilt and anxiety gave way to anger. "It takes two, you know. And I have no intention of hurting that boy."

Adam gave her a shake, his fingers pressing deep into the soft white skin of her shoulders. "Dammit, Laura! Will you listen to me! I..." He stopped and glared down at her in sheer exasperation, then muttered a disgusted "Oh, hell" and fastened his mouth on hers.

For a moment Laura resisted, but gradually, as he held her close and the heat from his body seeped into hers, as his kiss went from hard demand to tender persuasion, she yielded. With a soft sigh, Laura sagged against him. Slowly her arms crept upward to circle his neck and her mouth flowered open to his seeking tongue.

Lovingly, he explored the dark recesses of her mouth, probing the curving roof, skating over her teeth, stroking the delicate membrane in her cheek. When he would have withdrawn she caught his tongue and sucked gently, and Adam groaned and pulled her closer. The lush velvet of her caftan was warm and erotically smooth, and his hands roamed over her back in a sensuous caress. For long moments they clung together, lost in the ardent embrace. When at last he raised his head, Adam bracketed her face with his hands and looked deep into her eyes with a passionate hunger that made her quiver.

"Oh, Laura. Laura," he whispered raggedly, as his

thumb swept back and forth over her kiss-swollen lips. And then his hands glided down over her neck and outward over the smooth, gentle slope of her shoulders. Briefly, his fingertips played with the ruffled edge of the caftan, then, holding her gaze, he slipped them under the shirred elastic and eased it downward.

Laura stood immobile, her hands at her sides, her head tilted proudly, as the caftan flowed slowly down over her full breasts, the gentle slope of midriff and waist, the womanly roundness of her hips. Adam bent his knees and nudged the elasticized neckline beyond her fingertips, and the soft folds collapsed around her ankles in a circle of sumptuous blue velvet.

Easing back a half step, Adam simply stood and gazed at her. In the flickering light from the fire, Laura could see his eyes darken, his face tightened with passion, as he visually touched every line and curve from her head to her toes, and the quivering within her grew to a heavy throb.

"Dear God! You're exquisite," he uttered in an passion-choked voice.

Reaching out, he grasped her hands and drew her forward, and as Laura stepped over the pile of velvet he enfolded her in his arms. Instantly his lips found hers in a slow, burning kiss. The rasp of his warm callused palms against the satin smoothness of her skin was oddly pleasing. Tenderly, they roamed over her back, his fingertips tracing her delicate shoulder blades, the curving line of her spine, as their lips clung and the kiss went on and on.

And then they were sinking to the floor. Eyes closed, Laura held Adam tightly. As he lowered her to the rug she felt her back and shoulders sink into the thick, soft pile.

"Oh, sweetheart, I need you so much," he murmured against her neck while his teeth nipped her gently. "So much."

He lay partially over her, his bent leg hooked over hers. His warm breath dewed her skin as he scattered hot, delicate kisses over her neck and collar bone, before returning to claim her lips once again.

The abrasive rub of his clothing against her naked skin was both irritating and arousing, and Laura whimpered her protest into his mouth as she writhed sinuously beneath him. She snatched frantically at the back of his shirt, pulling it free of his jeans, and slid her hands beneath it. Adam jerked, then shuddered, as her flexing fingers began to knead his flesh.

Releasing her mouth, he raised his head and looked at her through half closed eyes. "All right, my love," he whispered, in response to her unspoken plea, and with a lithe movement, rolled to his feet.

In helpless fascination, Laura watched him shed his clothes and toss them onto the sofa. Through it all, his eyes smoldered over her, taking in the sleek, long limbs, the enticingly curved body, the gorgeous honey-colored hair spilled all around her lovely face. On one side, her creamy skin was gilded an orange-gold by the flickering fire, and cast in blue shadows on the other. Lying gracefully on the rich oriental rug, her eyes glowing with desire, she was breathtaking, alluring, the essence of provocative femininity.

As Laura watched the firelight play over his lean, hard body she felt a quiver of longing and anticipation ripple through her. Adam was the most beautiful, most desirable, most rawly masculine man she had ever seen. Love for him filled her to bursting, and when finally he tossed aside the last article of clothing she held out her arms.

He came back into them willingly, his groan of pleasure blending with her soft sigh at the first touch of warm skin to warm skin. "Oh, sweetheart, just the feel of you drives me wild."

Laura fought to catch her breath. "I...yes...oh, yes!"

Cupping palms shaped her breasts while his thumbs brushed the rosy aureoles, bring them to aching readiness. A soft sigh drifted through Laura's parted lips and she buried her fingers in his hair to hold him close, as slowly, maddeningly, his tongue lapped at first one, then the other. Her sigh became a moan when, at last, he drew a hardened bud into the warmth of his mouth and suckled gently.

The same loving attention was given to the other breast, while his hand slid downward over her flat belly, and the long, sleek curve of her thigh. His fingers played with the back of her knee, then trailed upward along the satiny smooth skin of her inner thigh to the thatch of honeyed curls.

"Oh, Adam," Laura gasped at his first probing, intimate touch. Helplessly, her body arched against his hand when he found the core of her desire. A feverish delirium gripped her, and she clutched his shoulders in mindless desperation, her nails digging into his flesh.

With every breath excitement built, tension stretched tighter, need grew unbearable. Breathing was difficult, almost impossible.

Adam kissed the silky valley between her breasts, then his head slid downward. Warm, moist breath filled her navel as he brushed his open mouth back and forth over it. His tongue drew a wet circle around the tiny cavity, plunged into it, withdrew and circled again. Laura writhed beneath his tormenting mouth, consumed with sweet agony.

But when Adam's head dipped to nuzzle downy curls at the apex of her thighs she gasped and clutched his shoulders. "Please, darling. I need you now. Now."

Lifting his head, Adam looked at her with burning eyes. He hesitated only a moment before honoring her pleading words and beseeching hands, sliding upward to move into position between her soft thighs. His face was taut and flushed with passion as he braced on his palms and stared down at her intently, and, with one slow, sure thrust, joined their bodies together.

He thrust deep, and stilled. Eyes closed, he caught his lower lip between his teeth and struggled for control, his face contorting with a pleasure so intense it was almost pain. Then Laura's hips began a subtle little rotation, and he opened his eyes and smiled. "Witch," he growled lovingly as his body matched the motion.

Smiling, Laura ran her hands up his arms and locked them behind his neck, urging him down to her. When his cloud of chest hair settled over her breasts she nipped his lobe and whispered, "Love me. Love me."

"Like this?"

"Yes. Oh, yes."

"And this?" he asked in a throaty whisper, sliding his hands beneath her and lifting more fully into his possession.

"Yes, yes, yes! Oh, darling! *Darling!*"

The end came quickly. Explosive. Cataclysmic. Glorious. A burning comet so bright and intense it sent them hurtling out into space, giving them a shattering glimpse of heaven that rocked them both to the depths of their souls.

For long minutes, as thundering hearts slowed, as breathing gradually returned to normal, they lay locked together, stunned by the sheer beauty of their loving. Finally Adam summoned the energy to move and stretched out on his side next to her. Reaching out, he stroked a damp curl from her temple and gazed lovingly into her eyes. "Oh, sweetheart, that was beautiful," he murmured in a ragged voice. "Perfect."

Overwhelmed by the depth of her feelings, Laura stared back at him, her wide brown eyes brimming with love. Her throat was tight and aching, but finally she managed to whisper brokenly, "Yes. Yes, it was."

Their feelings were too intense, the joy they had just shared too unutterably beautiful, and for several moments they just looked at each other, speaking without words, in the age-old way of lovers. The air between them was heavy with emotion, the silence poignant.

But no matter how beautiful, their loving had settled nothing, and gradually that painful truth intruded. Each saw it in the other's eyes.

As joy slowly faded into sadness Adam rolled onto his

back. Side by side, shoulders touching, they lay in silence, staring at the dark ceiling. The only sounds were the ponderous ticking of the grandfather clock in the entry, and the hiss and pop of the fire.

"What are we going to do?" Laura asked finally, in a low, pain-edged voice.

For a moment she thought he wasn't going to answer. Then Adam sighed heavily. "I won't sneak around, Laura." He addressed the words to the ceiling, his tone flat and implacable.

Rolling her head on the rug, Laura looked at his set profile, and this time she was the one to sigh. "And I won't flaunt our relationship under Mike's nose."

"Then we've reached a stalemate," he said grimly, still staring fixedly at the ceiling. "Any suggestions?"

She studied the shadow of beard stubble on his face, the sprinkling of silver hairs in his sideburn, the graceful whorls in his ear. Resisting the urge to touch him, she turned her head away and stared into the fire. If she told him the truth it would settle the matter once and for all. Once he knew who she was, most likely Adam wouldn't want to be around her any more than Mike did.

But no matter how her conscience prodded her, Laura simply couldn't do it. *It's not the right time,* she told herself. *We just made love, for heaven's sake.*

"I suppose we'll have to compromise," she said softly.

"How?"

"Well, I guess there's really no point in trying to keep our relationship a secret. We've been seen together several times." Shooting him an accusing look, she grimaced wryly. "And after today there can't be any doubt in anyone's mind."

An unrepentant smile curved Adam's mouth. "None at all," he agreed complacently. "So you see, it's too late to shield Mike. People are going to be talking about us. There's no way we can stop it."

"True. But I don't intend to rub salt in the wound."

"Meaning?"

"Meaning that there will be no more threesomes. We'll see each other only when Mike is not around." It hurt to say the words, but Laura knew it was the only option open to them. Even that, she knew, wouldn't be satisfactory to Mike, but she couldn't voluntarily give Adam up. Not even for her son.

"Dammit, Laura—"

"No, Adam. I mean it," Laura insisted, quickly cutting off his angry objection. "It's that or nothing."

Adam gave her an exasperated glare, opened his mouth to argue, then snapped it shut, and reached out and hauled her into his arms. "Come here, woman," he growled as he pulled her tight against him and settled her head into the curve of his shoulder. With his chin propped against the top of her head, he stared into the fire and ran his hand absently up and down her arm. "Okay. We'll play it your way," he said reluctantly after a moment. "For now."

Laura relaxed against him, releasing the breath she had been unconsciously holding. She had been terrified that he wouldn't agree, and now she was weak with relief. She turned her head and pressed a warm kiss on his chest. "Thank you, darling," she whispered as she closed her eyes and snuggled closer. *Oh Lord, it feels so good, so right, to be held in his arms. Surely it can't be wrong. I'll tell him the truth soon,"* she vowed silently as sleep began to overtake her. *Only, please God, let this last just a little longer. Please.*

An hour later, after carefully extricating himself from Laura's arms, Adam dressed by the light of the dwindling fire, then scooped her up and started for the stairs. Laura stirred sleepily in his arms once, but when he laid her in the big brass bed and tucked the quilts around her chin, she snuggled her face into the down pillows with a contented sigh.

He stroked the silky hair at her temple and smiled down

at her with loving indulgence, tinged with exasperation. He could wring her lovely neck for the stubborn stand she had taken...and yet...he couldn't help but be deeply touched by her concern for his son's feelings. How many other women in her place would be so understanding and generous? he wondered.

Tenderness gripped him as he studied the way her lashes lay like dark feathery fans against her cheeks, the tiny blue veins in her delicate eyelids. He wanted desperately to crawl into that bed with her, to hold her next to his heart while they slept, to wake with her in the morning. But he couldn't. Mike was undoubtedly already home from the movies.

With a sigh, Adam leaned down and placed a kiss on Laura's forehead. "Good night, sweetheart," he whispered.

Chapter Eleven

Being together only when Mike wasn't present was not the most satisfactory arrangement in the world, as the next couple of weeks proved. Adam was a loving and conscientious father who spent a lot of time with his son. On weekends they went hunting and fishing, and many evenings were taken up with extracurricular school activities. Football season had no sooner ended than Mike was into basketball. He was also on the debating team, and it seemed that Adam was either attending a game or chauffeuring Mike and his friends to a nearby town for a debating contest. And of course, when Mike had friends over, Adam didn't feel comfortable leaving them at home alone.

"I swear, if I didn't know better, I'd think he was wise to our arrangement and was just dreaming up things to keep us apart," Adam groused one evening when he had managed to steal a couple of hours with Laura while Mike was at the movies. "He's never demanded as much of my time before. And he sure as heck never had such a busy social life.''

Sharing his frustration, Laura had smiled and commiserated with him, while privately thinking that Adam was probably closer to the truth than he knew. Mike was a bright boy. It shouldn't be too difficult for him to figure out that the more time his father spent with him, the less he would have for Laura. He was probably even hoping that she would eventually get so fed up with the lopsided arrangement that she would break off the relationship. And if Laura hadn't loved them both so much, she might have.

But somehow she and Adam managed to be together. An hour here, a few minutes there. They lunched together as often as possible. When he could, Adam came by Laura's house early for coffee before they had to leave for work, or he would show up on her doorstep late at night, tired and frustrated and aching for her company, for the warmth and loving they shared. And once, they even enjoyed the sheer luxury of an entire evening together.

They couldn't go on that way indefinitely, Laura knew. Sooner or later something would have to give, and if the way Adam was chafing over the situation was any indication, it was going to be sooner. A confrontation was brewing. She could feel it in the air. And she hadn't the faintest idea how she was going to deal with it.

The problem nagged at Laura constantly, and one evening in mid-November, as she turned onto the country lane that led to her house, she was once again mulling it over in her mind. She was so preoccupied that when the beam of her car's headlights struck the huddled figure at the edge of the road, his presence didn't register at first. But then suddenly he was on his feet, running into the middle of the road, waving his arms frantically. Acting purely on reflex, Laura slammed on the brakes and brought the car to a sliding halt on the gravel lane. Her eyes widened when, in that split second before he ran around the driver's side of the car, she recognized the panicked face caught in the glare of the headlights.

"Mike! What are you doing out here?" she asked worriedly as she pressed the button on the armrest, bringing the window gliding down with a soft whirr. She darted a look around at the gathering dusk, then her eyes swung back to him. "What's wrong?"

"It's Molly! She's been hurt!" he cried hysterically, his face contorting with anguish and fear. "Please! You've got to help her! Please!"

"Calm down, Mike. Of course I'll help." Before she finished speaking Laura started to climb from the car. The moment she was standing Mike grabbed her hand and dragged her to where the dog lay by the side of the road.

Pitiful whimpering sounds came from the animal, and as Laura dropped to her knees beside her she caught her breath and bit down on her bottom lip. One leg lay at an obscene angle to the dog's body and blood ran from a long gash along her side. Even in the faint illumination from the car's headlights Laura could see the pain-glazed look in Molly's beautiful amber eyes.

"What happened?" Laura's voice was shaky. So was her hand when she reached out to tenderly stroke the silky mahogany coat.

"Pickup hit her. Trespassers," Mike blurted out in a breathless, incoherent rush. "They were hunting where they shouldn't be. We took 'em by surprise and they jumped in their truck and took off. Molly couldn't get out of their way."

"I see. Well, we're going to have to get her to a vet, fast. And in the meantime we're going to have to stop this bleeding."

Laura scrambled to her feet and whipped off her coat, letting it fall unheeded to the ground. Beneath it she wore a softly gathered, muted apricot and gray plaid skirt and a delicate apricot, high-necked, batiste blouse. With frantic movements she snatched the hem of the blouse free of her skirt and began to work open the buttons.

"What are you doing?" Mike cried when she slipped out of it and began ripping off the sleeves.

"I told you—we've got to stop the bleeding." Laura's apricot satin camisole gleamed in the harsh beam of light from the car as she once again dropped to her knees beside the injured dog. The chill wind whipped her hair around her face and raised goose-flesh over her arms and shoulders, but she barely noticed.

Knowing that an injured animal could hurt you without meaning to, Laura very gingerly tied one of the batiste sleeves around Molly's snout. The other she folded into a thick wad and shoved into Mike's hand. "Here. When we get her into the car press that against the wound and see if you can stop the bleeding."

"But your blouse!"

"It's just a blouse, Mike. It's unimportant," Laura said distractedly as she donned what was left of the garment and shrugged back into her coat. "Now run and open the back door of the car, so we can lift her in."

Mike sped away to do as she instructed and was back within seconds. "She'll bleed all over your upholstery," he warned, as they gently picked Molly up and started for the car.

"It doesn't matter," Laura grunted tersely, her concentration centered on causing the animal as little additional pain as possible.

Between the two of them, they managed to get the struggling dog onto the backseat. Mike scrambled in after her and knelt on the floorboard, desperately crooning soothing words.

"Press that cloth to the wound tightly," Laura instructed as she climbed in behind the wheel and slammed the door. She shoved the gearshift into reverse, whipped the car around, and stomped on the gas pedal. Tires spun and gravel sprayed the air as the Lincoln took off toward the highway with a powerful roar.

Laura made the short trip back to town so fast she nearly burned up the pavement. When she brought the car to a grinding halt before the veterinary clinic on the edge of town, it was in darkness, and Dr. Hanson was in the parking lot, just climbing into his pickup.

Three short blasts of the car horn brought him sprinting over. By the time he reached them Laura was already out and had the back door open. "It's an emergency," she informed him quickly, not bothering with social niceties. "Mike's dog was hit by a truck and she's in a bad way."

Dr. Hanson took over with rapid efficiency. Shoving a ring of keys into Laura's hand, he instructed her to go open the clinic door, then he turned to bend over his patient. As Laura sped away she heard him say, "Now then, Mike, I want you to keep that cloth pressed against the wound while I lift her out. That's it. Thatta boy. Easy does it. Easy now."

Laura had barely gotten the door open and flicked on the lights when Dr. Hanson came striding in with Molly in his arms. Mike was running along beside, doing his best to obey the doctor's instructions. "I'm going to need help," the burly man said as he shouldered open the door to the treatment room. "My assistant's home number is taped to the phone. Call him and tell him I said get over here on the double."

Shakily, Laura did as she was told. Once assured that the man was on his way, she then called Adam's house. When she got no answer she dialed his office, but no one was there either. Desperate, she called Harriet Beacher and explained what had happened, and asked her to try to locate Adam. Laura had barely hung up the phone when Mike emerged from the treatment room.

His face was chalky and there was a look of desperation in his eyes. "Dr. Hanson said I had to wait out here," he muttered, casting a resentful glance at the treatment room door. "He said I'd just be in the way."

"Well, I...I'm sure he's right, Mike," Laura began tentatively. "His assistant said he'd be here within three minutes. They'll know what to do for her."

"But she's *my* dog!" Mike cried stubbornly, his face becoming mottled with color as fear, frustration and anger overwhelmed him. "I should be with her!"

His mouth worked with emotion, and Laura's heart went out to him as his chin began to quiver. "I know, Mike. I know," she soothed. "But that's just not possible right now. Why don't you come over here and sit down," she suggested, leading him toward one of the vinyl-covered couches that lined the waiting-room walls.

Laura shed her coat, and when she sat down beside Mike she eased his off his arms and tossed it onto the chair with hers. He didn't seem to notice. Slumping forward, he propped his forearms on his spread knees and clutched his hands together between them, twisting them restlessly. As though willing it to open, he fixed his gaze on the door across the room. Anguish tightened his features and sheer terror glittered in his topaz eyes. His whole body was stiff with tension.

Biting her lip, Laura watched him anxiously. She hated to see him hurting so. She longed to comfort him, to reach out and stroke that rigid back and tell him that everything would be all right. But she couldn't. She didn't *know* if everything would be all right. But more important, she wasn't sure if Mike would accept an offer of sympathy from her. She felt so helpless! So useless!

"I raised her from a pup," Mike said out of the blue. "She was just eight weeks old when I got her." His voice was low and quavered with raw emotion. It brought an aching tightness to Laura's throat and she swallowed hard, blinking away the moisture that rushed to her eyes. "I trained her, took care of her. She sleeps beside my bed every night. And when I get off the school bus, she's there waiting for me.''

''Oh, Mike.'' The pain that etched his voice tore at Laura's heart. Unable to help herself, she put her hand on his hunched shoulder. ''I'm so sorry. So very sorry.''

He turned his head and looked at her pleadingly, his eyes swimming with unshed tears. ''She can't die, Laura,'' he said desperately. ''I don't think I could stand it if she died.'' His voice broke on the last word, and when the tears began to spill over onto his white cheeks Laura could stand no more.

With a soft cry, she put her arms around him and pulled him to her, cradling his head against her shoulder. Mike offered no resistance. ''Oh, Mike, darling. I know. I know,'' she crooned as she patted his heaving shoulders. ''Go ahead and cry, darling. It's all right.''

Laura squeezed her eyes shut and pressed her cheek against his head, but her tears could not be held in check. They streamed from between her lashes, spiking them and wetting her face, dripping into the corners of her mouth. She stroked Mike's black silky hair and stifled the sobs that rose in her throat as she rocked him gently. This was her child, flesh of her flesh, and she would have given anything to spare him this pain.

When Dr. Hanson stepped into the waiting room, Mike jerked out of her arms and sprang to his feet. Laura rose more slowly, fear clutching at her when she saw the grave look on the vet's face.

Mike's quick demand to know how Molly was made the older man grimace. ''Not good, son,'' he said sympathetically. ''I'm afraid there's no way I can save her leg.'' He studied Mike's stricken face for a moment, then added softly, ''For that reason, I recommend that we put her down.''

''*No!*'' Mike screamed the word, his eyes growing huge with horror. ''No, you can't! I won't let you!''

''Be sensible, Mike. It's either that or amputate. She'll

be crippled. Unable to run or hunt or play. Is that what you want?''

"I want her alive!" Mike shouted fiercely.

Sighing, Dr. Hanson ran his hand through his hair and down the back of his head to massage the tense muscles at its base. "Where's your father?" he asked tiredly. "I think this is a decision he should make."

Laura stepped close to Mike and put her arm around his shoulder. "I've tried to call his father, but I can't reach him. His aunt is trying to locate him now." She hesitated, then drew a deep breath and asked the question she knew had to be asked. "Do we have time to wait for him?"

Mike's head snapped around and he stared at her, shocked anew. She felt his whole body stiffen beneath her arm.

Dr. Hanson shook his head regretfully. "No." I'm afraid we need a decision now."

"Then I'll make it, Doctor. I'll take full responsibility." Laura looked at Mike, and her expression softened at the terrible fear in his eyes. Very gently, she cupped her hand against his jaw. "Are you sure this is what you want, Mike?" At his frantic nod, she turned back to the vet. "Do whatever you have to, but save Molly, Doctor," she instructed with quiet but firm authority.

He looked at her for a moment, then nodded. "Very well, I'll do my best."

"Thanks, Laura," Mike said shakily when the vet disappeared into the treatment room.

Laura smiled. "Come on. We might as well sit down. I think we're going to have a long wait."

Laura returned to the couch, and after a moment Mike joined her. They sat side by side, neither knowing what to say or do. The vinyl cushions crackled noisily as Mike fidgeted. He swiped at his eyes with the heels of his hands and sniffed loudly. Laura wanted to touch him again, but he was staring stonily at the floor, and she was afraid he was embarrassed over breaking down in front of her, so she did nothing. Then suddenly, without ever looking at her, Mike reached over and took her hand and laced their fingers together.

Laura's breath caught. As a welter of painfully sweet emotions swelled in her throat and chest, she closed her eyes tightly, savoring the moment. Tentatively, she squeezed Mike's hand, and after a moment, he squeezed hers back.

Fifteen minutes later, when Adam burst into the clinic, that was how he found them.

"Dad!" Mike was on his feet and hurrying toward his father before he could close the door.

"What happened?" Adam demanded, frowning worriedly at the distraught boy.

"Molly got hit by a pickup. Laura helped me bring her here." In a rush born of fear and nerves Mike babbled out the whole story, including Laura's decision to save the dog. It was then that Adam took a close look at Laura, and his eyes widened.

She had not bothered to retuck her blouse, and its wrinkled hem hung loosely around her hips. Her arms were bare to her shoulders, sticking out of ragged holes where the sleeves used to be. Her blouse was, or had been, a luscious Victorian concoction with a pin-tucked bodice, dainty pearly buttons, and a high, stand-up, lace-edged collar, but what was left of the exquisitely feminine garment was streaked with grime and what appeared to be dried blood. Laura's hair was disheveled and her face bore the telltale marks of tears and smeared mascara.

Adam had never seen her looking more lovely.

If he'd had any lingering doubts about his feelings, they were gone in that instant. Love for Laura welled up inside him like a gushing spring, filling his heart, his soul, his entire being, until he thought surely he would burst. He wanted to snatch her up in his arms and hold her close, to bury his face in that fragrant honey-colored hair, feel her softness against him, to tell her, and show her, all the things he was feeling. But now was not the time.

He led Mike back to the couch and sat down. Leaning across his son's lap, Adam picked up Laura's hand and gazed deep into her eyes. His smile was warm with love and gratitude. "Thank you, darling," he said huskily, giving her a look of such melting tenderness it brought the ready tears back to her eyes.

"You don't have to thank me, Adam," Laura said uncomfortably. "Anyone would have done the same."

His eyes ran over her once again, and his smiling look silently disputed her claim, but he merely said, "But you're the one who did it, and we're both grateful. Aren't we Mike?"

Mike hesitated only a second, then cast Laura an uneasy glance. "Yeah. Thanks, Laura," he mumbled self-consciously.

"Then you think I made the right decision?" Laura directed her question to Adam, her expression uncertain.

"Absolutely. A three-legged Molly is definitely preferable to no Molly at all."

The waiting was interminable. The minutes seemed to drag by like hours. Mike alternately fidgeted on one of the couches and paced the floor with his thumbs hooked in the back pockets of his jeans. Both Adam and Laura tried to distract him, but no attempt at conversation held his attention long, and finally they gave up. While Laura idly flipped through a magazine, Adam perused the prints of the hunting dogs that lined the walls, then finally resorted to counting the blocks of vinyl tile on the floor.

But at last the doctor emerged, and they all jumped to attention as though they were spring-loaded.

"Well, it looks like she's going to make it," he announced wearily. "I'll have to keep her here for a few days, but I think she'll be fine."

A look of utter relief passed over Mike's face, and for

an instant his whole body sagged. Then, straightening, he asked eagerly, "Can I see her?"

"Sure. She's still unconscious, but you can see her for a few minutes."

They were all smiling when they trooped after Dr. Hanson, but when they left the clinic ten minutes later, their expressions were somber. It had been a shock to see the lively Molly limp and helpless and swathed in bandages, and that awful emptiness where her leg had been.

In the parking lot, they quietly bid each other good night, climbed into their separate vehicles, and headed for home. When Adam's pickup turned into his drive, he honked the horn twice, and as Laura drove on by she returned the farewell.

The grandfather clock in the entry was striking ten when Laura let herself into the house, and suddenly she felt bone tired. She was torn between grabbing a quick bite or having a long hot soak. In the end, weariness won over hunger.

As she relaxed in the steamy, violet-scented water she allowed herself to think about that moment when Mike had picked up her hand and held it. She tried to tell herself that it meant nothing. He was just grateful. He would have been grateful to anyone who helped him. Don't read more into it than there was, Laura admonished herself severely. But when she thought about the way his palm had felt against hers, the way he had held on to her so tightly, a smile tilted her lips and hope welled up inside her in spite of all she could do.

Half an hour later, she was tying the belt on her cinnamon velour robe when the doorbell rang. The lateness of the hour and an awareness of her isolation caused Laura to tiptoe out onto the landing and peer cautiously down at the front door, but the silhouette visible through the frosted glass oval sent her scurrying downstairs.

"Adam! What are you doing here? Is something wrong?" she asked the moment she snatched the door open.

Adam stepped inside and immediately pulled her into his arms. When he saw the fright in her eyes, he felt a momentary pang. It was late and she had had an exhausting evening. He probably shouldn't have come, but dammit, he couldn't stay away. His heart was too full. He had to talk to her, had to tell her how he felt. Now. Tonight.

"No. Nothing's wrong," he said in a low, throbbing voice. "I just had to see you. Hold you." Cupping her jaw with his hand, he tilted her face up and kissed her with such sweetness, such slow, savoring warmth, it stole Laura's breath away. When he raised his head she was clinging to him like a limpet, her eyes half closed and heavy-lidded, her soft mouth parted and wet.

Adam smiled. "I can't stay but a minute. Mike's too upset for me to leave him alone for too long, but I had to tell you how proud I am of you. And to thank you again for what you did for Mike."

Uncomfortable, Laura lowered her eyes to his chest while her fingers plucked restlessly at the buttons on his shirt. "It wasn't all that much, Adam. No more than anyone else would have done. I just happened to be the one who came driving by."

Her reluctance endeared her to him all the more, and Adam's expression grew tender. "Honey, I can't think of many women who would give the shirt off their back—or should I say, the designer blouse—to help save a boy's dog. Whether you want to admit it or not, you're a pretty special lady." A pleased smile spread across his face. "And though he hasn't exactly said so, I think Mike's opinion of you has undergone an abrupt about-face in the last few hours."

"He's just grateful to me for helping him, Adam. That's all."

"Yes, he's grateful. But because of what you did, he's been forced to take a good long look at you and accept you for the kind of person you are. Kind and gentle, loving and generous. Forgiving. Not even a stubborn, fourteen-year-

old boy can help but like and admire those qualities."
Adam's eyes caressed her face and his voice dropped to a
low velvety rasp, barely above a whisper. "Those same
qualities are part of why I love you."

Laura's eyes went wide and for a moment her lungs
stopped functioning. At one and the same time his words
made her whole and tore her apart. Adam's love was what
she wanted above all else...and what she dreaded most. For
love demanded honesty and sharing. Openness.

"And I do love, you, Laura," he continued before she
could reply. "I love you very much. More than I thought
it was possible to love anyone."

"Oh, Adam," Laura whispered in a small, aching voice.
"Adam, this...this has been an emotion-charged evening.
We've all been strung out and overwrought and...and I
don't think you should...."

Adam chuckled softly, adoring her with his eyes.
"Sweetheart, I'm not in the least confused about my feelings, if that's what you're thinking. I'm grateful to you for
what you did, but I love you for what you are."

Feeling wretchedly undeserving, Laura lowered her head.
Her hair swung forward in a shiny curtain, and Adam
pushed it back, smiling as a tendril curled around his hand.
He loved its silky, rich texture, its sweet fragrance. "After
I lost Carol, I never thought I would love another woman,"
he said quietly, tipping her face up. "But then, I hadn't
counted on finding one like you.

"To be honest, what I felt for Carol pales in comparison.
We grew up together and our love was easy and comfortable, something we just drifted into. But I never felt this
excitement before, this kind of urgency." He cupped her
face with his big hands and looked deep into her eyes. "I
love you, Laura. Everything about you. I love your sweetness, your compassion, that genteel stubbornness that drives
you. The elegant little tilt to your head, and the way your
hips sway when you walk." He ran his fingertips over the
smooth curve of her cheek, and his voice grew deeper,

more intense. "Your goodness. Your warmth. Your honesty."

Laura almost cried out. His gentle, loving words flayed her, each one flicking her conscience raw. "Oh, Adam," Laura protested in a forlorn little voice. "Don't endow me with virtues I don't have. I'm...I'm not what you think. I mean...there's something you don't know about me. Something—"

"Hush." Adam placed four fingers over her mouth, halting her confession. Tenderness and love marked his expression and glowed from his eyes as he gazed down at her expectantly. "All I want to hear is that you love me," he whispered.

The storm of emotion that raged in Laura's chest almost suffocated her. She stared up at him with wide, teary eyes, joy and sorrow, hope and despair, tearing at her. Love him? Of course she loved him—more than she had ever loved anyone or anything in her entire life—but for a brief instant she considered denying it. Wouldn't it be more sensible? Safer, and in the long run, kinder to all of them? Mike included?

But sensible or not, when Adam's eyes began to cloud with pain at her hesitation, she abandoned the idea instantly. "Of course I love you, my darling," she managed, her voice vibrating with emotion. Turning her head, she pressed a warm kiss into his palm. "I love you so much."

"Laura. Laura." He breathed her name on a heartfelt sigh as his lips lowered to capture hers. The kiss was long and deep, rife with feelings too profound for words.

And when it was over, Laura closed her eyes and laid her cheek against his broad chest. Her arms went around his waist and held him tightly. Beneath her ear she heard the thunder of his heart, felt the heavy rise and fall of his chest.

Adam's moist breath filtered through her hair and tickled across her scalp as he kissed the top of her head. "I love you," he whispered again, as though driven to say it.

"And I love you," Laura choked. Hugging him tightly, she bit down hard on her lower lip. Tears squeezed from between her lids and streamed down her cheeks, wetting Adam's shirt and dripping from her chin to form dark circles on the cinnamon robe. Dear God. How could anything be so right and so wrong at the same time? Loving Adam, and having him love her back, was the most beautiful thing that had ever happened to her. But Laura knew, with a painful, heartfelt certainty, that she was going to pay dearly for this glimpse of happiness.

But not now. Not just yet. Please God, she begged fervently as she snuggled more tightly against his chest. She drew in deep draughts of air, savoring his virile man-scent, his reassuring strength, his warmth that enveloped her. *I'll tell him the truth soon. I swear it. But please. Let me have his love for just a little while longer.*

Chapter Twelve

It was almost closing time the next afternoon when Laura looked up from straightening a rack of clothes near the front window and saw Mike ambling across the square. She watched him avidly for a moment, until, with a start, she realized he was heading for her shop. Quickly, she turned away and busied herself fluffing the throw pillows on the settee.

At the jingle of the bell above the door Laura looked up and gave him what she hoped was a surprised smile. "Why, Mike. What brings you here?"

He stood just inside the door, his shoulders hunched, his fingers jammed into the back pockets of his jeans. Glancing around at the feminine trappings, he shifted uneasily from one sneakered foot to the other, a look of sheer male panic crossing his face. He glanced behind him at the door, as though reassuring himself it was still there, then looked at Laura. "I, uh..." He stopped and cleared his throat.

"I...well...I thought you might like to know that Molly's doing okay," he said with self-conscious reluctance.

Laura's face lit up. Stepping forward, she placed her hand on his arm. "Oh, Mike, that's wonderful."

"Yeah, well, I walked over to the clinic after school and stayed with her for a little while. She's weak and everything, but Doc Hanson says she's doing okay."

"I'm so glad," Laura said softly, giving him a warm smile.

A moment of awkward silence followed. Mike looked away, but when his eyes fell on a frothy nightgown, artfully draped over a small velvet chair, he jerked his gaze back to Laura. "Also, I, uh, I'd like to pay you for that blouse you ruined." Digging into his pocket, he pulled out some crumpled bills, but when he stretched out his hand to give them to her, Laura shook her head.

"No, Mike. I'm not going to take your money." Some of the joy faded from her eyes. She knew that it could be just his budding male pride that had prompted the offer, but she couldn't help but wonder if he were trying to pay off some imaginary debt so that he wouldn't feel obligated to her for anything.

"But your blouse—"

"Hardly matters," she finished for him. With a sad smile and a wave of her hand, Laura indicated the shop full of feminine apparel. "As you can see, one blouse more or less is certainly not going to wreck my wardrobe." When he looked like he was about to argue further, she added, "And anyway, Molly's recovery is all the repayment I need."

After subjecting her to a long, intent look, Mike nodded and stuffed the money back into his pocket. "Okay. If that's the way you want it." He edged back a step and put his hand on the doorknob. "Well, uh, I guess I'd better be going. Dad's waiting for me at his office. I got a basketball game in a little while."

Laura cocked one brow. Was this his not too subtle way

of telling her that she wouldn't be seeing Adam tonight? "Goodbye, Mike. Thanks for coming by."

He opened the door and started to step out, then hesitated and looked back over his shoulder. "Uh, if you want me to, I, uh...I could keep you posted on how Molly's getting along," he offered uncertainly.

The heaviness lifted from Laura's heart and a slow warm smile blossomed on her face. "Thank you, Mike. I'd like that very much."

With a quick nod, he was gone. Through the window, Laura watched him lope across the street and cut diagonally through the square toward Adam's office.

"What was that all about?" Racine asked as she came to stand beside Laura.

"I'm not sure," Laura answered distractedly, her eyes still on the retreating boy. "I'm just...not sure."

Over the next few days Laura's uncertainties and doubts slowly gave way to fragile hope. Every evening, just before closing, Mike dropped by the shop with news of Molly's progress. The meetings were short and often awkward, but there was none of the hostility that Mike had displayed toward her in the past. And though she told herself that it was probably wishful thinking on her part, it seemed to Laura that he was lingering just a little longer every time.

All day Saturday she half expected him to walk in at any moment, but as the day wore on with no sign of him her spirits sank. "Well, what did you expect?" she demanded of herself angrily as she locked up the shop. "Undying gratitude? That he would suddenly think you were the most wonderful person in the world? How ridiculous!"

Still muttering under her breath, Laura drove by the bank and dropped the day's receipts into the night deposit slot, then headed for home.

The phone was ringing when she climbed the back steps. Sure it was Adam, she hurried across the porch and fumbled impatiently with the lock, cursing under her breath when it proved stubborn, then giving a little cry of alarm when the door suddenly flew open and plunged her headlong into the darkened kitchen. By the time she had groped her way to the wall phone she had barked her shin twice, was out of breath, and not in the best of moods.

"Yes, hello," she snapped into the receiver, only to be met by absolute silence. "Hello, who's there?"

"Laura?"

In that instant the depression that had weighted her down for the past few hours floated away like thistledown, and she beamed a smile at the darkened ceiling. "Mike! I'm sorry I was so abrupt. I had to hurry to catch the phone and I was afraid you'd hang up."

"Yeah, well, I just wanted to let you know why I didn't come by today," he said in a gruff attempt at casualness, which he then spoiled by adding excitedly, "We brought Molly home this afternoon."

"Oh, Mike." Laura's voice was low and vibrant with emotion. "That's wonderful."

"Yeah." Mike laughed, then caught himself and abruptly cleared his throat. "Well...I just wanted to let you know. I'll, uh...I'll be seein' ya."

"'Bye, Mike," Laura murmured, but the dial tone was already droning in her ear. She hung up the phone slowly, and for several minutes just stood there, her fingers still wrapped around the receiver. Finally, tilting her head back, she closed her eyes, and there in the darkness, gave full rein to the joyous smile that had been tugging at her mouth.

The irrational feeling of elation lasted until Adam called a while later to tell her he would not be able to see her that evening.

"We brought Molly home today," he informed her, inadvertently wiping out any suspicions she might have had that he had told Mike to call her. "She's doing fine, but Mike is a nervous wreck, so I guess I'd better stay home with him. At least for tonight."

"That's all right. I understand."

"I don't suppose you'd consider coming over here?"

"No, Adam, I wouldn't," Laura said as firmly as she could, while shaking her head and smiling ruefully at his persistence. Adam had been delighted when she told him about Mike's visits to the shop, viewing them as proof that his attitude toward her had changed. He saw no reasons to continue "tiptoeing around Mike," as he put it. But despite her burgeoning hope, Laura wasn't convinced. Not entirely.

"Dammit, I miss you, woman," Adam flared angrily. "It seems like weeks since I've been able to touch you."

"I know, darling," Laura soothed. "I know." His vehemence and the raw hunger in his voice enveloped her in a wave of longing and set tiny pulses to clamoring in her most secret parts.

"Do you?" His voice dropped to a low, sensuous rasp that made her heart thump, her skin prickle. "Do you know that I want to kiss every beautiful inch of you? That I want to fill my hands with your breasts and feel you warm and naked against me?"

"Adam, please," Laura pleaded shakily.

"I want to be inside you, Laura. Right now. I want to love you slowly, all night long. I want to hear those sweet purring sounds you make, to watch your face go all soft and rosy with passion."

"*Adam!*" she groaned as the sensual torment brought a heated flush to her whole body. Her knees began to wobble and she slumped against the wall, her free hand pressed to her hot cheek. "You shouldn't be talking that way. What if Mike should hear you?"

"Then he'll know exactly how love sick his old man is," he said remorselessly. At Laura's shocked gasp Adam chuckled and took pity on her. "Don't worry. He's in his room with the stereo turned up so loud he couldn't hear a cannon go off right outside his door."

"You're shameless," she scolded softly.

"I know, but you love me anyway, don't you?"

Trembling with emotion, Laura closed her eyes and gripped the phone tighter. "Yes. Yes I do."

It wasn't until much later, as Laura tossed and turned in her lonely bed, that it occurred to her that perhaps now that Molly was out of danger, Mike would no longer feel obliged to keep up his daily visits. Realistically, she knew it had to happen sooner or later, but it was a depressing thought all the same, one that disturbed her sleep and stayed with her throughout the next day—right up until the moment Mike arrived.

Laura was sitting at the kitchen table, watching the wind swirl the fallen leaves through the yard, while trying not to think about how big and empty the house seemed, how terribly silent. Idly, she took a sip of hot chocolate, but as she returned the cup to the table a movement caught her eye, and she looked up just in time to see Mike climb through the back fence.

Before he could cross the yard she was at the door. When his footsteps sounded on the back porch she jerked the door open and stepped back with a smile. "Come in, Mike, before you freeze to death."

A fresh norther had blown in during the night, dropping the temperature into the mid-twenties. Mike entered the kitchen on a frigid blast of air, his cheeks and nose whipped red by the wind, his eyes watery. The crisp freshness of the outdoors radiated from him.

"Take your coat off and sit down while I pour you a cup of hot chocolate," Laura offered. She half expected him to refuse, but he tugged off his gloves and the knit cap that was pulled down over his ears and stuffed them into the pockets of his down-filled coat.

"Boy, it's cold out there," he said as he shrugged out of the coat and hooked it on the pegged rack beside the back door. He raked spread fingers through his mussed hair, then rubbed his hands together briskly. He sniffled, and Laura smiled as she saw him swipe at his nose with his sleeve. Catching her eye, he grinned self-consciously and slid into a chair.

"So, how's our patient today?" she asked, setting the cup of hot chocolate in front of him.

"Well, she still seems kinda weak and she sleeps a lot, but Doc Hanson says that's normal. He says it's going to take a while for her to recover from the surgery. But she's learning to hobble around pretty good on three legs."

"That's good. It will be difficult, but I'm sure she'll adjust."

They both fell silent. Laura stirred her hot chocolate while Mike nervously drummed his fingers on the oak table. After a moment he looked around the cheery kitchen and said, "I see you got the place all fixed up. It looks nice."

"Thank you. I'm pleased with it."

The silence stretched out between them again. Mike took a sip of the hot drink, then curled his fingers around the mug to warm them. "Actually, I came over to...well, to see if maybe you'd like to come see Molly," he said at last, staring fixedly at the wisp of steam rising from his cup.

For a moment Laura couldn't speak for the painfully sweet tightness that gripped her chest. He was offering an olive branch, awkwardly, tentatively perhaps, but she was well aware just how difficult the gesture must have been for him, and she was deeply touched. And very proud. Laying a hand on his arm, Laura gave him a misty smile. "I'd love to see her, Mike." She quickly downed the last of her chocolate and stood up. "Just give me ten minutes to change."

She was back in five. Excitement and a boundless elation pounded through Laura's veins as she and Mike bundled up and dashed out to the car. She had never been in Adam's house before, and she found the prospect strangely exhilarating. And to be invited there by Mike was sheer heaven.

The mile or so between the houses was covered in just a few minutes. When Laura and Mike rushed in out of the cold and slammed the door behind them, Adam emerged from the living room—and came to an abrupt halt. His jaw dropped and his eyes grew round and for a moment he just stared. But then shock gave way to sheer gladness. It flared brightly in his eyes like a Roman candle, then dimmed to a steady warm glow.

"Well, I wondered where you had disappeared to," Adam drawled as he strolled toward them with studied nonchalance. His words were directed at Mike but his smile encompassed them both.

"I invited Laura over so she could see for herself how Molly's doing," Mike explained sheepishly. He scrambled out of his outdoor gear and tossed it onto the brass coat rack by the front door, missing the look of happy triumph that passed between the two adults. "Come on, Laura," he said as he started toward the den. "She's in here in front of the fire."

Adam took Laura's coat and hung it beside Mike's, but when she went to follow the boy he stopped her. Grasping her shoulders, he looked at her lovingly, his eyes glowing with warmth. "Welcome to my home, my love," he whispered as he bent his head to kiss her.

His lips cherished hers with a depth of feeling that was almost frighteningly beautiful. With exquisite tenderness, he kissed her sweetly, deeply, telling her without words of his love and his profound joy. Laura's chest swelled with emotion and tears gathered beneath her closed lids. For a moment she thought surely her heart would burst from so much happiness.

Laura was trembling when he finally raised his head, and she looked up at him with her heart in her eyes, unable to utter a sound.

"Come on, Laura. In here," Mike called from the den.

Smiling ruefully, Adam brushed her mouth with a feathery kiss and slipped an arm around her waist, pulling her firmly against his side. "Come on, let's go before he comes looking for you."

When they entered the room Molly raised her head from the hearth rug and thumped her tail in welcome. Laura dropped to her knees, her heart squeezing with sympathy when the dog rolled her amber eyes soulfully. "Hello, Molly girl. You're looking a lot better now," she crooned as she stroked the silky mahogany head.

For several minutes Laura admired and petted the dog, while Mike sat beside her and related everything the animal had done since they brought her home.

When Adam offered her a cup of coffee, she accepted with alacrity, wanting to draw the visit out as long as possible. As she sipped the brew and listened to Mike's chatter her eyes wandered around the room.

It was large and filled with comfortable, homey furniture, done in earth tones with occasional splashes of brighter autumn colors for highlight. The walls were paneled with rich walnut, and dark massive beams spanned the width of the room. The huge stone fireplace that dominated one wall was flanked by floor-to-ceiling bookcases. Across from it the outer wall was made up almost entirely of glass, and looked out on a spectacular view of the rolling tree-covered hills.

It was a warm, inviting room with a feeling of permanence and security, a place meant for quiet evenings by a cozy fire. A place for a family, Laura thought wistfully.

She lingered over the coffee as long as she could, but finally it was gone. "Well, I guess I'd better be going," she announced as she stood up, trying to hide her reluctance behind a smile.

"Do you have to?" Mike asked, surprising her. "I mean, I thought maybe you'd like to stay for supper."

"Why, I..." Biting her lip, Laura looked at Adam, and behind Mike's back he grinned and gave her a thumbs up sign. She looked back at the boy and her voice came out husky and a bit tremulous, "I'd like that very much. Thank you, Mike."

* * *

It was almost midnight when Laura unlocked her front door and she and Adam stepped inside. The moment it closed behind them, he drew her into his arms. Leaning back within the warm embrace, she laced her fingers behind his neck and smiled up at him. "I really shouldn't have let you bring me home. I feel guilty about you getting out in this cold when I had my car."

"I'll pick you up in the morning and you can get it then. But in the meantime I needed an excuse to be alone with my lady." Adam's mouth curved in a wry smile. "I'm glad my son has finally come to his senses, but I'm tired of sharing you."

"Oh, Adam. I had such a wonderful time tonight," Laura said feelingly.

Adam's face softened as his eyes caressed her. "Did you, sweetheart?"

"Oh, yes." She slipped her arms around his waist, closing her eyes as she laid her cheek on his chest and hugged him tightly. "Oh, yes," she said again with a contented sigh and a dreamy smile.

It had been one of the most beautiful evenings of Laura's life. Amid laughter and good-natured bantering, she and Adam and Mike had cooked dinner together—a simple meal of spaghetti and salad that had tasted like ambrosia. After they had cleaned up the kitchen, Mike had issued a challenge and they ended up spending the evening sprawled on the den floor playing video games. And through it all, Mike had grown increasingly more relaxed and friendly.

"Well, I think you won Mike over completely," Adam said with a smile in his voice, laying his cheek against the crown of her head. "Any female who can zap eighty-seven alien space ships, sixty extraterrestrial monsters and an intergalactic giant all in one game is Mike's kind of woman. In fact, if I'm not careful, he'll be trying to beat my time, first thing I know."

Laura looked up at him and grinned. "Are you still sore because you lost?"

"I wasn't sore," Adam denied with mock indignation. "And anyway, I admit that I'm not all that turned on by space-age technology and electronic competition. My taste runs to more...earthy pursuits."

"Oh, really? Such as?"

Grinning wickedly, Adam rocked his hips against her. "Let's go upstairs and I'll show you," he suggested in a low, throaty murmur.

"But Adam, Mike—"

"Is sound asleep by now," he stated firmly as he tucked her against his body and started up the stairs. "And once he drops off it would take the end of the world to wake him. He'd never know if I got home at midnight or three in the morning."

"You're sure?" Laura asked, wanting to be convinced.

When they reached the landing Adam gave her a warm, wet kiss. "Positive," he whispered against her lips. Laura sighed happily, delighted to concede. They drifted down the hallway, each with an arm around the other's waist, Laura's head resting against Adam's shoulder.

In the bedroom Adam turned her to face him. Grasping the bottom of her cream sweater, he began to peel it up over her body. "I may not be a whiz with electronic lasers," he said conversationally as he drew the bulky knit garment over her head and tossed it aside. "But when it comes to the personal touch..." Using both hands, he touched her collarbone with the tips of his fingers, then let them skim downward slowly, watching her face as they grazed over the upper slopes of her breasts and swirled around the lacy cups of her bra, before deftly unhooking the front closure. "...I do have a certain...knack."

Laura shivered as callused palms cupped her breasts. Adam bent to nuzzle the rosy crests, his warm breath and wet tongue a loving torment. "Not...not just a knack," she choked, tunneling her fingers through his hair to hold him close.

"No? A flair then?" Adam dropped to his knees and

lifted first one foot, then the other out of her shoes before his hands returned to deal with the snap on her jeans. Slipping his fingers inside the waistband, and then under the top edge of her panties, he drew them down over her hips and legs to her ankles, and eased them off, while Laura clutched his shoulders for balance.

"No, it's...more than that," she gasped as Adam kissed his way back up her leg. "It's a...a definite...talent."

With the tip of his tongue he traced the angular junction at the top of her thigh, and Laura moaned, her fingernails digging into his shoulders as she swayed unsteadily. Adam rose in one lithe movement and eased her back onto the bed. She lay watching him, fascinated and unbearably excited as he shed his clothes with a slow deliberation that was meant to tantalize. He was beautiful, darkly tanned, big and strong, the essence of masculinity.

Adam's eyes never left her, sensual pleasure tinged with amusement glittering in their hazel depths as he noted the rapt enjoyment.

He stretched out beside her and grinned. "So, you think I have talent, huh?" he asked smugly, cupping her breast and brushing his thumb back and forth across the burgeoning nipple.

"Y—yes." Laura shifted restlessly and arched her back.

His hand glided downward and he pressed his palm against her flat belly. His face was taut with passion, his eyes glittering hotly, as he studied the contrast between her skin and his. Brown to ivory. Leather to pearl. Male to female. Slowly, maddeningly his fingers threaded through the honey-tinted curls at the apex of her thighs, and sought the delicate petals of her womanhood.

"Very much talent?" he asked softly.

"Oh, my darling," Laura managed on a ragged sigh as her hands clutched his shoulders, urging him to her. "You have a positive genius."

And there in the darkness, with love and tenderness, he proved it.

Chapter Thirteen

For Laura, the next two weeks passed in a blur of sheer happiness. Mike not only accepted her, he seemed to actually welcome her presence in their lives. He laughed and joked with her and teased her unmercifully at times. And, like a typical adolescent male, he bestowed on her a rough, offhand brand of affection: a playful punch on the arm, a tug on her hair, a poke with an elbow. And occasionally even a careless hug.

Laura loved every minute of it. But intense happiness was something new to her. New and wonderful...and scary.

Life had never been so full, so rich. Suddenly she seemed to have everything her heart had ever yearned for. Her son liked her—actually *liked* her—and she was loved, passionately and deeply, by a good man. It was more than she had expected. Much more than she had ever dared hope for. It seemed too good to be true. Too perfect to last.

Most of the time Laura was able to thrust her fears away and enjoy the miraculous turn her life had taken, savoring every minute spent with Adam and her son. But now and then something would remind her just how precarious was her hold on happiness, as happened Thanksgiving day.

They had the feast at Adam's house, and he invited his Aunt Harriet and Carly Sue and her husband to share it. The huge meal was delicious, the bantering conversation delightful. To Laura, it was the best holiday by far that she had ever known.

When the meal was over, the men escaped to the den to watch football, leaving the women to do the dishes. It was shortly after that, while Carly Sue was busy clearing the table, that Laura found herself alone in the kitchen with Harriet.

"Well, have you told him yet?" the older woman demanded in her brusque, no-nonsense tone.

Laura's hand stopped in mid-motion. Fear widened her eyes and drained her face of color. Swallowing hard, she shook her head. "No. No, I haven't," she admitted in a small voice. Laura turned her attention back to the dish she was holding, and with shaking hands, began to scrape the leftover candied yams into a smaller bowl. "I...I just haven't found the right time."

"There is no 'right' time to drop a bomb like that. You just pick a time and get on with it. The longer you let it drag out, the harder it's going to be." Harriet gave her a long, stern look. "I don't want to see my nephew hurt. For that matter, I don't want to see you hurt either. You're a fine woman, and I like you, and I think you're good for Adam, but you can't expect to build a future with a man and keep a secret like this from him. Tell him, Laura," she urged. "Before it's too late."

"I will. I promise." As though girding herself, Laura drew a deep breath and let it out in a long, unsteady sigh. "I...I'll do it tonight," she said, her mouth firming with grim resolution.

But that evening when Adam took her home he was clearly not in the mood for confessions, or conversation of any kind. The moment they entered Laura's house he pulled her into his arms.

His kiss was deep and soul-stirring, and Laura was powerless to resist it. She sagged against him, her body pliant, her lips clinging to his in soft surrender, the slow, evocative thrusts of his tongue and the warm caress of his hands driving every coherent thought from her mind.

But when his lips left hers a spark of sanity returned. "A–Adam," she said breathlessly as his nibbling lips caressed the side of her neck. "Adam, there is something I must tell you."

"Mmmm. I have to tell you something, too." His tongue traced a swirling pattern on the tender skin just behind her ear, then he nipped the lobe gently. "Did you know that all day I've been waiting to do this? That while we were eating, and later when I was pretending to watch television, I was driving myself crazy wondering if you were wearing that little nothing lace bra. The black one that's cut so low it shows the tops of your nipples." One of his hands moved up her ribcage and cupped her breast. His fingers flexed while his thumb swept searchingly. "Did you?"

"No...I mean, yes. Oh, Adam—"

His hand slid downward between their bodies to press against her flat abdomen. "And those matching panties with the naughty lace inserts?" he murmured hopefully as his marauding mouth moved along the line of her jaw.

"Adam. Adam, listen to me," Laura panted. "I have to tell you— Oh!"

Without warning Adam bent and lifted her in his arms. He looked down into her startled face, a sensuous smile playing about his mouth. "Are you by any chance trying to tell me that the house is on fire?"

"No! Of course not!"

"Good." He dropped a firm kiss on her mouth and strode for the stairs. "Because anything else can wait."

The Sunday following Thanksgiving was Mike's birthday. Laura baked him a cake, poignantly aware that this was the first time she had ever been able to do so...and that it may very well be the last.

Harriet joined them after church for a family birthday dinner. Practical as ever, her gift to Mike was a hand-knit pullover. Laura gave him a portable stereo radio, which he enthused over at length, but it was Adam's gift of a moped that thrilled him the most.

Laura viewed the vehicle with unease. It looked dangerous to her, and she hated the idea of Mike careening over hill and dale on the thing, even if it didn't go very fast. But since it was obvious that neither Adam nor Mike shared her concern, she didn't say anything.

Mike called his friends to tell them what he had gotten for his birthday, and shortly after his aunt left, several of them dropped by. When the boys trooped outside to see the moped, Laura found herself alone with Adam for the first time since Thursday night.

"Thank goodness," Adam said with a comical grimace the moment the door closed behind the rowdy teenagers. "The only thing more exhausting than a fifteen-year-old boy is several of them." He flopped down beside Laura on the sofa and leaned back wearily. Rolling his head to the side, he smiled up at her. "Hi," he said softly, infusing the word with a tender intimacy that squeezed at Laura's heart.

"Hi." Laura's answering smile wavered, then collapsed. She looked away, unable to meet the loving warmth in Adam's eyes, and stared at the blaze dancing in the fireplace. Her palms were sweaty and her stomach felt as though it were tied in a knot. *Tell him. Tell him now. You swore you would the first chance you got, and this is it.* Steeling herself, Laura drew a deep breath.

"Adam, there is something I have to tell you," she said shakily. "I tried to tell you the other night, but you wouldn't let me, but now I must."

"Okay, sweetheart, shoot." Adam reached out to take her hand but before he could, Laura jerked to her feet and walked across the room to stand by the window. She couldn't let him distract her again. Staring out at nothing, she crossed her arms over her midriff and rubbed her elbows in agitation.

"You're probably going to be angry," she began nervously. "I should have told you this sooner, but...well..." Her voice trailed off lamely and she drew another deep breath. "The thing is, I—" She stopped and frowned as Mike zoomed by the window on his moped, and immediately her taut nerves found an outlet, transforming fear to anger. "For heaven's sake, Adam," she snapped. "Whatever possessed you to buy him that thing? He's liable to break his neck. It scares me to death just to watch him."

A deep chuckle sounded just above her ear as Adam's arms slipped around her from behind. "You're adorable, do you know that?" he murmured, placing a warm kiss on her temple and pulling her back against his chest. "You're acting more like a worried mother than most real mothers."

Biting her lip, Laura closed her eyes against the pain. It felt as though there were a tight band around her chest, slowly squeezing the life out of her. She wanted to tell him that she was Mike's real mother. That she was afraid because she loved him, because she was terrified of losing him. But her fear of losing Adam was even stronger. Would he turn away from her if she told him? Would he look at her with disgust and loathing? Could she bear it if he did?

With his arms securely around her, Adam swayed with her gently, his chin propped on her head. "So, what was this urgent thing you had to tell me?" he asked in a teasing voice.

"I...I...I have to go to Houston on business," she prevaricated, silently cursing herself for a fool and a coward.

She felt him grow still, the arms that surrounded her stiffening. When he spoke his voice had cooled by several degrees. "Oh? When?"

"Tomorrow."

He released her and stepped away, and Laura shivered,

immediately missing the warmth of his body. She turned to find that he had retreated several paces, and now stood with his back to her. The rigid set of his shoulders sent a tiny frisson up her spine.

"I see," he clipped, his back still to her. "And how long will you be gone? Or do you even know?"

"A week. Ten days at the most." Laura watched him in worried confusion. What was happening? What had gone wrong? In trying to avoid the inevitable anger and hurt her confession would bring, she had somehow made a terrible blunder. His voice was growing colder with every word, and she could actually feel him withdrawing from her.

"It's business. Things have been piling up in Houston, things that my assistant can't handle. That I must attend to myself." It was not a lie. Sometime the day before, Diane had left a panicked message on her answering machine, and Laura had called her back only a few hours ago with a promise that she would be there by noon tomorrow.

She waited expectantly for Adam to comment. When he didn't, she added nervously, "Actually, I probably should have gone back before now. But I just didn't feel comfortable, leaving Irma and Racine in charge of the store."

Nothing.

Watching him, Laura ran her damp palms over her gray wool slacks. "Adam, what's wrong?" she asked finally, her voice low and edged with worry.

"Wrong? Why nothing," he said, swinging around to face her. His smile was as remote as his voice. "Nothing at all."

It wasn't true, and Laura knew it. For despite his claim, Adam's attitude remained cool and distant, so much so that by the end of the evening even Mike was shooting him puzzled looks. The restrained kiss Adam gave Laura at her front door, along with the fact that he showed not the slightest interest in making love to her, merely added to her growing anxiety. She didn't sleep well that night, and worried and fretted during the trip to Houston the next morning.

Laura called Adam as soon as she arrived, and again the next night, but the remoteness was still there. Worried, and anxious to get back to Oakridge so they could clear up whatever was the problem, Laura stepped up her schedule and tried to cram a week's work into the next three days. That necessitated long hours and late night meetings with her store managers, her Houston attorney, and her accountant.

Unfortunately, it was during one such meeting at her apartment, that Adam called.

As he counted off the rings his hand tightened around the receiver and his mouth flattened into a grim line. He was angry with himself for calling when he'd sworn he wouldn't, and angry with Laura for not being there when he did. Flicking a glance at his watch, Adam muttered a rude word. *Where the hell is she? It's almost eleven.*

He had counted eight rings and was just about to hang up when Laura picked up the phone.

"Hello."

Adam's heart took a little leap, and he cursed silently. "Hello, Laura," he replied quietly.

"Adam! Darling, what a wonderful surprise."

"I just thought I'd check and see how it was going," he said, striving to keep his tone indifferent.

"Fine. I've been working hard." There was a pause, and Laura added in a low, caressing voice, "I've missed you, darling. Very much."

A flicker of hope rose in Adam's chest, despite the small persistent voice that counseled caution. With a long sigh, he leaned his head back against the sofa and closed his eyes. "I've...missed you, too." He was about to ask how much longer she expected to be there when he heard a burst of masculine laughter and several voices in the background.

He sat up straight, jealousy piercing him like a hot knife.

"I'm sorry, I didn't realize you had company," he said in a freezing voice.

"No, no. I'm just having a business meeting. Don't worry, they can continue without me for a few minutes."

Business meeting. Adam gritted his teeth. *It sounds more like a damned party.*

Adam cursed himself for a fool. Hadn't he always suspected that it wouldn't last? That she would get tired of the quiet life? Hadn't he been steeling himself for the break? "That's okay," he said stiffly. "I don't want to keep you from your work. Good night, Laura."

Adam returned the receiver to its cradle with controlled violence, bolted off the sofa, and stalked across the room to stand in front of the fireplace. With one foot resting on the hearth, an arm braced against the mantle, he stared broodingly at the fire.

You're an idiot, Kincaid, he berated himself silently. Why in heaven's name did you let yourself fall for Laura when you knew this might happen? Tiredly, he ran his free hand through his hair and gave a rueful snort. Because you couldn't help yourself, that's why. Any more than you could help lying awake for hours last night, wondering why she hadn't called, tormenting yourself by imagining her in your arms, all soft and warm and pliant, smelling of violets and sweet, clean woman. Even now, just the memory of her soft voice brought a stirring warmth to his body.

Swallowing around the painful knot in his throat, Adam pressed his lips together, threw his head back and squinted at the ceiling. *God! How will I stand it if I lose her!*

The digital clock on the Lincoln's dash blinked to ten thirteen when Laura turned onto the gravel lane Saturday morning. Despite working until almost midnight the night before, she had gotten up at six thirty and been on the highway by daylight. The coiled-spring feeling in the pit of her stomach had tightened with each mile that brought her closer to Adam. Now that she was almost there, the

tension was so great she could barely stand it. Her anxious
nerves were aquiver with hope and fear. Adam had been
so distant every time she had talked to him over the phone,
and he had ended their last conversation so abruptly. But
he *had* called, she reminded herself. That had to be a good
sign.

Laura didn't even consider going home first. She turned
into Adam's drive, her heart lifting at the sight of the
sprawling house. Almost before the sound of the engine
stopped, she was out of the car and up the steps, her finger
jabbing impatiently at the doorbell.

The instant Adam opened the door Laura launched herself against him, flinging her arms around him and burying
her face against his neck. He was caught so completely off
guard, for a moment he just stood there, his arms limp at
his sides, his face blank with astonishment. But then his
stunned brain began to assimilate the fact that Laura was
actually there, hugging him tightly, making incoherent little
sounds as she pressed hectic kisses against his neck and
the underside of his jaw.

"Oh, God, Laura!" he cried as he crushed her to him.
"You're here. You're really here."

"Adam. Oh, darling. I'm so glad to be back," Laura
declared fervently, in between kisses. "So glad. I thought
this week would never pass."

Her words made Adam's heart lurch, and he captured
her face with one hand, lifting it to look deep into her eyes.
His own widened in wonder at the sheer joy he saw there.
"You really mean that, don't you?" he whispered in a low,
incredulous voice. "You're actually glad to be back."

"Yes, of course," she said, her face soft with love as
she gazed up at him. "This is where you are. And where
you are is where I'll always want to be."

"Oh, Laura. Laura." He breathed her name reverently,
humbly, his eyes drifting shut as he lowered his head and
caught her parted lips in a kiss so soft and sweet, so utterly
adoring, it pierced her very soul.

The hand beneath her chin trembled. Laura could feel his heart thundering against her palm, could sense the passion he was holding tightly in check, yet he continued the exquisitely tender assault on her lips, telling her without words of the depth of his love. Laura was so touched her heart swelled almost to bursting.

At last he raised his head and looked at her. "I love you, Laura," he declared in a deep, emotion-filled voice. "I love you more than I've ever loved anyone. More than life itself."

Laura gazed back at him with tears in her eyes and reached up to gently touch his cheek with her fingertips. Her lips were quivering and emotion clogged her throat, but finally she managed in an aching whisper, "And I love you. So very much."

Then he was kissing her again, deeply, hotly, all restraint gone. Laura accepted his passion eagerly, her own rising to meet it, as bodies pressed close and hands roamed in feverish excitement. The sweet poignancy of love became raging demand, boundless need. Their mouths rocked hungrily, their warm breaths mingled, tongues thrust, parried, entwined. They strained together, frustrated, enthralled, each wanting, seeking, more.

When Adam suddenly ended the kiss he was breathing hard and his eyes were glittering hotly. "I need you, Laura. Right now," he said in a gravelly voice. Keeping an arm around her waist, he pulled her tight against his side and started down the hall with long, urgent strides.

"B–but, Adam, Mike might—"

"Mike is at Tommy Wright's house. He won't be back until late this evening." Adam opened a door at the end of the hall, hustled Laura inside, and kicked it shut behind them. Even as he hauled her across to the king-size bed his fingers were working open the buttons on her blouse.

At the bed he turned her to face him, quickly ridding her of the silky garment and the lacy bra beneath it, then going to work on the hidden clip at the waistband of her slacks, his face wearing a burning, intent look. He was bent slightly forward, and Laura ran her hands over his shoulders and caressed the back of his neck as she nibbled greedily at his lobe. "This is really shameless, you know," she whispered shakily, her breath filling his ear with its moist heat. "It's the middle of the morning." But already her hands were sliding downward, and when they reached his chest her nimble fingers began popping open the pearl snaps on his western shirt.

"Uh-hmmm," Adam agreed as he hurriedly and methodically stripped her. Buttons, hooks, and zippers were dealt with swiftly. Within minutes she was stretched out on the bed, watching avidly as he snatched off his own clothes, and when he was done she smiled and held out her arms, and he came into them willingly, their soft groans of pleasure blending as warm flesh met warm flesh.

There was no time and no need for foreplay. The loneliness of the last five days, the uncertainties that had bedeviled them both, had built their desire for one another to a fever pitch. They kissed deeply, and as Adam rolled Laura to her back, her legs curved about his hips, each desperately seeking the reassurance that only their oneness could bring.

Their joining was swift and smooth and deeply satisfying, a homecoming, a restorative, a balm to their souls. For a moment they savored it in stillness. Eyes closed. Hearts pounded. Straining muscles quivered.

Then the movement began.

The age-old rhythm carried them quickly to their goal, and within moments they reached an explosive completion, a shower-burst of exquisite pleasure, made sublime by the love they shared. As they held each other in fierce possession, their joyous cries echoed through the bedroom.

For long moments after, sated, too replete to move, they lay fused together, pale flesh to dark, soft gentle curves to sinewed strength. Sunlight poured in through the window and stretched out over the bed in a bright rectangle, gilding their entwined limbs and sleek, sweat-sheened bodies with pale gold.

Finally Adam stirred and rolled to his side, settling her against him, her head cradled on his shoulder. Her fingers idly played with the damp hair on his chest as she lay with her eyes closed, her crooked leg intimately nestled between his.

"Laura," Adam said softly, as he rubbed his jaw against her temple.

"Hmmm?"

"Will you marry me?"

Laura's heart stopped beating for a moment, then started up again with a sickening lurch. She lay perfectly still, not daring to move. The astounding words seemed to echo loudly in the quiet room.

"M–marry you?" she finally ventured in a strangled voice.

"Yes. I've known for a long time that I wanted to marry you. The only reason I haven't asked you before now is I wasn't sure that you could ever really settle here."

Laura looked up at him, her eyes filled with surprise. Momentarily, she forgot the awesome problem that threatened their happiness. "But, Adam! I love it here. I told you that from the very beginning."

"I know, I know," he said, grimacing wryly as he stroked her cheek. "I guess it's just a hangup of mine. Because I know that I could never live in a big city. Carol and I tried it once. Years ago, right after we graduated from college, we moved to Dallas." He gave a mirthless snort of laughter and shook his head. "We were going to shake the dust of this town off our boots and become big-city sophisticates. And for more than a year, we gave it our best shot. We both landed good jobs with prestigious firms, met the right people, joined the right clubs, went to the right parties. Oh, yes," he said wryly, shaking his head in bitter recollection. "We played the game well, but we hated every miserable minute of it. When we finally admitted that to ourselves, we burned up the highway getting back here. And here is where I intend to stay. I couldn't go back to the rat race, Laura," he said softly. "Not even for you."

"I wouldn't ask you to," she replied, giving him a worried look. "But..."

"But what?"

The guarded expression that came over Adam's face pierced Laura's heart like a dull knife. Unable to meet his eyes, she pulled out of his arms and sat up. "It's just that...well...I...I don't think we should get married just yet."

"Why not?" Adam pushed himself up in the bed until he was leaning against the headboard. "I love you. You love me. Mike adores you. You seem to like living here. Where's the problem?"

Laura remained quiet, knowing she had no excuse but the real one. She sat hunched over, her arms looped around her updrawn legs, her chin resting on her knees. Smiling at her defensive posture, Adam reached out and drew his finger along her bowed spine, down to the shadowy cleft at its base.

"Are you afraid that people will think I'm marrying you for your money?"

The soft question brought Laura's head snapping around, and she looked at him over her shoulder, her eyes wide with distress that he would even think such a thing. "No. Of course not," she insisted.

"Then what is it? What's bothering you?"

Her expression agonized, she met his steady gaze. She had to tell him. She had to. She couldn't marry him with this secret between them. If he ever found out, he would think she'd tricked him into marriage just to have her son. Squaring her shoulders, Laura drew a deep breath. "I want to marry you, Adam," she said softly, then quickly held up her hand when his eyes flared and he opened his mouth to speak. "But...! When you hear what I—"

The sudden shrilling of the phone on the bedside table

brought her confession to a halt and drew a curse from Adam. He glared at it and looked back at Laura, and for a moment she thought he wasn't going to answer it, but when the ringing continued unabated, he finally snatched it up.

"Yes. What is it?" he barked into the receiver.

Laura sighed heavily, not sure whether she was relieved or irritated, but when Adam suddenly stiffened beside her all she felt was a terrible foreboding.

"What!" Adam's back came away from the bed, and he swung his feet to the floor. "How bad?" he snapped, and at the look of horror on his face, Laura knew real alarm. When he began to snatch up his discarded clothes from the floor and tug them on, she did the same, knowing without being told that something dreadful had happened.

She was stepping into her wine wool slacks when Adam slammed the receiver down and turned to her, his face stricken and drained of color.

"It's Mike," he croaked. "He's had an accident on the moped."

Chapter Fourteen

They burst through the doors of the hospital at a dead run.

The woman behind the reception desk looked up, startled, but when she recognized Adam, her expression changed briefly to one of sympathy before her smooth professional mask slipped into place. "Dr. Conrad said you were to go to ICU, Mr. Kincaid," she instructed briskly as he and Laura skidded to a halt in front of her desk.

The words struck fear in Laura's heart, but her little moan of distress was lost as Adam's grip on her hand tightened, and he turned and sprinted down the hallway, pulling her along with him.

The intensive care unit was at the end of the new wing, a four-bed room with a large plate-glass window overlooking the hall, which was now closed off with curtains. Dr. Conrad was standing just outside the door, talking to a weathered, middle-aged man and a young boy, but when Adam and Laura came running up he broke off the conversation and turned to them.

"How is he?" Adam demanded before the doctor could say a word. Both he and Laura were breathing hard, and the question came out on a ragged pant.

Dr. Conrad sighed. "I'm not sure yet, Adam," he admitted gravely. "He's still unconscious. He has a broken leg, and probably a concussion. We'll need X-rays before we'll know if he has any other internal injuries."

"Oh, my God!" Laura's alarmed cry was muffled by Adam's shirt as he pulled her into his arms and held her tight against his chest.

"I got him here just as quick as I could, Adam," the weathered man hastened to assure him. "My Tommy, he got me just as soon as it happened, and we put him in my pickup and lit out for the hospital."

"What the hell happened?" Adam's demanding gaze swept back and forth between Tommy Wright and his father.

"We were ridin' our mopeds through the pasture when all of a sudden Mike just went flying over the handle bars," Tommy explained in a shaken voice. "I think he musta hit a stump in the tall grass."

Adam turned back to Dr. Conrad. "May we see him?" he asked anxiously, his face taut with strain.

The doctor's brows met in a reluctant frown. "Well...I guess you can, Adam, for a few minutes." He glanced at the weeping woman in Adam's arms. "But I'm afraid, since Mrs. Phillips isn't a relative, she'll have to wait out here."

Laura pulled out of Adam's arms and whirled around. Her tear-streaked face was pale, her eyes wide and beseeching as she gripped Dr. Conrad's arm. "But I *am* a relative!" she cried, on the verge of hysteria. "I'm Mike's natural mother."

The statement had the explosive impact of a bomb. In the startled quiet that followed Laura realized what she had blurted out, and her hand flew to her mouth. Dr. Conrad's face was blank with shock, as were Tommy's and his dad's.

The two women behind the nurses' station were watching avidly. No one moved, or said a word.

Laura turned to Adam, and fear clutched at her insides. He was staring at her, his eyes wide and wild, filled with shock that was rapidly turning to rage before her eyes.

"You bitch!" he hissed through clenched teeth, taking a menacing step toward her, and Laura flinched at the smoldering hatred in his face. His hands were balled at his sides and a muscle jumped along his tight jaw. "You conniving little—"

"Adam! Adam, get a hold of yourself!" Dr. Conrad commanded as he stepped between them and grabbed Adam's arm.

"This is neither the time nor the place to straighten this out." He tipped his head toward their interested witnesses, his grim expression urging discretion. "You can use my office later. After you've seen Mike."

For several tense seconds Adam fought a battle with himself. He glared at Laura murderously, his nostrils flared, his mouth so tight there was a white line around it. "All right." He pulled free of the doctor's restraining hold. With a cold, nasty smile, he gestured for Laura to accompany him. "By all means, Mrs. Phillips, let's go see *our* son," he said in a voice that dripped with sarcasm and loathing.

In a daze of pain Laura moved past Adam on shaky legs and stepped through the door that Dr. Conrad held open.

The next few minutes were the worst in her life. Laura didn't know which hurt more, the sight of Mike, pale and unconscious, with one side of his face horribly swollen and discolored, or the hostility she felt radiating at her in waves from the man she loved.

They just stood there in silence, side by side, watching Mike. There was nothing they could say. Nothing they could do. Except pray. Dr. Conrad took Mike's pulse, listened to his chest, then peeled his lids back and examined his eyes. When he was done he looked at them and shook his head. "No change."

The door opened to admit a technician pushing a portable X-ray machine, and Dr. Conrad motioned that it was time for them to leave. "I'll let you know the results just as soon as the pictures are developed," he said as he escorted them down the hall. "But for right now, I think you two need to do some talking." He stopped at a door that bore his name on a discreet brass plate, unlocked it, and pushed it open.

When the door clicked shut behind them, Laura gathered her courage and turned to face Adam, her eyes pleading. "I was going to tell you, Adam," she said in a small reedy voice. "Honestly I was."

"When? When Mike was grown and gone from home and there was no longer any reason to keep up the pretense?" He was leaning back against the door, his arms folded across his chest, piercing her with a stare as cold as ice.

"No! I...I've tried to tell you many times. I was about to tonight when...when the phone rang."

"Sure you were." He gave a scornful bark of laughter that cut her to the bone. Then he was glowering again, his eyes full of hatred and disbelief. "You don't honestly expect me to belief that, do you? Why would you spoil a good thing with the truth? God! What a gullible fool I've been. You batted those big brown eyes and sashayed that delectable body, and I went trotting after you with my tongue hanging out. You must have been laughing yourself sick. To think I was practically begging you—*begging* you—to share my life. Your scheme worked perfectly."

Tears streamed down Laura's face. "It wasn't like that, Adam. There was no scheme."

"You lying bitch!" he snarled, pushing himself away from the door and stalking toward her. He shoved aside a chair that was in his way, sending it toppling over, but his pace never faltered. A few steps away he stopped and glowered down at her, his face almost as rigid as stone. "Don't try to tell me that it was pure coincidence that you picked this town to move to. You picked it because Mike was here, didn't you? *Didn't you, dammit!*'' he roared when she didn't answer immediately.

"Y—yes, but—"

"You came here to regain the child you gave away. You knew my wife was dead, and you saw a heaven-sent opportunity to get your son back with no legal hassle, no expense, no publicity. No strain, no pain. You just get the poor sap of a father to fall in love with you, marry him, and slip in the back door, and no one's the wiser."

"No, Adam...please believe me. It wa...wa...wasn't like that." Choppy sobs shook Laura's whole body, and she stopped for a moment, fighting for control. "I...I didn't know about Carol. I swear it. I just wanted to...to become your friend so that I could...could get to know Mike. See him once in a while. I...I didn't count on fa-falling in love with you, b—but I did. And the only r—reason I didn't tell you was I was afraid you would think I was just trying to t–trick you," Laura cried plaintively. But even to her own ears, her story sounded feeble, and when she saw the sneering disbelief and repugnance in Adam's eyes she knew it was useless; he would never believe her.

"You scheming little slut." Adam spit the words out bitterly, as though they left a foul taste in his mouth. "You're not capable of loving anyone. Not even Mike. Fifteen years ago you gave him away. What happened?" he jeered. "Did you decide it might be fun to play Mommy for a while?"

Laura's chin quivered pathetically as a fresh torrent of tears poured down her cheeks and silent, convulsive sobs shook her shoulders. Though his words cut her to the quick, she was painfully aware that she deserved every one of them. She had known he would react this way if he found out who she was. If she had told him the truth in the beginning, she could have spared them both this horrible scene. Instead she had deceived him—not with malicious intent—but a lie by omission is still a lie. Laura could not blame him for thinking the worst.

"God!" Her silent misery brought a look of utter scorn to Adam's face, and he swung away in disgust, as though he couldn't bear to look at her another minute. He stalked to the window and stared out, his whole body stiff with fury.

Outside, the day had turned bleak, the sun now hidden by a murky gray overcast, and to Laura it seemed depressingly appropriate. In the space of just a little over an hour, her life had gone from glorious ecstasy to the depths of despair. Through the blur of tears that still flooded her eyes, Laura watched Adam with infinite sadness, remembering how it had been between them just a short while ago: the tenderness, the beauty of their loving, the closeness, the heart-stopping intimacy that had seemed so perfect, so right, that it had touched her soul.

Would things have been different if she had told him early on? Maybe. Maybe not. The only thing certain was, it couldn't have been worse than this. Desolation and hopeless love filled Laura's eyes as she studied Adam's rigid back. He was angry and hurt, his pride wounded, maybe beyond healing. She ached for him. For them both.

Tight-lipped, Adam glanced at Laura over his shoulder. "I guess you know that this whole sordid story will be all over town by nightfall. At least a half dozen people heard your little slip of the tongue. There's no way in hell we can keep it from Mike." He laughed cruelly at her stricken look. "What's the matter? Hadn't that occurred to you? Hell, you know what this town is like." His eyes narrowed and his voice dropped to a harsh command. "So you better damn well tell him before someone else does. Just as soon as the doctor says he's well enough."

Laura felt sick. Never had she even considered telling Mike. God! What would his reaction be? "You're..." She stopped and swallowed hard. "You're going to let me see him?"

"I sure as hell am not going to do your dirty work for you. Besides...I doubt that I'll have much choice." He impaled her with a look that shimmered with bitter resentment. "Mike has grown fond of you, and when he finds out that you're his natural mother he's bound to be curious, if nothing else. I can't stop you from seeing him. I won't even try. But do it when I'm not around."

Adam dug into the pocket of his jeans, pulled out a ring of keys, and tossed them to Laura. Reflexively, her hands plucked them out of the air. "Now I want you out of my sight. Out of this hospital."

Laura looked down at the keys in her hand and realized they were for his pickup. "But...how will you get home?"

"Your concern is touching, but don't worry, I'll get a ride with someone. Even if I have to walk, it's better than being around you."

Each word was like a stone striking her heart, but Laura managed to quell the cry that rose in her throat. For a moment she gazed at Adam's hard, unforgiving face with pain-filled eyes, then, with fragile, wounded dignity, she walked silently out of the room.

"What's this I hear about you leaving?"

Laura looked up from the purchase she was sacking and found herself the object of Harriet's demanding stare. Calmly, she folded the top of the sack down, stapled the receipt to it, and handed it to her customer. "Thank you, Mrs. Dumas. I hope you enjoy the sweater," she said with a smile.

Mrs. Dumas looked from Harriet to Laura, then walked away slowly, obviously reluctant to miss out on the exchange about to take place. When she had gone, Laura turned her smile on Harriet. "It's true. I am leaving."

"You mean you're going to let the tittle-tattle of a bunch of sanctimonious busybodies drive you away?"

"No. No, it's not that," Laura replied, chuckling softly at Harriet's vehemence. The gossip had been bad, some of it downright vindictive. The reactions of the local people had run the gamut of outright hostility, wariness, curiosity, and occasionally, scornful amusement. In the past weeks Laura had endured more cutting looks and snide comments than she cared to think about. Ironically, the only supporters she seemed to have in town were the two women who were closest to Adam: his aunt and Carly Sue.

"Then why are you leaving? Why are you just giving up?"

Laura moved to the antique display case and began to needlessly straighten the artful clutter inside. "Because I'm just making everyone miserable by staying."

Harriet pursed her lips and looked at her intently. "By everyone, I take it you mean Adam and Mike?" At Laura's quick nod, she asked, "How did Mike take it when you told him who you were?"

"Very well, actually." Maybe even too well, Laura told herself silently. Throughout her entire confession, Mike had just lain there, his face calm, his fingers absently pleating and unpleating the sheet across his chest. She had told him the bare facts, and said that they would discuss it more fully when he was well. Expecting him to protest, he had surprised her by merely smiling politely and saying, "Yeah, sure." After that, though she had visited him every day, by tacit agreement, they avoided the subject.

"But you haven't seen him since he got out of the hospital, have you?" Harriet probed.

"No. But then, he's not very mobile at the moment. I can't expect him to walk the mile between our houses on crutches."

"Mmmmm." Harriet studied Laura's downbent head, then asked quietly, "Have you seen Adam?"

Laura's head snapped up, and she gave her a wry look. "You've got to be kidding. He avoids me like the plague. And anyway, even if I did happen to run into him, it wouldn't do any good. At Adam's request I went to the hospital when I knew he wouldn't be there. But once he

was coming out of Mike's room just as I was going in."
Laura paused and looked out the front window, remembered pain clouding her eyes. "He looked right through me
as though I didn't exist," she said tonelessly.

"He's still hurting, Laura, but he'll get over it, eventually."

Laura shook her head sadly. "No, Harriet. Not as long
as I'm here. Staying here is like rubbing salt in his wounds.
I won't do that to him," she said quietly.

Harriet argued further, but Laura was adamant, and in
the end the older woman stomped out, muttering something
about stubborn fools who needed their heads knocked together.

That afternoon Laura left the shop early. She wanted
Racine and Irma to get used to running it without her, and
now was as good a time as any to start packing her things.
Her heart was heavy as she stuffed books and mementos
into cartons but she swore to herself that she would cry no
more tears over what simply could not be. It was a resolution that she came perilously near to breaking when she
found the two gaily wrapped Christmas gifts. Mike's was
a radio-controlled model airplane, Adam's a suede hunting
vest. She had picked them up in Houston, but when she
had finally returned home that disastrous afternoon, almost
four weeks ago, she had pushed them to the back of the
closet beneath the stairs, unable to bear the sight of them.
Christmas had come and gone, and she had forgotten about
them.

Laura was still contemplating the two foil-wrapped
boxes, wondering what she was going to do with them,
when she heard a series of thumps on the front porch.
Frowning, she struggled to her feet and started toward the
door just as the doorbell chimed.

"Mike! What are you doing here?" Laura cried, her eyes
going wide with alarm when she opened the door to find
him there, leaning on a pair of crutches. "Surely you didn't
walk all this way on those?"

"Naw, a friend of mine drove me." He jerked his head toward the driveway, where a young man not much older than he was sat behind the wheel of an old jalopy.

"Well, aren't you going to ask him in?"

"No. I, uh...I want to talk to you in, uh...in private," he said uneasily. "Bryan said he didn't mind waiting."

"I see. Well, won't you come in?"

The heavy thump of Mike's crutches as he followed her into the parlor matched the beat of Laura's heart. The time had come for the talk she had been dreading. Mike had had weeks in which to brood and wonder, and now he wanted answers.

Mike stopped short at the sight of the cartons littering the parlor floor. He stared at them for a moment, then looked sharply at Laura. "What's all this? Are you leaving?"

"Yes, Mike, I am. I'm moving back to Houston."

"Why?" The word shot out of him, angry and tense.

Laura drew a deep breath. "Because by staying here I'm making life awkward and uncomfortable for your father. Seeing me, just knowing I'm here, is painful for him. So for his sake, for all our sakes, it's best if I leave."

The anger left Mike's face, and he stared down at the intricate pattern in the oriental rug, his shoulders hunched defensively over the crutches. "I thought maybe you wanted to get away from me."

"Oh, Mike," Laura said in gentle reproach. "How could you think that? I came here because of you."

He took two swinging steps toward the window, then turned back and looked at her searchingly. "Why did you give me up? Didn't you want me?" he asked in a quavering voice that tore at Laura's heart.

She looked at his young, vulnerable face, at the hurt and hope that swam in his topaz eyes, and her own filled with tears as the terrible pain and sadness of the past fifteen years overwhelmed her. She shook her head, her expression growing infinitely soft and loving. "Of *course* I wanted you, sweetheart," she assured him in an aching whisper. "I wanted you so much I thought I would die when I had to give you up."

"So why did you?" His chin was quivering as he asked the question, and he swallowed hard against the emotions that were clogging his throat.

"I was not quite seventeen when you were born... frightened and confused. The boy I loved had turned his back on me, and my parents threatened to do the same unless I gave up my baby. They were shocked and outraged and humiliated by my..."—one corner of Laura's mouth twitched in a pathetic little grimace—"...my fall from grace."

Memories from that time flooded through Laura and she could no longer hold back her tears. They streamed from her eyes and dripped down her face unheeded as she stared beseechingly at her son, silently pleading for his understanding, his acceptance...his forgiveness. "I was a child, Mike. I hadn't even finished school. All I had to give you was my love, and I knew that just wasn't enough."

Mike's hands were clenched at his sides, his slender young body rigid. The muscles in his face worked as he struggled to control his emotions. "Do...do you know where...where my fa...where the man who fathered me is?" he asked with a quiet dignity that made Laura's heart ache for him.

"No. Within days after I told him I was pregnant, he and his parents left town. I never heard from him again."

"And your parents? My...grandparents? Are they still alive?"

"Yes. Though I don't see much of them." Shaking her head regretfully, Laura sighed. "You see, they're very rigid in their views. I suppose they tried, but they never really managed to forgive me, not even after I married and became 'respectable' again. When they retired they moved to California. We speak on the phone once or twice a year, but that's about it."

"Is that why you came here? Because you have no one?"

"Partly," Laura admitted. "But mainly because I could no longer stay away. All these years I've yearned for you, but I knew I didn't have the right to reclaim you. I moved here thinking I could at least see you now and then, maybe get to know you, but I never meant to disturb your life." Regret and sadness entered her eyes and she turned away and placed her hand on the back of a chair. As she absently traced a pattern in the velvet upholstery she murmured softly, "But I hadn't counted on falling in love with your father. I'm sorry, Mike. I should never have come here. I've just made problems for us all."

"No! No, you haven't!" he denied hotly, and Laura looked up, surprised by the anguish in his eyes. "Please, don't go, Laura! I don't want you to go!"

For an emotion-choked moment, Laura could barely breathe. They stared mutely at each other, then, as Mike's tears slowly overflowed, her face crumpled, and she stepped forward and pulled him into her arms.

Mike clutched her fiercely and pressed his face against her neck, his bony shoulders shaking. With her eyes squeezed shut, her teeth clamped over her lower lip, Laura hugged him to her and stroked the back of his head tenderly.

"Oh, Mike. Mike. Sweetheart, I'm sorry. So sorry." She crooned in a pain-filled voice as she rocked him back and forth. "I didn't mean to hurt you. I didn't mean to hurt anyone." Drawing a deep breath, Laura released him and framed his tear-streaked face between her palms. "But don't you see? I have to go. My presence here is just making your father's life miserable." She smiled gently and smoothed a lock of dark hair off his face. "But—provided your father will allow it—you can visit me any time you'd like."

Mike sniffed and swiped at his nose with his sleeve. "Promise?" he asked as he attempted manfully to recover his composure.

"Promise," Laura assured him softly.

Chapter Fifteen

He heard Mike enter the house, heard the ponderous thump, slide, thump of his crutches as he maneuvered through the foyer, but Adam remained where he was, standing by the glass doors in the den, staring broodingly out at the bleak winter landscape. He had been surprised when he arrived home to find Mike gone, but not alarmed.

He's been to see her. Adam's hand tightened around the glass of bourbon and water he was holding as the thought stabbed through his mind. Dammit! Why can't he just forget about her, as she did him, fifteen years ago? Leaning a broad shoulder against the door frame, he took a long pull on his drink and grimaced as it burned going down. The sigh that lifted his chest was heavy with self-reproach. *For that matter, why can't you, you sap?*

Even now, knowing what she was, what she had done, he couldn't get her out of his mind. Or out of his heart. He missed her with a deep, dark longing that was a constant dull ache in his chest. Muttering a vile curse, Adam tipped his head back and squinted at the pewter sky. Why, out of all the women in the world, did he have to fall in love with Laura?

Adam heard Mike enter the room and stop just inside the door, but he did not turn around. "Have a nice visit?" he drawled, unable to keep the biting sarcasm from his voice.

"She's leaving." Mike flung the bald statement down like a gauntlet.

Adam stiffened and turned slowly, carefully keeping his face expressionless. "Who's leaving?"

"You know who I mean," Mike shot back. "Laura, that's who. She's packing right now. She's going to move back to Houston." He was glaring accusingly at his father, his expression belligerently aggressive.

A burning pain twisted at Adam's gut, but he managed a negligent shrug and drawled indifferently, "So?"

"So, are you just going to let her leave?" Mike demanded.

"Why should I care one way or the other?" Adam snapped back, torn between pain and anger. "For that matter, why should you? She didn't care enough about you to keep you."

"For Pete's sake, Dad! She was just a kid. Only a little older than I am. She was in love with this guy and thought he loved her, but when she got pregnant he dumped her and took off. Her parents gave her the choice of giving me up or leaving. What would you have done in her place?"

Adam looked away from his son's angry glare and downed the last of his drink in one long swallow. The thought of Laura, young, alone and frightened, aroused a whole new set of feelings, ones he didn't even want to think about at the moment. Taking refuge in anger, he snarled back, "All right, all right! That part of it I can understand. What I can't forgive is her deceit. Laura doesn't love me, Mike. She never did. She wormed her way into my life and my heart, but she was just using me to get you back."

Mike looked at him steadily, his young face thoughtful. "If that was all she wanted, then why is she leaving? We're friends now. She could see me any time she wanted." With that calm statement delivered, he swung around on his crutches and thumped out of the room.

Adam remained perfectly still, staring after him. For several moments his face mirrored the doubts that seethed in his mind. Then suddenly he slammed his empty glass down on the coffee table, strode out into the foyer, and snatched his sheepskin jacket off the brass coat rack.

For the second time in less than an hour, Laura received a shock when she answered the doorbell's summon.

"Adam!" His name came out on a startled gasp, and then her throat closed up on her. Adam seemed similarly afflicted, and for a timeless moment they just stared at each other.

Unconsciously, Laura clutched the doorknob until her knuckles were white. She drank in the sight of him like one dying of thirst, her heart booming in her chest. He was thinner, and there were lines in his face that had not been there before. But to Laura he looked wonderful. She wanted, more than anything, to fling herself into his arms.

"Hello, Laura," he said at last. "May I come in?"

"Yes. Yes, of course." As he stepped inside her senses were assaulted by his familiar masculine scent, and she felt her insides tremble.

Laura shut the door and gave him a wan smile. She had to force her wobbly legs to carry her into the parlor. "Won't you have a seat?" she invited nervously as she shifted a box off the settee to make room.

Adam, as Mike had done earlier, stopped just inside the room and surveyed the jumble of cartons. Slowly his gaze came back to her, questioning and intent. Tension crackled in the air between them. "Mike said you were leaving."

"Yes." Laura rubbed her sweaty palms on her jeans and looked away, but as though drawn by a magnet, her eyes went back to him. Her body's response to his presence was strong and uncontrollable. Her breasts swelled with emotion. Pulses throbbed.

"Why?"

"I...I would think that's obvious."

"Tell me."

"Because my being here is just making things worse. This is a small town, for heaven's sake. We're bound to run into each other from time to time. And I know you don't want that. You can't keep avoiding me for the rest of your life, so the best thing would be for me to leave."

"It's my problem. Why should you care?" he probed relentlessly.

"Oh, Adam. You know why," Laura said in a small, defeated voice. But his silent stare demanded that she say the words, and she looked at him reproachfully, wondering why he was putting them through this when they both knew he wouldn't believe her. "I care because I love you. I can't bear to cause you any more misery than I already have." She stared down at her hands, twisting them together in front of her, not wanting to see the derision in his eyes.

"Do you mean that?" His voice was deep, rough with emotion.

Laura hazarded a glance at him and was surprised to find his eyes were glittering and his face wore a look of desperate hunger. A flare of hope burst in Laura's heart, but she subdued it. "Yes, I mean it," she said in the barest whisper, watching him.

Adam's throat worked convulsively. "I hope you do, Laura. Because, God help me, I can't let you go."

Before she could move, he crossed the room and snatched her into his arms, burying his face in the fragrant, honeyed-colored waves at her neck. "I love you, Laura," he groaned hoarsely, his voice tinged with desperation. "I've been so miserable without you these past weeks."

"Oh, my darling. So have I. So have I!" Laura cried. She clung to him fiercely, her restless, caressing hands learning anew the texture of his skin, the firmness of his hard flesh, the silky smoothness of his hair. She had not expected to be in his arms ever again. It was sheer heaven.

"Oh, Adam, I'm sorry. So sorry," Laura whispered. "I should have told you who I was in the beginning. I know that now."

"I'm sorry, too. I shouldn't have said the things I did." Adam raised his head, and their eyes met in a long look that spoke of past pain and regret. "I didn't mean all those things, Laura. I wanted to mean them, but I didn't. Not deep down."

Cupping his face with her hand, Laura smiled at him, her eyes soft with understanding and love. "I know, my darling," she murmured, stroking his cheek with her fingertips. "I know." They stared at each other silently, hungrily, all that they were feeling plain in their eyes. Their hearts were full to overflowing. There were a thousand things they wanted to say—a million that could not be expressed.

Adam's eyes dropped to her mouth. Laura's lips parted. Her eyes fluttered shut.

And then the heady anticipation was over.

Their mouths met and blended softly. Beneath the agonizing sweetness, the kiss was rife with hunger, but it was held in check for the assuagement of a far greater need. Lips rocked together gently, breaths mingled, as, with exquisite care, each sought and granted forgiveness, offered solace, and pledged their love anew.

When at least their clinging lips parted, Adam raised a hand and cupped her jaw tenderly. Warm and intent, his gaze roamed over her face, touching each feature as though trying to absorb her through his eyes. Laura trembled under that possessive look, her body turning to hot liquid. "I need you, Laura," he said huskily. "I need you so very much."

In answer, she stepped back and took his hand in hers. With a beckoning smile on her lips, she led him from the room and up the stairs.

In the bedroom Adam took her in his arms and kissed her deeply, giving full rein to the pent-up hunger that throbbed within them both. His hands roamed her back, pressing her close, letting her know the strength of his need. Looping her arms around his neck, Laura fitted her body intimately to him and rocked her hips gently. Adam groaned and tore his mouth from hers. "I didn't know how I was going to live without you," he whispered against her neck.

"You won't ever have to," Laura vowed fervently, stroking the hair at his nape with urgent fingers.

Adam stepped back and gripped the bottom edge of her sweater in both hands. He pulled the soft russet knit over her head and tossed it aside in a single motion. Beneath it was only the smooth, fragrant skin that had haunted his dreams for weeks.

Silently, his eyes devoured her. A flame leaped in their hazel depths. There was a disturbed cadence to his breathing. "You're beautiful." With shaky hands Adam lowered the zipper on her slacks and pushed them off her hips. Dropping to one knee, he pressed his face against her stomach above the tiny triangle of her pink bikini panties. "Absolutely beautiful," he murmured passionately as he alternately licked and kissed the silky skin.

A delicious quivering started deep inside Laura, and she clutched his head, tunneling her fingers through the warm silk of his hair to hold him close. Laura closed her eyes, awash with emotion. Her love for him was boundless. It swelled with painful sweetness in her chest, then seemed to overflow her heart and spread through her body in a warm tide.

As his mouth and tongue continued to worship her, Laura's hands glided down his neck and gripped the bunched muscles in his shoulders, drawing intense pleasure from the silky brush of his hair against the undersides of her breasts, the rough caress of his callused palms against her thighs.

His fingertips slipped beneath the top edge of Laura's panties, and with a smoothing motion, the scrap of pink silk and lace was eased down to her ankles. Adam slipped them over her feet, then peeled away the warm socks that hugged her feet and calves, and thrust them aside with the rest of her clothing. Gripping her hips for leverage, he stood up.

For a long moment he simply stared at her, and Laura quivered, desire streaking through her at the hot look in his eyes. His lips curved in a slow sensuous smile, and he bent and placed a kiss on each breast, then eased her back onto the bed.

His own clothes were removed with haste, and within minutes, he was stretched out beside her, pulling her into his arms. Their mouths met and meshed in a searing kiss that sought to make up for the long lonely days they had been apart.

Laura's breasts were flattened against his hair-covered chest, her nipples turgid buttons of desire, and against her soft abdomen she could feel his arousal. "Oh, Adam. Adam. I've missed you so." Her hands ran over him in a restless caress, glorying in the feel of him.

"And I've missed you. So much. So very much." Eyes closed, Adam trailed kisses down her neck, across her shoulders, and finally down into the valley between her breasts. He lavished attention on the lush, womanly flesh, stroking the budding nipples with his tongue, sucking greedily, until Laura trembled and cried out.

His hand trailed over her ribcage and waist to her flat belly. His fingers kneaded the quivering flesh, then moved downward, threading through the nest of honey-tinted curls to find the heart of her desire.

Laura moaned and arched into the caress, her body shuddering as liquid heat shot through her. "Love me, darling. Please!" she cried as she gripped his shoulders and urged him to her.

"Yes." Adam uttered the word in a gritty voice as he

moved into position between her silky thighs. He braced above her, and as their gazes locked he made them one, joining their bodies with a slow, powerful stroke that wrung a cry of joy from Laura.

Rapture claimed them. Nothing existed but the extravagant pleasure of loving and being loved. In the gathering darkness, soft moans and dark velvet words were murmured, while stroking, sensual hands brought shudders of delight. Trembling, they clung to one another as their bodies tightened in anticipation and need. The sweet, sweet pressure gripped them, building, expanding, until suddenly the world seemed to explode in a throbbing, consuming burst of ecstasy.

It was a long time before either of them stirred, but finally Adam raised up and braced himself on his fore-arms. Laura lifted her lids lazily and gazed up at him with smoky topaz eyes. Her smile was one of sensual pleasure. She felt boneless, replete, deliciously sated.

The smug contentment on her face brought a smile to Adam's lips, and he leaned down and kissed her slowly.

"I love you," he whispered, gently smoothing a lock of hair from her cheek.

Tears of happiness gathered in Laura's eyes. Her face glowed with love as she laced her fingers at the back of his neck and whispered unsteadily, "I love you, too."

"Enough to marry me?" he asked, his face serious and touchingly anxious.

The tears welled and spilled over, running down to wet the hair at Laura's temples. She stared up at him with diamond-bright eyes, her chin wobbling as happiness overwhelmed her. "Yes, I'll marry you, my darling," she choked out finally through quivering lips. "I'll marry you any time you want."

"Tomorrow?"

Laughter mingled with the tears as she shook her head. "Oh, my darling," she chided in a gentle, loving voice. "I don't think it can be done quite that soon."

"All right, then. We'll get the license tomorrow, and have the wedding next weekend."

"If that's want you want," Laura replied happily.

All the tension seemed to drain out of him at her agreement, and he released a long sigh. He kissed her once more, then framed her face with his big hands and smiled. "In that case, we'd better get dressed and go."

"Go?" Laura's brow furrowed in puzzlement. "Go where?"

Adam's eyes grew warm with love and his smile deepened. "To my house," he replied in a husky voice. "To tell our son."

* * * * *

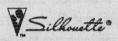

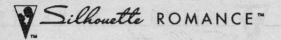

What's a single dad to do when he needs a wife by next Thursday?

Who's a confirmed bachelor to call when he finds a baby on his doorstep?

How does a plain Jane in love with her gorgeous boss get him to notice her?

From classic love stories to romantic comedies to emotional heart tuggers, **Silhouette Romance** offers six irresistible novels every month by some of your favorite authors! Such as…beloved bestsellers **Diana Palmer, Annette Broadrick, Suzanne Carey, Elizabeth August** and **Marie Ferrarella**, to name just a few—and some sure to become favorites!

Fabulous Fathers…Bundles of Joy…Miniseries… Months of blushing brides and convenient weddings… Holiday celebrations… You'll find all this and much more in **Silhouette Romance**—always emotional, always enjoyable, always about love!

WAYS TO *UNEXPECTEDLY* MEET MR. RIGHT:

♡ Go out with the sexy-sounding stranger
   your daughter secretly set you up with
   through a personal ad.

♡ RSVP yes to a wedding invitation—soon
   it might be your turn to say "I do!"

♡ Receive a marriage proposal by mail—
   from a man you've never met....

These are just a few of the unexpected
ways that written communication
leads to love in Silhouette Yours Truly.

Each month, look for two fast-paced, fun and
flirtatious Yours Truly novels
(with entertaining treats and sneak previews
in the back pages) by some of your favorite
authors—and some who are sure to
become favorites.

YOURS TRULY™:
Love—when you least expect it!